"Splendid And Bizarre... It's A Helluva Book!"

—The National Observer

"What would you think of a mountain-fed river that harbors marlin as well as trout? Of runt-size mastodons and ducks that rise in clouds, so that even the lousiest shot is sure to bag his limit? Of unicorns rampant on the hilltops, and yellowskinned bandits on the river bottoms? Of a fugitive Nazi and girls so nubile that they insist on a roll in the hay without formal introductions? You've got 'em all, plus the fabulous Ratnose, beside whom Paul Bunyan pales . . . IT'S THE MOST OUTRAGEOUS OF STORIES . . . A WRY PAEAN TO UNSPOILED NATURE AND THE OUTLAW LIFE WHERE EVERYTHING FROM SEX TO FOOD IS FOR THE TAKING, WHERE KILLING IS CASUAL AND MACHO IS EXALTED AS THE ULTIMATE END . . ."

—Newsday

"ONE MARVELS AT THE TALENT THAT CREATED IT, HOPES FOR ITS HEALTH AND SAFETY, AND FEELS A COMMAND TO URGE OTHERS TO SHARE ITS DISCOVERY!"

—The Washington Post

Blood
Sport

«‹‹◉››»

Robert F. Jones

A DELL BOOK

For Louise *(who liked it)*,
Leslie *(who hated it)*,
and Benno *(who may yet have to live it)*.

Published by
DELL PUBLISHING CO., INC.
1 Dag Hammarskjold Plaza
New York, New York 10017

Just as the water of the famed Hassayampa renders those who drink of it incapable of telling the truth . . .

—SPARSE GREY HACKLE

Part 1

1

The Hassayampa River, a burly stream with its share
of trout, rises in northern China, meanders through an
Indian reservation in central Wisconsin, and empties
finally into Croton Lake not a mile from where I live
in southern New York State. Over the years, my son
and I have hunted and fished most of its length. On
the opening day of trout season, there is usually a
fine, translucent collar of ice along the edges of the
larger pools, and when my son was younger I would
build a small fire on the bank and he would heat
stones in it. While I fished, with only the most sporad-
ic of success in the cold brown water of that early
season, he placed the hot stones on the ice and squatted there, Indian fashion, until one stone, then another and another melted its way through the ice and
sank to the bottom. The bubbles, he tells me, often
were trapped beneath the clear ice—bubbles of steam
that shrank as they cooled.

"They writhed and changed shape and moved
around beneath the ice like germs under a micro-
scope," he said. "You had your trout and I had my
bubbles."

2

Because of its length and the immense range of country it traverses, the Hassayampa yields an incredible variety of flotsam. Playing along the river as a boy—I was Tarzan and Shif'less Sol Hyde, Bomba or Broken Hand, Markhead, Og, The Last Man off Wake Island—I collected a representative sampling of its gifts. They occupy four shelves in my study, the collection loosely divided into "Natural Gifts" and "Unnatural Gifts."

Among the Natural Gifts: eagle skulls, turtle shells, pumice stones warped by time and water into the heads of cretins; seeds of all colors and sizes—some as bright as a chickadee's eye, others as dull as tennis balls; driftwood snakes and driftwood dragons; a single driftwood tit, its erect nipple as pink and smooth as a petrified rose petal; jawbones with teeth in them; the slender saw of a fox mouth, the crosscut weaponry of a freshwater shark; the weathered pizzle of a wild ox (how it survived the water trip I do not know, but even today it is as hard and smooth as mahogany; perhaps it drifted down on an ice floe); a rat nose; some leg bones, ribs, pelvises large and small, spines and beaks and shards of skulls whose eyelessness says "O"—the river is a floating abattoir.

Among the Unnatural Gifts: bamboo flutes and willow whistles; crossbow bolts; a bent and rusty belt buckle, tediously restored with oil and lacquer, that reads GOTT MIT UNS; bamboo flutes adorned with copper wire from World War II Japanese armatures; a set of nesting bowls cut from human skulls—prime, adolescent, infantile—and decorated with the symbols of an indecipherable, interlocking geometry that some of my more learned friends say comes from another star; ax handles; a snakeskin condom; a rotting Ho Chi

Minh sandal sliced from high-grade rubber and bearing the phrase VITESSE RAPIDE; a set of wind chimes strung on copper wire from World War II American armatures; a gill-net float of tarred white pine into which someone carved the stylized face of a rodent; a cigar box containing a mummified hand still clenched around the hilt of a samurai sword that had been broken off short against the guard . . .

I found the cigar box on a winter's morning, down on the Hassayampa where I had come in search of steelhead. The big, searun rainbows had arrived under a sleet storm the previous night. I could see them working their way up through the riffles, dark and agile in the grooves of the outer banks where the current had cut freeways beneath the roots of the maple-and-hemlock shore. The fish held in the soft spots where the current broke itself on those dying roots, shadowed by fiber and blue in the occasional clouds of marl that broke from the banks above. Casting into the head of the riffle to drift my spawn sack, orange and slimy, wrapped in a square of hairnet, down to the lounging trout, I snagged the cigar box. The hand, when I opened the box, was so small and crisp that at first I could not identify it. It was the sword's haft that gave me the clue. If it's holding a sword, it's got to be human. . . .

The Hassayampa as a burial ground.

Shortly after my son had mastered the fly rod, I took him on a long backpacking trip into the Altyn Tagh mountain range, where the Hassayampa rises. The trip would be good for him, I reasoned. He was a bit of a sissy—crying when his mother refused to make waffles for his breakfast, a master of the repressed snivel, relying on a combination of charm and hurt feelings to wheedle things out of his elders. He prefers not to fight, though like the proverbial rat, he will when cornered. Still, it is difficult to find the right corner for him. When asked what he would do if he were to be drafted into a war, he says he would move to the city, change his name to Joe, and get a job as a bus driver. What if he were caught? He would join the Marines, because they have tough uniforms and teach their men karate. Often he lies awake at night contemplating such spooky concepts as infinity and eternity. What are his feelings during these sleepless nights? He shudders and says he would rather not talk about it.

If naiveté is an open sore and cynicism a scab, the Hassayampa should put a few scars on him. On the first night out, I thought it only fair to warn him that the upper river was far different, indeed far more dangerous, than the stretch he and I had fished near our home.

"There are bandits and predators," I told him. "Even some ghosts."

We were camped among pines in a shallow swale on an eastern slope, so as to be awakened at first light. The pine fire popped and guttered, but the shadows it cast were yellow and warm. I took the 9mm Luger pistol from my pack. Its leather holster gleamed in the firelight; the weapon itself, when I drew it, glowed.

"Do you think we'll need it?" my son asked, his eyes the same color as the Luger. "Where do you shoot for on a predator? Or on a bandit? Or on a ghost?" I told him, and then we drank some cocoa and went to sleep. The next morning, after he fetched the water, he told me remorsefully that he had dreamed of neck shots and head shots.

4

My father died on the Hassayampa the month before I was born. He was cutting timber in the dark—hardwoods, my mother said. I have a photograph taken of him at the time. In it, he is wearing knee-length lace-up boots, stagged trousers and a heavy wool shirt with a checked pattern. His hair is windblown, and he is smiling under his moustache. He is a tall man, lean, with strong hands. There is snow on the ground, and a whiskey bottle stands on a tree stump in the distance. In those days, you could get $50 for a black walnut tree, $35 for a maple, $22.50 for a chestnut.

Some say he was crushed by a falling tree; others, that he fell through the ice and drowned. A friend of mine, a physician, feels it may have been a heart attack. But he has never seen the photograph. My uncle, who tends to exaggerate, has always maintained that he was murdered by the Outlaw Ratanous. When I was young, I preferred to believe my uncle's suspicions: it was pleasant to fall asleep vengeful. Now I'm not so sure.

I had many copies made of the photograph. Some are wallet-sized; others are suitable for framing. When I am bored or unhappy, I take out the photograph (or else stare at the one on the wall) and wonder what my father was smiling about. After a while, the answer always comes: the Hassayampa.

On the second night of our trip to the Altyn Tagh, my son and I made camp early so that we could get in a little fishing before dark. We pitched our tent on a sandy point at the foot of a long chain of rapids. I explained to the boy that if it rained upstream during the night, we might get washed out by a rise in the river, but that it was worth taking the chance since the sky to the west, where the weather usually originated, was clear and the late sun was reddening. On the point, we would not be so badly bug-bitten. He said that was okay. On his first cast with a small bucktail into the main pool, he hooked a fair-sized fish that jumped and tail-walked its way clear across the dark, marbled surface of the Hassayampa. The drag sounded like a wounded crow.

"Oh, you sumbitch!" my son yelled as the fish started grey-hounding up the pool.

"It's a striped marlin," I told him. "Next thing, he'll sound."

My son cast me a doubtful glance—a freshwater marlin?—but kept the pressure on the fish. Sure enough, it sounded. For the next hour and a half, my son pumped and reeled, pumped and reeled, with the fish stripping back all the line the boy had gained before it could dry on the spool. "Shit!" he said. "I think he's foul-hooked. Or maybe tail-wrapped. I can't move the bastard!" I told him to take it easy—we had plenty of time. He began to sweat, and a sullen twist came to his lips. Finally, though, we saw color—the blue-and-silver flash with the wobbly black stripes.

"I'll get the gaff," I told him.

"No," he said. "Let's just bill him and release him. They're not worth eating anyway. What the hell would we do with two hundred and fifty pounds of marlin meat?"

The trip was a gift to the boy, so I let him have his way. I billed the marlin and cut the leader. I could just make out the white blur of the bucktail in the side of the fish's jaw as the light failed and his rough bill slapped back into the Hassayampa. That night we dined on Spam and beans, but it didn't rain.

Above the pool where my son caught the freshwater marlin, the river grew wicked. Cliffs impeded our progress; swamps stuck their mosquitoes up our noses. We swatted steadily at blackflies. Briers caught and cut. Our sweat—the venom of civilization—stung in the wounds. We could hardly wait for night.

In the evenings, we read to each other beside the campfire from our few favorite books. We had packed them along regardless of the extra weight. I read to my son from Myerson's massive tome, *Strange Waters: The Hassayampa Through Time & History* (Macmillan, 1923, 847 pages): "No less an American than Jefferson seriously believed that prehistoric creatures long since pronounced 'extinct' by science, the mastadon and the sabre-toothed tiger among them, still survived on the upper reaches of the Hassayampa. Indeed there is evidence to support Jefferson's contention. To this day, Hassayampan hunters sipping their gruel in the smoky *wats* of Tor and Hymarind occasionally mutter dim yarns concerning massive animals—vague and awesome shapes, importunate but hesitant as well—that appear betimes through the shifting, chilly gauze of a vernal blizzard to trumpet in the dark beyond the last bright tongues of the campfire. Perhaps they are merely yaks, but . . ."

"Hey, listen to this!" my son chirps in the smoky, shifting gauze of our own campfire. " 'Tom slammed the ship into hyperdrive and soon they were alongside the hulk of their erstwhile enemy. 'Gee,' said Tom, in a voice tinged both by pride and horror, 'We really zapped 'em.' The alien spacecruiser had been ripped open like a can of paint by their lasers. Out of the ragged gashes in its hull, the six-limbed bodies of its far-travelled crew spun like rimless wagonwheels to gleam in the sickly light of nearby Betelgeuse . . ."

There was a crunch in the alders beyond our campfire. Then we heard a faint whinnying. My son whipped out the Luger and shot into the dark. Something whimpered and crunched back into the alders. The boy looked at me, frightened.

"Okay," I said finally. "You only wounded it. Because of the dark, we don't dare follow it up right now. We'll wait until morning."

"It had teeth, I know that much," he answered.

At dawn we followed the blood trail up through the alders into a meadow high above the Hassayampa. The few trees in the meadow had been heavily browsed, and the yellow grass was trampled flat in their shade. It was stiflingly hot. As we rested in the shifting shade, we watched a praying mantis as it waited for a kill, high on a heap of dung. When we resumed our tracking, the blood trail was dry. Ants had found it and were carrying away large flakes of dried blood.

The animal itself lay dead at the edge of a stream, its head in the purling water.

"It's a mastodon," my son said as we neared the body.

"Let's wait a minute," I said. "It may not be dead." I handed him the Luger and told him to put a bullet back of the animal's ear to be sure. The flies flushed at the shot. As mastodons go, this one was a runt—only four feet high at the shoulder—but we chopped out its ivory and peeled the tender meat from the backbone. Already buzzards were circling, and ticks waddled from the cooling orifices of the mastodon's ears. We carried the ivory back down to the Hassayampa and cached it under an uprooted willow tree, to pick up on the way back home.

"Gee," said the boy, in a voice tinged by both pride and horror, "Myerson's right."

Now and then, sleepless in my mummy bag as the fire died, I could not be certain that I had come up the Hassayampa on so innocent a mission as the outdoor education of my son. Sometimes I thought I was making the trip in pursuit of Ratanous. Over the years I had come to call him Ratnose. In the shallows of sleep I could see him dimly, thin in his fur coat (wolfskin? ratskin?) with his arms extended sideways, only his sharp nose highlighted by the fading fire. Occasionally I caught a whiff of him: sharp, sour sweat and rotten teeth, knifing through the smell of warm ash; my heart would pump crazily the way it had when I was a child and Ratnose lurked in my closet, or behind the attic door across the hall from my bedroom.

Ratanous had been hanging around too long. I thought we had killed him years ago and dumped his body, throat-shot, into the icy Hassayampa. But he kept turning up, or seeming to turn up. I could not even be sure he existed, except that other people whose judgment I trust seem to think they have seen him here and there. I saw him once at the end of a dark alley in Nagoya, standing in a group of transvestites, and another time walking up a road on Mount Kenya with a band of Wakamba, but both times he got away before I could reach him. I did not even know how he came by his name, or when I had first heard it, who told it to me or whether perhaps I had given it to him myself. He had never harmed me, but I knew without doubt that he could. (Not necessarily that he would, but I couldn't be sure.) I would have to kill him, or try to kill him—that was clear enough. Maybe he was up the Hassayampa. It would be his kind of country, as it was mine: empty and high and bleak, full of ruins and large animals.

The backstraps of the mastodon consumed, we searched for more meat. I knew there was a vast, warm lagoon only a short distance from the Hassayampa, near the foot of Mount Pyngyp, and that we were certain at this time of year, on this most southerly loop of the river, to find waterfowl there for our larder. Canvasbacks and blue-winged teal, mallards and sprig, perhaps a few brant or a family of Canada geese. We would not need skiffs or blinds or decoys or retrievers: the Hassayampans in this vicinity hunted their waterfowl the hard way. We would do the same, wading the lagoon up to our armpits amid the snakes and the caimans, flighting the birds with our gunfire and killing them high overhead in their panic.

We slogged through the swamp toward the lagoon, inhaling mosquitoes, spooking birds and snakes ahead of us, our boots accumulating the foul fecal mud with every step until our feet resembled the root balls of transplanted saplings. "It's only a little ways more," I said. "Anything for meat. Just think: Half a dozen fat mallards stuffed with wild celery turning on the spit! Goose liver! Tender little teal that we'll eat in two bites, bones and all!" My son grunted and spat out a mouthful of entomology.

The lagoon spread before us like hammered steel, its horizontal tension cut by sprays of spring-green reeds. We could hear the waterfowl gabbling: the gibberish of duck talk interrupted now and then by the crabby complaints of the geese. There was continuous motion over the lagoon. The family feuds of the duck folk—*Anas discors, Anas platyrhynchos platyrhynchos, Histrionicus histrionicus pacificus*—are open-ended, and always the subclans and cliques were flying away in high dudgeon, bitching as they sculled their

way through the air to another part of the swamp like
so many outraged in-laws. A duck in flight is always
in a sulk. "Okay," I said, "you wade on around there
to the right—take it slow and easy and look out for
the potholes. With all that ammo in your pockets,
you'll sink like the *Bismarck*. I'll ease on around to the
left. When I shoot, the ducks will get up all over the
lagoon. Wait until some of them start moving over
you and then cut loose. Pick up your dead and your
crips right away and stick their heads through your
belt loops, but keep your eyes peeled because they'll
keep coming as long as we keep shooting. And don't
worry about the snakes—they'll get out of your way."

He said okay and started moving off, with the warm
water already up to his belly button. I pushed into the
deeper water. It was like wading through a caldron of
live bouillabaisse: bluegills and tilapia spooked out of
the weeds; shoals of minnows and darters fled from
the bow wave of my chest.

For an hour we had splendid shooting. Never were
there fewer than a hundred ducks in the air, often as
many as a thousand—the Yeatsian antithesis, the
tightening gyre: a dozen teal caught between the
guns, their delicate formation shattered and shifting
to the impact of our chilled shot, turning inward and
inward until only three are left to wing it out low on
the deck, dodging to safety through the reeds.

I watched my son take a final double—mallards,
duck and drake—that swept in behind him as he retrieved a crippled teal. The boy heard their wing
beats, that zipper rip of ducks in full flight, and
wheeled to face them. The couple banked in panic,
but it was too late. *Pow, kapow!* and they folded,
bouncing and skipping upside down across the hard,
flat water. The drake lay finally on his back, his orange paddles flailing good-bye to the sky. When I
looked at him later, I saw that the shot had nipped off
the top of his skull, exposing the minuscule brain, and
his lower mandible dangled like a shoe tongue. The
boy held him high and grinned at me.

Wading back to our camp, we stopped to rest on a dry, brush-grown embankment. The sun was sloping down toward the slumped shoulders of Mount Pyngyp, and we admired its light on the iridescent blue specula of the dead ducks. A long snake slithered past us—the longest snake I had ever seen, until I saw that it was actually two snakes, one in pursuit of the other. They were of the same species—about four feet long, with green and tan lengthwise stripes and black masks on their oval (nonpoisonous) heads. *Ranera*—frog snakes. As the first snake raced up the branch of a low bush, the second snake raced up the first snake's back and locked its jaws behind the first snake's head. Instantly the snakes coiled around each other. I looked down the twist of snake bodies and saw that one of the snakes had a little serpentine pecker about three quarters of an inch long sticking out of his belly. It was a hard-on, sure enough, and he was trying to stick it into the other snake.

But which snake was doing it to which? I went back up to the heads and traced down the body of the snake that was holding the other in submission. Wouldn't you know it, he was the one with the pecker! He screwed for about ten minutes with slow, steady thrusts that sent undulations up his back clear to his jaws. When he came, a little ooze of snake semen bubbled out around his donglet. He released his partner, and she zipped away. The rapist shot his black tongue a few flicks and then did likewise. I sat there smiling, and then looked around to see how my son had taken it.

He had pulled a toy dump truck out of his game pocket and was *vroom*-ing it around in the mud, building a freeway around the butt of his shotgun where it leaned against a shrub.

It was too hot now for much travel during the middle of the day. The sun worked its way through the triple canopy of the rain forest like a gobbet of worms through a dung heap. The morning ground fog that turned the Hassayampa's coils into a pearly Turner seascape was devoured two hours after dawn by the warming sun. The fog was our ally, and we walked through it beaded and cool, laughing at the sudden, shocking *splat* of the drops that fell on us from the waxy riverside trees. But the laughter was tinged with hysteria. Through the trees, we could see the river moving under the rainbow gray of the fog, carrying mute messages of upstream disaster. A fragment of thatching from a hut built too close to the eroding bank. A shattered sampan. A dog so bloated with death that it might have been an ox, with its stiff legs poking upward like the toothpicks in some obscene plate of canapés. Once a dead man in green military fatigues, gone almost black with the river water, an amphibious vulture riding his belly as pompous as a sea captain. Through the fog, this flotsam appeared magnified, distorted into things monstrous, and at first my son clung close to me as we walked. But when the fog lifted and the imagined monsters resolved themselves into the merely dead, he grew bolder. He forged ahead and scouted out a level piece of ground where we could lie up during the heat of the day.

Yet as we lay there, in some cool bamboo thicket, dozing or absently watching the trotlines, I often wondered what was going on deep down in his head. Was the trip really toughening him, as I hoped it would? Or was the mix of rot and beauty too strong for him—would it ultimately put him off of the wilderness for good? I would let the thought twist slowly in my mind, a philosophical spirochete common to the male human parent.

Is my son a coward?

Why do you ask?

Because perhaps I myself am a coward?

How can you be a coward with all the chances you take?

Don't cowards often throw themselves in front of buses?

My son lies naked on his sleeping bag, his head propped against his pack frame, his body stained with fly dope and ridged with thorn cuts, lumpy with bug bites. But the disfigurations of the moment cannot disguise the fact that he is handsome.

The spirochete wriggles another quarter of a turn.

Too handsome?

Thick, dark hair that falls well below his ears in the androgynous style favored by his generation. Large, dark eyes. Long lashes—woman's lashes? A straight, almost delicate nose, over a cupid's bow mouth. The chin is strong enough; the neck long and thick; the shoulders wide; a flat, hard chest. Only a hint of the baby belly—a memory long gone before this trip is out? No hips to speak of, and well hung for his age. Long, straight legs that give promise of a man of size—legs strong enough to walk me into the ground.

Too handsome? Too graced, too blessed with the cosmetic virtues of this cosmetic age?

Will the women of his life murmur at his knees?

The sun crawls slowly over the river. The shadow of the bamboo crawls slowly over my son's sleeping body. What do I want him to be? I want him to be tough. Tough as well as beautiful. Is there a contradiction there? The bamboo is tough and beautiful. . . .

My son rolls over and wakes up. He listens to the Hassayampa gurgling at the edge of the bamboo, then walks over and urinates into the river. He stretches. He pulls in the trotlines and unhooks a string of peacock bass, caught on salamanders that he captured under the rotting logs of the riverbank.

"Why don't you clean the fish right now?"

"Naw," he says, yawning. "I'm still sleepy. All this heat, it really knocks me out. Anyway, I hate to put a knife in them when they're still fresh and flipping."

The first hint of a late-afternoon breeze is whispering upstream, a taste of walking weather. I open my knife and clean the fish. My thumb and fingers work deep into the gills, holding the fish in submission as the knife does its bloody work.

"Goddammit," I say to him, "I want you to brush your teeth—and right now!"

The more I thought of it, the more certain I became that I had indeed once met Ratnose—that, in fact, I had helped a friend of mine to kill him.

That was back in the old days, when I used to trap this stretch of the Hassayampa. It wasn't big-time trapping, of the sort one still finds in Canada and the mountain West, but it helped me to flesh out my fantasies. The only furbearers we took were muskrats, raccoons, opossums, and sewer rats. My trapping partner was a kid named Ron Fertig, a dirty-minded youth whose father was a renowned gynecologist. In those days, Ron and I always had sex on our minds. We lay in wait like tomcats for a chance to peek into one of his father's medical textbooks: flip it open to any page and there was a shaggy slot staring you in the face. All the women in the pictures, of course, were pregnant, and the contortions of their faces were those of labor, not lust. But we weren't looking at faces. "I Learned to Masturbate From a Medical Textbook!"

Trapping, I suppose, was our surrogate for snatch: we took pelts, literally. Mainly we trapped the sewer outlets of one of the Hassayampa's tributaries, the Menomonee. We looked for fresh sign in the mud at the culvert's mouth and then set a No. 1 or a No. 1½ steel trap along the run, covering the boiled steel with leaves that took no scent from our smoked leather gloves. During the noon hour we ran down through the fields from school and checked the traps. If there was an animal in the trap, we clubbed it to death with the nearest branch and skinned it out right there. Often the male raccoons would undergo an orgasm while they were being clubbed. The opossums and muskrats were too stupid to get any sexual thrill from death. The raccoon was the most consistent of the ani-

mals we trapped in biting through its own leg to escape. Ron and I both developed an affection for raccoons. Since it was impossible to release them, because
of their ferocity, and since we caught more raccoons
than any other furbearers, we soon gave up trapping.

But not before we had trapped the Hassayampa itself. Having heard that there were mink and otter in
plenty along the big river, we took a week of Christmas vacation to pack in and trap there. Neither of us
read the newspapers much at that time, but if we had
we might have known there would be trouble—human trouble—along the middle reaches of the Hassayampa. This was in the winter of a war year, and
the government was still cleaning up on the warlords
and bandits whose last stronghold was the moun-
tainous watershed of the river. A few bands of outlaws had drifted down to the wild, impenetrable bottoms of the Hassayampa not far from where we were
trapping.

We first became aware of the bandits late one gusty
afternoon while tending our traps along the river. The
sunset, obscured by fast, lean clouds, had turned the
snowy woods red and black. We were wet and cold,
our hands stiff as we prized the warm bodies of mink
from the steel. Then we heard horses snorting and
stamping. There were six of them, scrawny pinto ponies carrying scrawnier men dressed in cotton quilting
and rat skins, their rifles—those skinny, long-barreled
Jap .25s—slung muzzle down like broomsticks on
their backs. On one of the packhorses sat a prisoner, a
dark and flat-faced man with a bloody rag tied over
one ear under his leather cap. His hands were chained
to the high wooden pommel. Our only weapon, a .22
Colt Woodsman, was back at camp—Ron was afraid
of losing it in the river—and it was toward our camp
that the horsemen were proceeding.

"Maybe they won't see the camp," Ron whispered.
"And even if they do, maybe they won't find the pistol. I left it under my sleeping bag." We cached our
mink in a hollow tree, pissing on the trunk and the

ground around it to warn curious animals away. Then
we followed up the bandits' trail. They had found our
camp all right, and we watched from the woods, belly
down in the snow, as they devoured our furs, which
had been scrupulously salted down and were drying
on willow stretchers near the fire. The hungrier bandits ate the stiff hides fur and all, while the more fin-
icky shaved off the hair with their machetes. "Listen,"
said Ron: "they haven't looked in the tent yet. While
they're still eating, I'm going to sneak into the tent
and get the pistol."

It was getting dark fast now, and by using the
available brush and snowdrifts to good advantage,
Ron made it to the back of the tent. Then he pulled
his hunting knife and cut a slit in the tent wall just
opposite the head of his sleeping bag. He groped for a
long moment, and I saw that he had the gun. What he
did next I wasn't prepared for: after checking the
magazine and pulling the slide to put one round in
the chamber, he stepped out past the side of the tent
and leveled on the bandits. He had the lanyard
around his neck and the pistol extended at full arms'
length, both hands white-knuckled on the grip and
the bead smack on the forehead of the bandit leader.

"All right, you gooks!" he said. "Drop those furs and
put your fucking hands on your fucking heads." The
leader's jaw dropped open, his wispy beard quivering
with outraged disbelief. He had only one eye, but it
pierced us like a javelin. A few slippery clots of mink
fur spewed from his lips as he tried to speak. "Feelthy
gringos!"—and he started to rise. Ron popped him
through the throat (he hadn't followed up the man's
rise fast enough), and the bandit leader fell backward
over the log, vomiting mink the way a cat might a
bloody fur ball. Ron popped the next man through the
forehead. I ran over and grabbed one of the rifles
stacked near the drying rack to cover the others,
checking the Mauser action quickly and surreptitiously to make sure I understood it. The flat-faced
prisoner still sat his horse, hands chained to the pom-

mel and immobile except for the flapping of his hat brim in the wind.

"You speak English?" Ron asked him. "You want get freedom?" He pronounced the last word in two gong-like syllables. The man said yeah, he wouldn't mind getting loose, and that the bandit leader had the key to the lock in his upper breast pocket. I fetched the key; the bandit leader was nearly dead now, and besides puking blood all over his shirtfront, he had crapped his pants: the inoffensive little .22-caliber hollow soft point bullet must have fragmented on his neckbone and sent a needle of lead up into that portion of the brain that controls evacuation. Perhaps, in his last moments, he was reassuring himself with memories of the outhouse. I unchained the prisoner and handed him a rifle. He smiled briefly, flexed his wrists, and then shot one of the bandits through the lower abdomen. The bandit stepped back, hip-shot, and then sat down in the mud around the campfire, hissing softly. The remaining bandits tensed up, their eyes dancing away from the muzzle, then back to it again. "We'd better, you know," said Ron. We gunned down the rest of them then and there.

Still, it didn't bring back our mink pelts. The bandits had swallowed or badly gnawed every one of the hard-won furs before Ron got the drop on them. We dragged the bodies down to the Hassayampa, where the skunks and the crows would make short work of them before winter was out. The Indian told us his name was Johnny Black—Timmendequas in his native Wyandot: Black Lightning—and that the bandits had jumped him while he was jacking deer two days before up the river. "Obviously they heard the shot when I nailed a plump little doe," he said, "and tracked me back to camp. Since I knew the country, they decided to keep me for a guide rather than kill me out of hand." He paused and poked the fire, where a kettle of hunter's stew was simmering, then smiled rather playfully. "They weren't bad guys, you know. They were the enemies of the Chinese Communists—

real believers in the free-enterprise system. They sure had an appetite for mink. And free-dom."

Ron's mouth dropped open, just as the bandit leader's had before Ron shot him.

"Cripes," he said, "I thought all bandits were Commies."

We turned the ponies over to the Indian. He told us to drop by and see him anytime, he was beholden, and then we headed for home. The minks we had cached in the hollow of the tree had been discovered by a bold and voracious skunk; nothing was left but a few grease spots and a scattering of rich brown fur. All told, the expedition had proved unprofitable. We had not a single hide to show for our frigid work, and for months afterward I shot bandits in my dreams, bandits who refused to die. Worse yet, even the medical textbooks had lost their prurient charm. My sexual fantasies turned to slim teen-aged girls, where they lie, locked and writhing, even today.

A reading from Myerson's *History:* "The collusion of officialdom both here and abroad in keeping the mysteries—nay! the simple but delightful truths—of the Hassayampa from the public extends a civilized man's concept of modern criminality beyond the point of rupture. This marvelous river, marvelous in the true sense of the word, in that its indigenous wildlife far exceeds in variety and antiquity any existing on the Earth's other waterways, is denied even its proper name on the maps of the world's so-called 'geographical' societies. Peiping, though it admits the existence of a river called the H'sa Yang Po (Hassayampa) rising from the Kunlun massif, shows that river on its maps as a mere tributary of the Yangtse. No mention is made of the exotic reptilian life known to exist on the upper Hassayampa, nor of the immense profits which, according to the reports of the few European travellers who have penetrated beyond 'the forbidding face of Mount Pyngyp,' may be derived from the drugs and ivories extricable from the carcases of those 'dragons.'

"A recent enquiry directed to the League of Nations regarding the indefensible and no doubt calculated obscurity of the Hassayampa's promise elicited the following response: 'We have not been able to determine the location of the Hassayampa River, no more than we have that of the so-called South African Diamond Fields, lately so much in the news.' Proof enough of collusion!"

The woods along here were filled with the ruins of failed farms. Every mile or so we spotted a barn, leaning red and rickety in on itself, its roof cocked sideways, the tarred shingles flapping in the wind. Nearby would be a cellar built of fieldstone, with an iron stove flaking away its rusty half-life amid the shards of polished random-width floorboards. We often camped in an abandoned farmyard. There was an abundance of firewood, for one thing, and depending on the time of year, we might find asparagus or stray tomatoes—the latter sometimes green but still delicious when sliced and fried; or sweet corn that had outlived its planter's ambition; sometimes potatoes; and, in the fall, usually apples or pears, runty and worm-eaten but sweet. Woodchucks felt the same way we did about the abandoned orchards, so now and then we shot a couple under the trees where they rooted in the buzzing fruit rot and had roast groundhog for dinner, stuffed with sliced apples. We always built our fire in the lee of a stone wall, and leaned back in the reflecting heat while the meat popped and sizzled over the burning floorboards. I wondered about the women who had polished those floors and sweated their dainty sweat into them year after mindless year: perhaps the fire burned blue and brighter because of that salty, pointless effort.

My uncle and I had hunted birds and deer up here when the farms were still working. He knew many of the farmers and had defended them in court back in the days when the railroad was trying to buy up the countryside along the Hassayampa in anticipation of a major China trade. My uncle claimed that he had won nearly half the suits, and in the other half had usually gotten the farmers a better-than-average settlement for their land. Then one night a railroad goon squad had caught him on the River Road and broken his leg as an earnest of their belief in monopoly rights.

"They built a roadblock that consisted of an old LaSalle sedan and six railroad ties," he told me. "I was too dumb to double back, and when I stopped they didn't even wait to talk. They dragged me to the railroad ties, laid my ankle over the top of them, and cut loose with a tire iron on my kneecap. Fortunately, it was my right leg they hit, so when I dragged myself back into the car I could still lay the weight of my foot on the gas pedal and work the clutch and the brake with my left. That got me home, and it kept me out of court against the railroad from then on."

It seemed to me my uncle had said that the leader of the goon squad had worn a fur coat . . . Ratanous? I could not be certain of my memory, but if it had been Ratanous, that would place him on the upper Hassayampa after my first encounter with him. A chilling thought. I threw some more floorboards on the fire and took comfort in reason: how could I be certain it had been Ratnose? I might very well have added the fur-coated goon leader to my uncle's story; childhood memories are imprecise; they overlap and cross-fertilize one another; there is no Ratanous, only my imagination.

But then, why do I have this clean, hard certainty that I must kill him?

12

We were lonely now. Two weeks on the river with only ourselves for company—it was time for a town and some different people. We broke from the river and hiked north over the Porcupine Mountains, a day's march. From the height of land that formed the watershed, we could see a big lake spreading like a rain cloud and the town flashing its windows at us in the late-afternoon sun. The woods gave way to pastures, then to barbed wire and surly polled cattle. We thumbed a ride into town in the back of a pickup truck that smelled of pigs, but to our socially deprived nostrils it was the best of domestic cologne. "Do you know where Hasslich lives?" I asked the farmer when he let us off. "Otto Hasslich, the old Kraut?"

"Yeah," the man said, "but you're bound to find him in Tilly's over there." He pointed to a tavern just up the main street. "Hasslich's always in there on a Saturday night." We hadn't known it was Saturday. We walked over to the tavern. Two dogs were screwing in the parking lot, and the male—a scruffy-maned orange chow—looked over at us and rolled his eyes, his purple tongue lolling happily out of his grin. It was the first time I had ever seen a chow smile. My son asked me what they were doing and I replied with the Noel Coward line: "The one in front just went blind, and its friend is pushing it to the eye doctor's."

The tosspots in the alehouse were watching a rerun of *Green Acres*, scratching their asses and yukking it up. Hasslich was at the end of the bar trying to make out with a woman the size of a steamer trunk. His clean, ruddy, ancient face gleamed with sincerity, only to be called a liar by his weedy white moustache. The woman chuckled at his pleas and removed his horny hand from her crotch as if she were discarding

a Tampax. I slapped Hasslich on the back and asked
him how were his *Wie geht's*. *"Na ja, der junge Grac-
chus!"* he cried, "what brings you again to the North
Country?" I told him that my son and I were prospect-
ing for uranium—*Oranien*—up in the Porcupines,
and that we'd come into town to register a tailing
we'd found. "No money in uranium," he said with a
sniff. "Have a beer! Better yet, have a shot and a
beer!"

Otto had been a boatswain in the Kaiser's navy during the Great War, and later was briefly married to
my mother's mother. Perhaps he had not actually
been married to her, but everyone in the relationship
maintained that he had. They remembered him as a
cruel, miserly autocrat whose favorite admonition to
my mother and her sister and brothers was: *"Ich bin
der Baas; du bist die Rotznase."* I'm the boss; you're
the snot-nose. Too mean and nasty to be tolerated in a
city, Hasslich had built himself a cabin in the woods
on the edge of the Porcupine forest. I had visited him
there years before. The interior of the cabin resembled the crew's quarters in his old ship, the battle
cruiser *Frauenlob:* tidy, compact, smelling of clean
steel and the onions festooned on the ceiling (Otto
was boss now only to the onions and spuds he raised
in the sour soil of the Porcupine watershed). He had
a hammock; a table that folded neatly against the
bulkhead; an icebox chilled by gritty blue blocks of
ice which Otto himself sawed out of a nearby pond.
At the top of a ladder leading to an alcove at one end
of the compartment was a wooden crapper with a galvanized tin bucket under the handcarved wooden
seat. Otto was a firm believer in the utility of night
soil. Though he was nearing eighty, he still came to
town once a month to get laid. "Draws off the poison,"
he said with a wicked little smile.

While Otto talked of the onion crop and refought
the Battle of Jutland, I sipped my brandy and beer,
enjoying as always the easy hopsy atmosphere of a
Saturday-night saloon. My son munched a cheeseburg-

er and watched teevee. The woman's name was Helgard the Laundry Widow. "My *Kinder* all went off to Ishpeming," she related with an air of regret. "My husband sawed a tree down on himself." The Germans will have even their tragedies in the proper order. But she was a handsome woman, though over fifty—solid and ripe, with a scent of laundry soap and woman sweat, and her mammoth tits looked as firm as a brace of biceps. "Show him how you box with them," said Otto proudly. Making sure the bartender wasn't looking, she lifted her blouse and threw a jab with her left tit, then a quick right cross with the other. A few long black hairs fringed the aggressive aureoles. I felt my pecker stiffening: we'd been in the woods too long. "I saw a stripper once in Saint Louis who could counterrotate her tits," I told the woman, "but I never saw anything like that. What else can you do?" Otto said that she could shoot a Ping-Pong ball clear across the street if you aimed her cunt properly. She blushed but didn't deny it. I had a sudden dark image of Otto aiming her like the Kaiser's cannon.

Drunk enough and lonely enough, one will diddle anything, so after a few more brandies and beer I found myself bird-dogging Otto's old lady. "Listen," I said finally, "why don't we go over to Helgard's laundry and have us a little orgy?" I pronounced it with a hard g so that they would understand. Otto seemed doubtful. "Look," I told him, "you're too old to make it more than once, if that. If I'm along, we can at least give her, you know, a decent hosing." We left the boy watching the tube and walked over to the laundry, which was just across the street from the movie theater. *Billy the Kid Meets Frankenstein's Daughter.* I belched and tasted the beer bubbles in my nostrils; the brandy roughhoused behind my eyes. The laundry smelled warm and fresh, illuminated by the hard white light of the marquee across the way, the shirts and sheets and pillowcases on the sorting table filigreed with indecipherable blue shadows. Helgard stripped and lay back on the table, her firm, broad cheeks glowing red as Otto messed with her muff. I sat on a mound of gravy-stained business suits and sipped from the pint of peppermint *Schnapps* we had brought along.

Otto was having an old man's problem getting it up, but then he took a boatswain's pipe from his shirt pocket and began blowing reveille. *Tooo-eee . . . toooooooooo-eeeeeeeeee-ooooo* . . . As his pecker slowly awoke from its wrinkled lethargy ("What the fuck's happening?—I ain't got the watch until the four-to-eight"), I noticed that it was tattooed like a barber's pole. It expanded further and I recognized the faded, frowning visage of Lloyd George tattooed on the glans.

Then Otto removed his shirt and I saw that he had a hunter tattooed on his chest. The hunter was leaning over Otto's shoulder and shooting down his back at a tattooed rabbit which was just about to disappear down Otto's asshole. The rabbit gazed apprehensively at the muzzle of the shotgun.

When Otto finally came, the shotgun went *pow!* and the rabbit tumbled dead and kicking onto the laundry table. At the report, placid Helgard flew into a rage. "I tell you how oft not to do that?" she shrilled as she thrust the old man away from her. "Now you mess up my shirts and linen again!"

Thus ended our orgy.

We left Helgard muttering, elbow deep in suds and wet wash. As we walked back to the saloon, Otto handed me the dead rabbit as a consolation prize. Its face bore an uncanny resemblance to the late Admiral Beatty, Victor of Jutland. A few droplets of blood were beaded on the whiskers, and the face looked ineffably sad, with inky little wisdom wrinkles weeping from the eyes. "Who did this tattoo work?" I asked Otto. "It's damned good."

He sighed and smiled. "Some old Chink on the Reeperbahn in Hamburg," he said. "You can't get a good military tattoo anymore, and that's a rotten shame. With good art, there is no defeat."

Back in the saloon, my son was leaning with his elbows on the bar writing something on the back of a napkin. He had the stub of a black cheroot in his teeth and a glass of draft beer in front of him. His cap was cocked over his eye like a pool-hall tough's. "I was thinking about when I caught my first bass, and how it nearly pulled me into the pond, and how Uncle Henry helped me land it," he said. "Then I got thinking about how the Visigoths killed Uncle Henry and I wrote down this poem."

> *Silens is not much of a city.*
> *Not like the city of laghter*
> *Or the city of noise.*
> *But silenc is dieing.*
> *Noise and laghter are taking over.*
>
> *Silens is Bleak jagged peaks,*
> *Dull grey colors.*
> *But once it was noisy,*
> *Then it died.*
> *But silence is getting rare.*

I told him it was a nice poem. "Yeah," he said.

We spent the night in Hasslich's barn, warmed by burlap sacks in the hayrick, and awoke to the calling of bobwhite quail at daybreak. Otto was already out in the onion fields. We could see him scuttling erratically along the rows, a blueblack insect working a weedy menace through the light ground fog. While I fried the rabbit on Otto's wood stove, my son split pine chunks in the barnyard, pausing between strokes of the ax to whistle back and forth with the quail. *Bob-white! Bob-bob-white!* Then the flash of the ax blade, and the white wood opening as easily as a prayer book.

This was the loneliest morning of the trip so far. I had dreamed of home, and awakening, I felt my guts jellied with the memory. The heads of animals adorned the walls—a waterbuck from Africa, an elk from Montana—staring down dolefully, forever, the essence of homecomings gone. A bright morning outside, with birdsong and the trout moving in the stream behind the house, rising now and then to a wayward fly. In the dream, I could hear the garden growing: bush beans, kohlrabi, dill, beets, sorrel, peas, radishes expanding toward the cracking point underground. The weeds taking over. My asparagus patch, dug at such great sweat, stalking uncut toward the sky. My wife, in league with other women, was letting it all go to seed.

She had said, when we left: "I know you can't take me along, but why not take your daughter? She loves to fish; she can shoot a gun; she loves the woods and the river."

I could not answer her with logic. I muttered something about the "dangers" of the river and then turned ferocious to prevent further questioning. But I remembered an incident that made it clear, in my own mind at least, why my lovely, learned daughter could not make the trip.

It was a sunny, dry morning, first light, and my girl was only three. She woke up and saw the day, and she wanted to get out into it. My wife and I were sleeping, so she chose not to disturb us. She opened the front door of the house and walked out into the morning. I can imagine it: a low and silvery sun, the dew cool on her bare brown feet, birds racketing in the early light, and the land empty, sleeping all around. But when she returned to the door, it was locked. She could not get back in to bed and love . . .

I woke up that morning hearing her sobs outside the door. At first I couldn't tell what it was—a strange bird singing? But I went to the door and found her there, crying sadly to herself on the front porch, certain that she had locked herself out of heaven forevermore. I picked her up and said some hearty things. I fixed her a good breakfast—but it was too late. From then on she was tied to the house, to her room, to her dolls and toys and records and her womanness.

Another time, fishing, she had hooked herself on a lure, through the skin of her thigh. I pushed the hook through and clipped it off at the barb. She never cried through the whole ordeal, but she looked at me gravely. She lived in her own world, and it was not the world of the Hassayampa. . . .

And at this moment, the world of the Hassayampa looked pretty frightening to me, too. This would be a good time to turn back. After all, we had killed enough fish and game to justify the journey. I was lonely for my wife and my daughter, for my house, my trophies, my garden. I was even lonely for my dogs—the big yellow retriever with his happy grin and my stupid, quick pointer with his empty eyes and his liver-colored nose that could tell where I had been, could interpret every meal I had eaten, by a simple sniffing of my moustache after a week-long trip. I wanted it all, now. Bed, talk, hugs, kisses, pats

on the head, possession, the foods we all liked together, the roles we so enjoyed playing with each
other: daddy, mommy, loving daughter, faithful son,
honest servant, even though canine. Ahead there was
none of that.

"Let's eat," my son said, slamming the ax into the
chopping block. "Time's a-wastin', and the river is a
long way off." We ate the rabbit and left the stack of
firewood as repayment to Otto for his hospitality. The
quail sang as we walked away.

We angled up through the Porcupines on an old mining road, aiming to rejoin the Hassayampa far to the west of where we had left it, thus avoiding the crags and billygoat trails of the Hsien-ho Gorges. As a boy I had often canoed this stretch of the river during the spring runoffs. My friends and I would take our departure from the railhead at Boxley, on the Buffalo River southwest of the Gorges, then drop down the Buffalo under the dripping limestone cliffs and flurries of falling dogwood blossoms until we reached the Hassayampa just above the beginnings of white water. It took half a day to run the Gorges—a wet, cold millrace in the shadow of the crags with tombstones under the eyelid and flashes of sunlight splintering on the mica as we skidded our way through the rapids—but it took three days to line our canoes back up. I had no desire to walk those slippery cliffs again, even without a canoe to drag behind me. Our return trip would be another matter. Perhaps we could trade for a canoe or a bullboat up near the Hassayampa's headwaters. Even a light sampan would do if the water was high enough.

The mining track we followed over the Porcupines had eroded in places into matching, man-deep gullies; catbrier and popple had reclaimed much of the road where it ran through the wet bottomlands. We jumped a few ruffed grouse dusting in the warm, dry ruts on the sunny slopes, and my son dropped two of them for our supper: clean kills as the birds rose roaring from the dust with that sprint-car acceleration that stops the heart and then folded to the report of the 20-gauge, tumbling with legs and primary feathers agrasp as if to clutch for the last time some invisible ladder in the air. I picked up one of the birds and pressed my face into the hot bronze-and-gunmetal feathers of its ruff, inhaling the last of its energy. "Sometimes when you're hunting without a dog you can smell them before they jump," I told the boy. "It's a hot, musky smell like someone sweating from hard work, only drier. As if all that potential energy created a kind of aura, and when you walk into the edges of it you can feel the hair rise on the back of your neck." The boy looked at me: Wow, the old man is really queer for birds. To confirm his suspicions, I licked a drop of blood from the down-curved beak.

With the black-barred grouse fans tucked into our hatbands to dry, and the skinned carcasses of the birds themselves cooling as they dangled from our belts, we hiked on, two lummoxes playing at Mountain Man. That night, leg-weary and crisp with a caking of dust and dried sweat, we camped on the banks of a stream that drained into the Hassayampa. We stoned ourselves on its icy water, then stripped and swam away the day's grime. My son found a cartridge case wedged in the rocks on the bottom of our camp pool: a .44 Magnum. "Who the hell would shoot that heavy a round in this country?" he asked as we warmed up again beside the campfire. A potful of grouse and rice stewed on the dingle stick.

"There used to be wild cattle in this country," I told him. "Not the longhorns that you still find out West, but the giant aurochs—the ancestor of all our domestic cattle. They stood about ten feet tall at the shoulder, and you needed a big soft bullet with plenty of foot-pounds to drop them. Back before the uranium miners came into this country, there was still a good-sized herd of them in the Porcupines. I had a buddy named Moonbeam whose folks had a cabin up here, over near Kurlander, and we used to hunt them.

"Moonbeam was a big kid, about six foot three, with kinky hair and a wide, I'm-a-dummy grin plastered on this round face of his and . . ."

"Yeah-yeah," said my son. "Get on with the hunting part. You're like a war movie where they give you all the training and character development and love interest and then only ten minutes of action at the end."

"Listen," I said, "I don't have to tell you this story at all. That's the trouble with you kids today—you want instant action, and when the world gives you a little bit of detail around the action you get bored and start shooting up. You think that killing is a simple act. The right weapon at the right place in the right cause. Well, it isn't. Killing is one of the most difficult things you can do—even more complex than love, because with love you create the potential for more love. With killing, the whole affair takes place in a few moments—a whole life in the crack of a trigger. Okay, end of editorial. Where was I?"

"You were making a short story long."

"Yeah, Monty Moonbeam and the Giant Ox. You've never seen Kurlander and you never will, because the whole town burned down a long time ago in a forest fire. When the fire came into town, the people tried to save themselves by wading out into the river up to their necks, but the fire storm ate up all the oxygen in town and they suffocated anyway. For weeks afterward the river kept disgorging bug-eyed corpses with the hair and eyebrows singed off.

"It was the winter before the fire when Moonbeam and I drove up to Kurlander in his 1934 Ford sedan to hunt the giant aurochs. Six feet of snow on the ground—the woods looked like a bed of green crocuses poking up through the snow, and the muskegs that would suck you down in the summer like a trout might a mayfly were frozen stiff. Which was just fine for our purposes. You hunted these wild oxen on snowshoes, running on top of the stuff while the bulls with their sharp, narrow legs had to wallow through it by main force. It was easy enough to wear them down; then you shot the poor bastards through the spine so as not to mess up the trophy. The hard part was dressing them out in the snow; the blood froze on our mittens, and the heavier cuts of meat tended to melt out of sight. But the hardest part was dragging the meat and the trophy out of the woods on a tobog-gan—those horns were six feet from point to point, and one point or the other always snagged in the undergrowth and tipped the toboggan. But we took strength from the smell of blood.

"When we got into Kurlander, for what proved to be our last hunt, it was already dark. We stopped at the pool hall for a beer and a bratwurst. Most of the people in Kurlander were Finns—the sons and grandsons of the loggers who had cut down the old white pine forest fifty years earlier. Sallow, scrawny, surly, with those bulbous foreheads that make you think of poisonous mushrooms. I'll tell you this, though: they handled their pool cues as neatly as their ancestors handled an ax or a peavey hook. There was an old man sitting in the corner with scabs for eyelids and snot caked on his whiskers—Blind Herman; he'd blown out his eyeballs with a blasting cap while dynamiting stumps years before. Moonbeam went over to talk to him. 'Monty,' the old man said, 'you're growing taller than the trees!' He was feeling his way up Moonbeam like you might if you had to turn on a floor lamp in the dark.

"Blind Herman told us that a real trophy bull had his harem yarded up in a tamarack swamp not far from Moonbeam's cabin. The local boys hadn't killed it yet because they were still getting over their Christmas hangovers. 'Crazy Joe will show you the place,' the old man said. 'I'll send him over to you in the morning, before first light.' Crazy Joe was a younger man who took care of Blind Herman—a loony who had gotten that way when a bull tossed him and stomped on his head as he was crossing a pasture, coming home drunk one night from a dance. As a result, Crazy Joe was still drunk and always would be. That part of it was all right, as far as I was concerned, but every now and then he would launch into a polka —hard going to those who followed him on snowshoes.

"We had to leave the car on the highway and hike in to Moonbeam's cabin—the tote road hadn't been plowed—and the cabin was so cold that it took a cord of firewood, three blankets apiece, and a pint of gin to get to sleep. The last thing I saw as I dozed off was the stained-glass eye of a mounted aurochs winking at me in the firelight.

"Crazy Joe came mushing up out of the dark as we were frying ham for breakfast. He was short, swart, and jolly, bellowing the Beer Barrel Polka at the top of his lungs, belching and farting until the icicles cracked from his moustache. 'Monty,' he said, 'you growin taller dan da trees!' I figured that that was what they said to you in the Kurlander country when they wanted you to feel good.

"While we were getting our guns and gear together, Crazy Joe staggered around the cabin, still in his snowshoes, hiccuping and singing in a slurred lush's voice. Now he was singing 'Show Me the Way to Go Home.' Then he went on a crying jag: something about his poor old ma—that nobody ever understood her. I offered him a slug of gin, but he turned it away with a broad gesture of the hand, his lower lip extended in self-righteousness. 'Never touch the stuff,' he said. 'Drunk enough without it, hic!' Then he got his snowshoes stuck in the doorway. He acted drunk, but he sure didn't smell it.

"It took us about an hour of heavy hiking to reach the swamp where the aurochs were yarded up: first over the lake, where the snow was compact and frozen like waves and squeaked under our snowshoes until I thought we would spook every living thing out of the country for miles around; and then into the tamaracks, where the snow was deep and quiet but the going was harder. It was getting on towards first light, and we saw sign in the snow where an owl had taken a grouse. There was a perfect imprint of the grouse's body in the snow, wings and fan spread, and then overlaid on that the wide kind of fingertip prints where the owl's wings had hit the snow. The owl must have knocked the grouse off the limb where it was roosting and then hooked it just as it hit the snow, and then flown off with it. Monty and I circled around the mark—it was too beautiful to wreck with our snowshoe prints—but Crazy Joe lost his balance in his drunken way and stepped on it. He sniveled a bit and kept saying, 'Sorry, boys, sorry, boys,' until Monty told him to shut up, we didn't want to spook the aurochs.

"We heard the aurochs before we saw them. It was that cowlike whuffling that you hear when you go into the barn at dawn to milk them, but it bore as much relation to the whuffling of domestic cattle as a lion's purr does to a house cat's. We could see steam rising in rings and wreaths from the herd, as if someone was holding a convention of extinct locomotives down there in the swamp. We could see the heads and horns of the bigger cattle, and the enormous head and horns of the bull weaving kind of slowly blue and boulder-like in the middle of the yard, and over it all this *chuff-chuff-chuff* sound, and the steam rising.

"The trick to hunting those bastards was to seal off the alleys that led out of the yard, and then to stampede them before they could see you. What we usually did was to locate the alleys and build fires in them—there were only two or three alleys at the most—and the smoke from the fires would panic the herd and send them stumbling into the deep snow, where you could run them down. That we did on this fine rosy morning, with the frost ticking in our nostrils and the pine smoke drifting down to mingle with the steam of the wild cattle. They went off through the tamaracks with us in pursuit, stumbling and cursing.

"Monty and I had rifles—my Model 94 Winchester and his .300 Savage—but Crazy Joe had only a lance, the traditional weapon of the country: a wide two-foot-long carbon-steel blade mounted on a peeled maple sapling. Monty and I each managed to put a round into the big bull's hump as he went wallowing through the drifts with his head swinging from side to side, staring back at us with eyes like fog lamps, but then the bastard gave us the slip in the alders at the edge of the swamp. Joe stayed behind as we worked into the purple alder jungle. Unfortunately, they were the same color as the bull, so we had to take our time, he being still fresh and likely to be lying up in ambush anywhere in the thicket. Then we heard Joe yelling and the bull whuffling behind us—the bastard had circled, as they sometimes do—and went flip-flopping back out as fast as we could, the snowshoes inevitably getting stuck again and again in the thick alder stubs.

"By the time we got out, the bull had punched Joe down into the snow about six feet deep. All we could see was his snowshoes, broken, with the webs all tangled, waving on either side of the bull's muzzle. The bull looked up as we came out, and Monty put a hollow soft point right up his snot locker—a great splat of blood and mucus—and the bull reared back and died without a moan. Joe's lance had bent against the bull's shoulder blade: so much for primitive weapons.

"Fortunately, the man himself wasn't bent near as badly. When we dug him out, we found he had only a couple of cracked ribs and a few hoofprints on his forehead where the bull had trampled him. The soft snow had saved his life. On a hard surface, the bull would have mashed Joe flat. We butchered the bull out with the ax and meat saw we had brought along and then wrapped Joe in the hot, bloody hide and dragged the whole reeking lot back on the toboggan. Joe kept mumbling, 'My God, he was taller dan da trees, taller dan da trees.'

"The funny thing was, from that day on Joe wasn't crazy drunk any more. The stomping he'd gotten from the aurochs had snapped him out of it. But as the winter wore along, he got surlier and surlier—even when he chug-a-lugged a bottle of *Schnapps* he couldn't get drunk. The next summer he went off into the woods alone, out to the west of Kurlander. It was from that direction that the great forest fire came burning a few weeks later, the fire that wiped out the town. Monty often wondered if Joe hadn't set it on purpose, out of resentment for anything that was taller than the trees."

My son blinked at the end of the story, not having realized there could be any such connection. We ate the stew and read for a while in our sleeping bags, and then spun out into the deepest corners of sleep.

15

In the evenings, I found myself thinking more and more about Ratanous. It seemed to me that I had read many books about him, years before. At the time, I didn't take them seriously—they seemed like just so many pages of amusement. Now they were anything but amusing: the man might attack us at any moment. Or so it seemed in the dark, with the wind howling high in the trees beyond the campfire. I wrote down some of the titles of books I had read that might have been about Ratnose:

>Ratnose the Relevant
>Ratnose & The Pillars of Wisdom
>The Beasts of Ratnose
>Ratnose's Wanderings in Africa
>Ratnose: Eye of the Woods
>Ratnose & The River Demons
>The Jungle Tales of Ratnose
>Ratnose: The War Years (1914-1921)
>Hilda, Daughter of Ratnose
>The Guns of Ratnose
>Ratnose's Revenge
>Ratnose Goes Beatnik
>The Way of Ratnose
>Run, Ratnose, Run!
>Commodore Ratnose
>Ratnose at the Circus
>The "Other" Ratnose
>Ratnose Meets the Press
>The Complete Short Novels of Ratnose
>Ratnose on Hunting & Fishing

That was as far as I got with the list. I think Myerson wrote most of them, fictionalizing from legends rampant on the Hassayampa in the late nineteenth century, and after his death the ongoing saga was picked up by his daughter, Leona Myerson Peterman. The books were immensely popular during the first half of this century, but fell out of favor with librarians after the war. My son, at least, could never find them in the children's section of our local library. Though I don't think he looked that hard.

16

I woke at first light thinking of my wife. Somehow, she and I were on the same clock. It happened over and over: when I came back from a trip she'd say, "I woke up at five-thirty Wednesday and couldn't get back to sleep; I just tossed and turned." As well she might, for at eleven-thirty the previous evening in Kirun or Helsinki I had turned down a whore's proposition and retired righteously to think of hers. Now it was the butt end of night, the peepers creaking, and I had my wife's titprints on my bowels, the invisible imperception of her warm curple fading from my hairy belly, when I heard the horse snort.

I shuddered out of the warm memory into cold fear: Ratnose!

Then the horse snorted again—a kind of gentle wheeze from the same direction. I lay back on the sleeping bag and waited. The fire was barely glowing under a blanket of ash. The light came very gradually, as it will at daybreak under normal skies, like water mixing slowly into an ink bottle. Green, then yellow, with the blackness not exactly fading but rather disasserting itself in the manner of a mother weaning an insistent child. Black and white together. The outlines of the hills back of the Hassayampa took shape. Movement on the ridge. A horselike figure, importunate, pawing and neighing. Pronged.

"There's a unicorn up there on the ridge," I told my son when he awoke. His eyes cleared of sleep; he reached for the Luger. I nodded approval, and he bellied his way into the bushes, shedding his sleeping bag like a cocoon. I listened for a while, watched longer, but heard nothing. Then I dozed off again. . . .

I awoke to the shot, two shots, and then stoked up the fire with a few pine stubs left over from the night before. The water was hissing when he returned, stumbling naked down the hill with the Luger spinning in easy gun-fighter loops and counter-loops from his trigger finger. He flicked his long hair out of his eyes with the gunsight.

"Wasn't worth the powder," he said as he pulled on his pants. "They're supposed to have gold horns and stay put only for virgins. I reckoned that I could score on the last account, but when I threw down on her, she only smiled. 'I'm a tinhorn unicorn,' she said. 'Born during the Depression. My folks dint have no bread.' She was nice-looking sure enough, and we had a nice talk, but she wasn't worth the powder."

"Then why did you shoot twice?" I asked him.

"Wolves," he said. He put down the Luger on my sleeping bag. "Where's the coffee?"

17

We had run short of food, and the land was spare of game. Even the Hassayampa had nothing easy to offer. My son turned over a downed tree and extracted three weak leafworms from the rancid soil—two of the worms broke in half as he tugged at them. The river here was strangely patterned: feeder streams came in at direct, ninety-degree angles to the main flow, which at this point was slow and stagnant. The water looked olive with algae, slippery. It smelled like those old cars you sometimes find away off in the woods, wondering how anyone ever had the nerve, much less the roads, to get them there; kind of a stale plastic scent—"fusty, peanut-smelling," Sylvia Plath called it.

"Worms ought to get 'em if they're here," my son said with confidence. He slipped the longest of the worms onto a No. 10 hook and flipped it squirming into the current, or what little current we imagined. Nothing. He jigged the worm a bit and reeled in. Stop. Nothing.

The sky had been heavy with strange smells all day long. Now it smelled of hot dogs—perhaps our hungry imaginations? Old grease, the puke of a drunk.

"Where are we?" my son asked.

I thought about that for a minute, maybe more. I knew I'd never been on this stretch of the Hassayampa before, yet it seemed familiar. Then I remembered . . .

"Oh, yeah. Wait a sec." I dug around, groggy, inside the big pack and came up with a tan plastic lure box. "Take that worm off of there and try one of these. They're special for this part of the river."

My son reeled in and looked at the worm. It was soggy, dead, unnipped, already rotten.

"Cut off the hook and tie a snap swivel on there," I said. He did. Then I handed him the first lure: it was an electric-blue Camaro Z-28 with a gold racing stripe, B. F. Goodrich steel-belted street radials, an STP sticker on the right rear windshield, and a pimply blond teen-age driver in a T-shirt that read SHYTTE in Old English script, the whole lure measuring only two inches in length and weighing three quarters of an ounce, exclusive of the stainless-steel treble hooks that dangled fore and aft. The young fellow who was driving looked bored.

"Why the stainless on a freshwater lure?" my son asked.

"You'll see when you try this water," I said, "if you haven't smelled it already. Now just flip it out there into the feeder stream and bring it in fast along the bank, with a lot of jigging motion. When you get to the corner here where the feeder hits the Hassayampa, snap it on around and reel in at top speed until the lure is about six feet away from the rod tip. Then let it sink."

He flipped the lure up into the feeder stream. As he reeled in, twitching the rod tip as he retrieved, I could hear the faint squeal of tires underwater. Like hearing street rodders dragging on the state highway ten miles off in the fog before dawn; almost like foxes barking in the spring when you're camped out away from the roads, but not that far away, and the chickens are still clucking over the ridge, the screech owls hunting along the ravine, and you can't tell in your slumber if it's really foxes barking or just chickens or hunting owls or kids laying rubber over on the State.

The water was too opaque to see if he had a follow, but when the angle of the line said the lure was at the corner where the feeder hit the Hassayampa, my son snapped it around and cranked furiously; then he let the lure sink. Then—*bang!* A terrific hit. I could hear the *clank* of the metal, the explosions of tiny Police Specials, whines and sirens, a far cry of pain. My son struck, struck again, and the rod tip bent. Line screamed off the reel, stopped, screeched, stopped; then the line began moving in toward the bank. My son reeled in fast, keeping the pressure on, angling the rod from his wrist, and pretty soon there was a splashing in the dusk under the bank. I netted it.

A Plymouth Fury II squad car, fully four and a half pounds in weight and about nineteen inches long, maybe twenty. Hooked solidly in the right front tire. The green lettering, NYPD, was almost obscured by the algae that had grown scumthick on the cream band of its background. The two cops had already split, but the pimply kid in the lure was slumped awkwardly out of the Camaro's shattered window. The rear end of the Camaro was bent up so that the spoiler kissed the radio antenna, and the pimply kid's teeny-tiny feet were bent against the fire wall. The engine in the Fury was still growling, so when I unhooked it, I slammed the car against a rock. The car shuddered and went quiet. A couple of shotguns fell out, each about as long as a toothpick.

"Well," said my son, "the lure is wrecked, and I don't see how we can eat a cop car."

"Okay," I said, "but it was a good, game fight, wasn't it?"

"Sure, but I'm hungry." He kicked the dead police car back into the river, where it caught among the weeds and then floated, belly up.

"Try this," I told my son. I handed him a two-ounce, slightly chewed Yellow Cab with a treble hook mounted on the front bumper. "Just cast as far as you can and retrieve quick."

Inside a minute, he had three wiggling pedestrians on the hook, none of whom put up much of a fight. One was a girl in a patent-leather suit, hooked lightly through the lip, so we released her. The other two—a banker and a hippie—we put on the stringer. On the next three casts, we added a spade pimp, an elevator inspector, the clubfooted editor of a monthly insurance-company newsletter, and three prostitutes, all of them plump and well over the legal size limit.

Switching to a feathery, quarter-ounce dildo, we caught two faggots and a tiny old lady who said her father was or had been a candlestick maker.

"I don't know if we should keep the hookers," my son said.

"We'll boil them," I told him.

"What about the elevator dude?"

"I'm told that they're edible."

By the time it was dark, the stringer was thrashing in the black water. I dressed out the catch on the bank, working the knife in mostly by feel, then cutting up to the point of the chin. A secondary pair of cuts along the outer opercle, then a quick rip downwards removed the entrails neatly. I left the reeking innards on the bank for the carrion dragons. Or maybe the mink.

"That Yellow Cab lure is dynamite for small stuff," my son said as we walked back up through the dark toward camp. "Why do they hit so good on that?"

"They feel they have to run across the stream ahead of it," I said. "They're always in a hurry when they see a cab coming down the street. It's a status thing—dangerous. Some of them actually suck other ones out in front of the cab, like Judas goats, unconsciously of course, but the effect is the same as if they were planning to kill. The ones who follow the unconscious leaders think it's safe, and then—zip—the hook in the front of the cab snags 'em. It's not really sporting, in a river like this, but we're hungry, right? You noticed that the only one who really hit at the cab was that chick in the leather, on the first cast? The one hooked through the lip? Well, we might have made a mistake letting her go—she might very well breed a whole new school of pedestrians who hate cabs, who try and avoid them. But I like to let them go when they're game."

We walked on into the dark, cursing as we barked our shins on boulders, whimpering when we ripped our arms and faces on the briers. Then we reached camp and my son got the fire going. I peeled and boiled the pedestrians and skimmed off the goop from the top of the pot (it smelled like turpentine), and we dined al fresco. With the fish course we had Jerusalem artichokes, dug only the previous day, sliced and quick-boiled in popping water, Japanese style. Then a cup of tea, a smoke, the fire dying into that web of red and gray that broadens into sleep.

"Why don't they take worms?" my son asked, finally, just before we dozed off.

"You can't run across the street ahead of an oncoming worm," I yawned. "No virtue in it."

18

Back in the days of the Mao Mao Emergency, the government surreptitiously organized bands of hunters, trappers, and retired military men to track down and kill the insurrectionists on the upper Hassayampa. Members of these "pseudogroups," as they were euphemistically called, became masters of disguise, sometimes to the point of psychological confusion. They wore the slouch hats and surplus army greatcoats affected by the insurrectionists—those long, olive-drab woolen cloaks under which each man packed a Sten gun and a razor-sharp kukri, optimum weapons at close quarters. Before going out, they blackened their hands and faces with burnt cork or walnut juice, depending on the length of the mission. (It took weeks for the walnut stain to wear away. I recall my uncle saying, on his return from one mission: "You go out a nigger, come back a Digger, and a month later you're still a Chink.")

More importantly, each pseudogroup member had to know the habits of the enemy down to the most banal detail. "You had to figure that you were under observation all the time," my uncle said. "Our favorite tactic was to walk into a Mao Mao camp at nightfall, pretending to be a new batch of recruits joining the cause. If our acting hadn't been perfect up to that climactic moment, we'd likely as not be greeted with lead and steel. If we'd actually fooled them, we could walk right up to point-blank range before whipping the Stens out of our overcoats and opening fire.

"It was the little things that betrayed you most often. Your Mao Mao buck always ate fruit and vegetables with his bare left hand. He ate meat with his right, cutting and spearing it with a butcher's knife. But if he was eating fried ants—you know those big

white ants that live in dead stumps up on the Hassayampa?—he'd eat with the fingers of his right hand
but wipe away the grease with his left sleeve. Many a
pseudogroup went under by failing to eat ants in the
proper manner. Another thing: when a Mao Mao took
a leak, he never touched his dingus. He spread the
tails of his overcoat and hunkered down like a
woman. I was in one group led by a fellow called
Freddy Palmer. We were up in the foothills of the Altyn Tagh late one summer, up at the edges of the
bamboo where the main force of the Mao Mao was
hiding out, and one morning Freddy forgot to squat. I
remember I was sitting next to the cook fire waiting
for the tea to boil—the Mao Mao loved tea, scalding
hot and with plenty of condensed milk and sugar—
when I heard something hissing. It wasn't the pot. It
was Freddy, standing there at the edge of the light,
sleep still thick on his fat black face, his dong in his
hand, wee-weeing into the dawn. I was about to whisper a warning to him when—*brrrrrttt!*—someone cut
him down with an AK-47. Then two grenades hit the
camp, *whump-kerwhump*, and we had a hell of a firefight for about ten minutes. When the firing stopped
and we could hear them crashing away through the
bamboo, I bellied on over to where poor Freddy was
lying. He was sure enough *kufa*—dead as they
come—and his poor pale peter still draining. He
hadn't even stained it black like we were supposed to.
Some inhibition, I guess, about being black to the
roots of his manhood—something silly like that. Anyway, he couldn't have drawn their fire more effec-
tively if he'd stood there singing, 'God Bless America'
and waving the Stars and Stripes."

During the last year of the insurrection, my uncle
took me up the Hassayampa for a Mao Mao hunt. "I
know a camp up there that hasn't been hit in years,"
he told me. "We should be able to count plenty
coups." He told my mother that we were going par-
tridge shooting upstate, but when he came to pick me
up in the Jeep before dawn one snowy December
morning, he winked and pointed to the gear piled be-

hind the seats. The overcoats smelled of mud and jungle and the sharp reek of cosmoline on the Sten guns underneath them.

We drove up the Interstate in the dark, my uncle sucking on a cold bottle of Pabst while I sipped coffee from the thermos, listening to the radio. "I'm sending you a big bo-kay of roses . . ." I was sixteen that winter and madly in love with a girl named Wendy Winchester, so the music and the dark worked their poignant magic all too well. Wendy Winchester had been run over by a car a few weeks earlier and badly injured. She'd live but she might lose a leg. I sat there listening to Eddie Arnold, wishing that it had been a Mao Mao that had hurt her and that I was on my way to get revenge, but it had only been a drunken Polack from the South Side.

The car, an Olds 88, had hit Wendy and four other girls where they stood on a street corner after a high school football game, waiting for the light to change. The other girls bounced off the fenders and escaped with cuts and bruises, but Wendy had been driven back up the hillside under the car, crushed into a privet hedge back of the sidewalk. It took half an hour to get her out from under the car. "All I can remember is the sound of those bushes crackling around me," she said one evening when I went to see her after she'd gotten out of the hospital. "At night now, when I hear a car crunching through the ice and snow . . ." She shivered, lovely and wounded.

My uncle and I stopped at Chicane for ham and eggs, then went back into the men's room of the diner to put on our disguises. "Rub that walnut stain in as smoothly as you can," my uncle warned. "And don't forget your pecker—remember what I told you about the late Captain Palmer." After he had stained himself properly, my uncle slipped a short Afro wig over his wavy white barrister's hair and pulled an *Amos 'n Andy* face. "How's Ah look, Bruthah?" I told him he looked "right on," or whatever they say. "You let me do the talkin'," he said.

When we came out in our slouch hats and overcoats, our hides as black and glossy as the diner's griddle, the counterman reared back in mock fright. "Goin' after Mao, are you?" he said. "Well, you shoulda been here last week. A few of the local boys went up in the hills just after that light tracking snow and nailed two of 'em. The bigger one dressed out at two hundred and fifteen pounds."

My uncle said that he had never hunted anyplace where it hadn't been better last week.

"Good luck," said the counterman as we left. "And don't you come back no Mao—haw!"

Off the highway, my uncle put the Jeep into four-wheel drive and we bumped into the hills on a tote road that soon faded into a mere trace. All too often I had to jump out and pull a wind-downed tree off the road. "That's a good sign," my uncle would say, dragging alternately on his cigar and on a fresh beer. "Nobody's been through here in a long time."

We made camp that night in the snow of the Altyn Tagh foothills. I pushed down into the alders with my 12-gauge Stevens and jumped two spruce grouse. I killed the first bird clean on a straightaway shot but missed the second and went on after it, hoping to jump it again—we were far enough away from the Mao camp for the shots to go unheard. As I came out of the alders, I spotted the silhouette of a grouse, motionless in a tree ahead of me. This was meat hunting, so I shot the bird off the limb, but when I went to pick it up, I found that it was long dead and already rotted almost hollow. It sure wasn't the bird I had flushed.

Walking along into the woods, I saw many grouse dead in the trees, toes locked in rigid death grips on their roosts. I shook a few out of the trees and all of them were light, dry, almost mummified. I broke one open, as one might a fortune cookie, and its body cavity was crawling with shiny red beetles. When I opened the bird that I'd killed earlier, I found a spongy pink mass of larvae in its craw and stomach. I threw it away with a shudder and went back to camp.

"You didn't have to throw it away," my uncle said when I told him about the beetles. "The meat was still good. Those beetles only eat the guts and the stomach lining of the grouse, and they aren't a parasite of man in any case." He was leaning back in a camp chair next to the fire, with a brandy-and-soda in his hand and his ample belly toasting in the heat. "But it doesn't matter anyway. While you were out beating the bushes with the old fire stick, I hobbled on down to the stream and picked up these." He lifted a stringer from beside his chair and showed me six fat Dolly Varden trout, not a one of them under fourteen inches. "If you want to catch bull trout," he laughed, "send a bullshitter." We dined on trout and fried potatoes, along with a bottle of Schwarze Katz Liebfraumilch chilled nicely in the snow.

The next morning we ate a breakfast of scrambled eggs and cold trout, locked up the Jeep, and started the long walk up into the foothills. At first light, my uncle pointed out a pall of blue smoke that hung over the hills to the southwest. "The Mao Mao are making charcoal up there," he said. "It's a good sign." The going was slow—my uncle's game leg held us back, and he was no longer in top shape thanks to all the booze and cigars he consumed—but by late afternoon we were within the perimeter of Mao activity. Whole hillsides had been stripped of brush and second-growth forest to feed the charcoal fires, leaving the land open to erosion (and also creating excellent fields of fire through which we had to crawl on our bellies, using the gullies caused by the autumn rains to maximum advantage).

When we came within sight of the main camp, it was almost sundown, and we lay up behind a brush pile to work out our plan of attack. The camp consisted of half a dozen teepees clustered around a low, log-built blockhouse. A few horses—seedy pintos, mainly—were corralled at the edge of the camp, and we could see women walking back and forth through the snow, their easy Nigger stride thrown off just a touch by the heavy boots and cloth wrappings they wore to fend off the cold. They were handsome women, many of them with shaved skulls, and those without overcoats were also bare from the waist up; their heavy tits swung glossy and gourdlike as they walked. I thought of Wendy Winchester's budding breasts, tender little pink-tipped things that bore about as much relation to these women's breasts as young strawberries might to plums. I suddenly realized I was hungrier than I was scared.

"We'll make our move when most of the men are in from the woods," said my uncle. "We'll come in out of the dusk, real casual. Keep your overcoat unbuttoned and hold the Sten inside it, down your leg, through the pocket slit. When we get up close—you'll feel it when they realize we're not legit—just up and cut loose. Keep your fire low; these pieces have a way of walking up on you even when you hold them sidewise. And stay low yourself in case they shoot back." He handed me two frag grenades and an incendiary. "When you've shot out your first magazine, flip one or two of these into the teepees and lay low while you reload. Now, I'm going to stay here while you belly on over to the right, toward the next brush pile. You're skinnier than I am, and quieter, so they won't see or hear you moving. Position yourself so that you can see me, and when I get up and start walking in, you do the same. That'll be about ten minutes from now. Got it?"

"What about the women and children?"

"You get the same ten bucks for any ear, regardless of age or sex."

"I mean, should we, like, kill *them* too?"

"I'd prefer not to, but it's hard to distinguish in the dark, and anyway, the women and kids shoot just as straight as the men if you give 'em the chance."

I went silent and looked away.

"What's the matter?" my uncle whispered. "Squeamish? Remember, all of these people—the grown-ups, at least—have killed at least one other human being as part of their oathing. Many of them have killed more. They kill their own wives and parents and children as part of the oathing, and then stuff them down wells or sewers. They believe in rape and torture and public ownership and free dope and poaching, and they have too many babies and a whole hell of a lot of clap."

"Okay," I said, "but where do we meet in case we get separated?"

"Wait for me at the Jeep if you can," he said. "You know where the rest of the ammo is cached. But if you can't wait, head on back to the highway. I'll see you back in town, unless I go under."

When I got over to the other brush pile, I checked out the Sten gun. It felt cold and greasy, and the *snick* of the slide as I put a round in the chamber sounded too loud to go unheard. I looked up, scared, like a kid caught looting a comic-book stand. I found myself struggling to stifle a giggle: it was crazy, two of us taking on an armed camp of overt oathing murderers, some of them with the biggest tits I'd ever seen. But now the men were drifting back into camp, swinging their axes and brush hooks with that happy Nigger rhythm, slapping their chests and thighs and calling out in falsetto voices to their wives and horses.

When my uncle rose and began limping into camp, I fired a burst from the Sten up into the sky and took off back down the mountain.

As I ran, I could hear his gun chattering, his grenades whomping, and the slower, heavier chug of their firearms. The horses screamed over the gunfire. I was too fast—too much in motion—to feel any regret.

A few nights later I was in Wendy Winchester's living room, drowning my doubts in Cherry Heering and enjoying one of Wendy's exquisite hand jobs. She was fascinated with my walnut-stained pecker. "It looks so much stronger," she said, stroking away delicately. Her ruined leg was up in its cast, covered with inscriptions that said things like GET WELL SOON, GIMPY!, and the scars on her face were healing into tender pink grooves that matched the avidity of her lips. It was Christmas Eve—her parents were out visiting relatives—and the only light in the room was the rainbow light of the tree. Just as Wendy went down on me—oh, ecstasy!—I heard a Jeep pull into the driveway. Ice crunched under its wheels, and she shivered.

It was my uncle, back from the dead.

"Hey, you little shit-head," he yelled as I came out of the house. "I thought I'd find you here." He was staggering with brandy, and his white roach of lawyer's hair waved merrily above his walnut-stained and smiling face. "I brought you a present," he said, opening the back of the Jeep. "Merry Christmas!"

Inside the Jeep . . .

19

By now we were deep into Ratnose's country. My
night sweats told me so, if my compass didn't. His
presence rattled the trees around our campfire,
bounced off through the brush with loud, white-tailed
leaps. Wind and deer, perhaps, are the essence of Ratnose. To shore up my determination—it was eroding
fast—I opened Myerson and looked for references,
hoping they might reassure me. I found them, all
right, but they did little to bolster my courage.

"Bandits abound on the upper Hassayampa," he
writes in Chapter XXXIV, entitled "Tristesse on the
Tributaries." "Indeed, local legends resound to the
screams of slaughtered peasants, of missionaries evis-
cerated and forced to devour their own reeking bowels, of explorers and military men cooked over slow
fires. The high peaks and precipitous valleys of the
region provide excellent cover for robber bands; the
abundance of game, both birds and beasts, offers sus-
tenance even in seasons when weather prevents
travellers from transiting the region. According to the
myths of Medieval Islam, the Old Man of the Mountains and his infamous Assassins *(Hashishins)* were
wiped out long before Marco Polo crossed the dry
heights of Persia enroute to his historic sojourn with
Kubilai Khan. Not so. They merely moved east, into
the country of the Hassayampa. To this day, hemp
and horror dominate the countryside, one taking
strength from the other.

"Historical evidence of the banditry endemic along
the upper Hassayampa dates at least from the Tenth
Century, when the Arabic adventurer Masudi of
Baghdad, records the slaughter near Tor of 'full half a
thousand infidels' by the 'murderous Minkhar il Jerbouk, most bloodthirsty of the region's robber lords.'

Masudi, whose travels in the course of a roving life-time took him as far afield as Ceylon, East Africa, the Aral Sea and even perhaps Cathay, avers that in all his wanderings he 'never met Minkhar's like' when it came to sheer, imaginative butchery.

" 'Physically this Minkhar is unprepossessing—small of stature, one-eyed, sharp-featured—but his looks be-lie an intellect exceeded only by his innate and rather magnificent aura of evil,' writes Masudi. 'His favorite tortures involve not just the mutilation of the flesh, but of the mind as well.' Masudi spares us further de-tails, but three centuries later we gain an insight into the specifics of Hassayampan cruelty. David of Ashby, the Dominican friar who visited the region circa 1250 A.D., was captured by 'the Robber Rhinoskiouros' in the mountains west of Hymarind and spent a fearful winter with the band. 'This heathen cut-throat,' writes Friar David, 'hath concorde with Beelzebub, and from him taketh the following power: that when he and his robbers are bent on rapine and pillage, he worketh a spell by satanic craft through which the day waxeth dark as the devil's hindermost parts, and his victims can scarce see their hands before their faces. This darkness he spreadeth over a distance of a fortnight's journey. Though Rhinoskiouros himself is but half-sighted, he possesseth the eye of the cat, and the darkness is to him like unto the day at meridian. His victims thus captured like blind men on the High Street, he delighteth in perverting the young to his wicked ways, pitting them soul to soul against their elders, so that finally the young destroy their loving parents . . . mutilating them in heart and limb alike . . . while their new satanic master laugheth with wicked glee.'

"Ashby was finally released by this monster, but only after he consented to having 'carnal knowledge of a large, dead fish.'

"Other travellers in later centuries were less fortu-nate than the English Dominican. Nikolai Nevski, a descendant of the sainted Alexander, ventured into the Hassayampa country from Novgorod in the 15th Century on a trading mission, only to have his entire party slaughtered and devoured by 'the 10,000 slaves of the Bandit Mishlitsa,' who was also known as 'The Gnawer.' This outlaw demonstrated his strength of jaw by personally biting off all of Nikolai's toes and then releasing him to limp back to Russia over the mountains . . .

"Even as recently as the late war between Russia and Japan we hear of banditry and murder most foul on the upper reaches of the river. In the winter of 1904-05, an entire Japanese battalion was captured east of the Hsien-Ho Gorges by a warlord named Hananezumi, who cunningly coerced the officers to renounce the code of *bushido* by which they lived, then reported this betrayal to their enlisted men, who thereupon turned on the officers and emasculated them. 'Afterward,' writes the sole survivor, a sergeant named Takahashi who escaped down the river by hiding under a drowned cow, 'this long-nosed devil Hananezumi wore as a monocle in his empty eye socket a dried testicle cut from our commanding officer. The rest of us he skinned and ate.'

". . . It was this last bit of gruesome information that got me to thinking," Myerson writes at the conclusion of this chapter. "All of the Hassayampa's most infamous outlaws were one-eyed; all of them were described as small and sharp-featured; all were possessed of a morbid wit. With the aid of friends better versed than I in linguistics, I discovered that all of the bandit leaders bore roughly the same name. Minkhar il Jerbouk translates from the Arabic as "Nose of the Rat.' Rhinoskiouros from Greek as "Nose-Squirrel.' Mishlitsa as 'Mouseface,' from the Russian. And Hananezumi, from the Japanese, as 'Ratnose.' Perhaps the position is hereditary, or perhaps . . ."

I could read no further. Ratnose had been around for a long time. He would doubtless still be here.

20

I find it amazing that the lower animals should hunger for ice, an element quite alien to their diets. Yet I have seen ice please so many animals. My dogs beg ice cubes on hot days. The gray bears of the Upper Hassayampa tear great, splintery mouthfuls of it from the rotting snowbanks of the Altyn Tagh, gagging and drooling as it shatters in their jaws. Often they rip their gums and palates on the hard, green ice that lies in the lee of the windy ridges: quite a sight, the shaggy cave bear in his summer coat, rancid with the grease of the carrion he has eaten, the long, gay loops of blood, clotted with ice, festooning his grizzly mandible. At moments such as these, tucked away in some hunter's cranny in the hills, watching the gray bear at his uncaloric snack, I can understand my own appetite for ice. I develop a sudden thirst—no, rather a hunger—for a Scotch-on-the-rocks. Ah, the rocks! The clear shards flavored ever so faintly with whiskey, crunching between the molars. Aggression and harmlessness all in one act.

So it was that late one afternoon, with the Altyn Tagh looming brown and white in the distance, I developed an irrational craving for ice. The river swept west, but ahead of us rose a wave of foothills on which the last few snowbanks of the previous winter lay melting—wastefully, it seemed to me. There was still a full quart of Johnny Walker Black Label somewhere at the bottom of my pack, and the urge for an iced whiskey rose as persistently as the mountains themselves. "Let's cut up there into the hills and get some ice," I said to my son. He looked up from the dwarfed birches of the riverbank to the soft purples and greens of the foothills and pondered.

The climb to the ice was anything but chilly. Once

we left the shade of the Hassayampa's alpine shrubbery, we were fully exposed to the steady heat of a cloudless subarctic sky. The sun filled half of that heaven with a hard white light that bled the blue from the rest of it. Only the withered gorse retained a hint of the soft yellows we usually associate with the sunlight of more southerly latitudes. As we climbed the ridge, which appeared gentle from the riverbank but was in fact so steady in its upward surge as to prove deadening to our legs, we found ourselves sweating in spurts, gasping, despising the sweet stink of crushed heather that rose from our boots. We tacked our way up the ridge on ancient caribou paths, steering by the cairns that dominated the skyline—Neolithic burial mounds, Myerson called them, though to us they appeared the fortresses of trolls, or maybe bears, or maybe both.

We paused often in the course of that hot afternoon to take coffee breaks in the shade of the smaller monuments. The stone was cool and smooth, with a scent—imagined or real—of hair and decay issuing from the gaps between those gray molars of the past. Below us, the Hassayampa wound its clean curves through the riparian forest. Now and then we saw squadrons of strange beasts rise from the Hassayampa's strand—griffins and mandiggers, perhaps, wasplike at this distance, their wings glinting in the hard white sun and their crowlike squalls reaching us long after they themselves had settled out of sight on the farther bank. Of course we could not hear their cries while our little gas-burning stove was on, heating the water with its dragon roar of a voice, but often we heard them while we sat there breathing the comfortable aroma of our coffee.

There were artifacts to be found around the cairns, and my son quickly learned to dig for them. Kicking with his boots and poking with his hatchet, he turned up seven flint fleshing knives, four bronze ewers, three rotten axheads, a cloven helmet of a cuprous alloy, three quarters of a ceramic pisspot decorated with backwards swastikas, a delicately carved but pornographic toothpick probably hewn from a subhuman shinbone, and the skull of an animal which I tentatively identified as a Loocritter.

"You can't go wrong by digging into the past," I told him when he came up with the skull in his hands. It was brown, crumbling around the slash that had taken the Loocritter's life centuries earlier, but the single unbroken band of ivory that comprised the animal's dentition, top and bottom, was still intact. "This animal, I think, was the Loocritter, or Leucrota as it used to be called. It's extinct now, but my grandfather's father used to hunt them up here shortly after the Civil War. They ran in herds, like antelope and horses, and they were damned quick. The only way to take them was with bait. You couldn't run them on a good pony—even with a lead, running down off a hill. If you drove them into a corral, most of them would chew their way out in a matter of minutes"—I showed him the sharp curves of ivory that armed the Loocritter's jaws—"but if you put down a good load of horseshit in the corral, they'd stay. They loved to eat dung. Sometimes you could nail them just by putting down a few yards of well-aged manure. They'd nose on into it and just stand there, munching away and rolling their eyes at you while you primed the rifle and sighted and shot. They'd even keep chomping after they were dead, or so my grandfather said. He knew a hunter who had his fingers bitten off by a dead Loocritter when he went to drag it away by the nostrils."

"What did they shoot them for?" my son asked.

"They'd knock out the ivory jaw bands for shipment back to Philadelphia. There was a market for them there. Chastity belts, something like that."

At the top of the ridge we found the first tailings of snow—gray and grainy, but underlaid with a layer of clean green ice. While my son chipped away at the ice with his belt ax, I prowled on up the ridge in search of sign. I had the Luger in hand, a round in the chamber for fear of gray bears—no, not fear exactly, but rather anticipation. The heat of the climb was in my throat and up my back like slivers of steel. Waiting to satiate the hunger for ice, I was hungry for conflict. From this height of land, I could see the Upper Hassayampa in its entirety, and I knew what lay along that sinuous, seductive coil of river.

In the snow just over the top of the ridge I found the sign of three horses. They had been shod quite recently, judging by the sharp edges of their iron, and they were rather small horses, carrying light loads. I slipped and skidded over the wet black rock of the ridge, backtracking them for half a mile. When I found horse droppings, I stopped to break them open, to smell them—like a Loocritter, I thought wryly. The droppings were very poor in quality: the horses had been eating the sparse browse of these mountains. There were none of those rich, crumbly oat hulls that we associate with the well-fed horses of our Eastern valleys. These were hill ponies, hill-raised and hill-fed, but shod at some expense and effort to their owners.

Then, in the silky snow of the lee ridges, I found a spot where a rider had dismounted to take a look-see and to urinate. He had walked up the back of the mountains to peer down on the Hassayampa—perhaps to observe the climb that my son and I had undertaken that very afternoon. He had worn, on his feet, my eyes told me and my memory affirmed, the crimp-laced, knee-length moccasins of the Mountain Wyandot, and there was blood in his urine. A sick and desperate savage, I thought. Probably ahead of us—with a companion and a packhorse, or with two packhorses, or maybe with two companions. No, not with two companions—not this far out from home and with no packhorse. If they were that desperate, they would have ambushed us long since. Probably two men and a dwindling supply on the third horse.

I slid back down to where the boy was cutting ice. The bottle of whiskey was already chilling where I had buried it in the snow. I mixed his Kool-Aid with some ice water in my snow-chilled canteen, added more ice, and then poured myself a tall, strong whiskey in the other aluminum cup. I dropped four chunks of clean, green ice into the whiskey. Then I loaded the Winchester pump gun with Double-O buckshot and stood it upright against the ancient grave beside me. By then, the whiskey was ice-cold.

21

We spent the night in the lee of the cairn, without a fire. There was no firewood, and even if there had been I would not have burned it for fear that the flames might draw unwelcome guests. We boiled some jerky over the stove, melted a slab of goose fat over that, and added the last of our dehydrated potatoes. It made a palatable stew, particularly tasty thanks to the thin, cold mountain air. We finished the meal with a chocolate bar and cups of steaming Ceylon tea—mine laced with whiskey.

"Did you see any bear sign up there on the ridge?" my son asked me as he ate his chocolate.

"No," I said, and I told him about the horse tracks. And their implications.

"Why don't we get up early and try for one of those bears?" he said. "We're short of meat, and with the weather getting colder the way it is, we could always use the hide."

"I don't think we should risk it," I said. "The gunfire might attract those horsemen to us, and I'd like to avoid a fight this far from home. If one of us gets hit . . ."

"You don't have to worry about gunfire," he said. "Look what I found in the cairn while you were up on the ridge." He reached behind his backpack, which was propped at the head of his sleeping bag, and came up with a crossbow. The stock was of weathered oak inlaid with ivory; the bow itself, short, recurved, and carved from what seemed to be the flexible jaw band of a giant Loocritter. The string and the trigger mechanism were made of a copper alloy, though the nut that released the string was carved from ivory. The inlays on the stock showed bearded men on snowshoes killing a great cat—probably an ounce, or snow leopard. Maybe a mountain tiger. They were using crossbows of the same design. The cat was crouched in the shelter of a wind-warped fir tree, its fangs bared and one paw cocked to lash out at the shuffling hunters. Crossbow bolts bristled from the cat's side and throat. The creator of this scene had been a miniaturist of no mean skill: puffs of ivory steam issued from the mouth of the largest hunter, obviously the hunting chief giving orders to his men, and a nimbus circled the cat's head like a frozen halo.

"What about quarrels?" I asked. "Did you find any in the grave?"

"Quarrels?"

"The arrows you shoot from a crossbow are called quarrels. They're shorter and heavier than longbow arrows, and the heads aren't barbed."

"Like these?" He held out a handful of green arrowheads, some with rotting wood still set in the cavities.

"Great," I said, "but what do we do for shafts?"

"How about the wooden rods we use for cleaning the shotguns? I could whittle one of them down, or even both of them. We'll be back into the woods along the river soon enough and we can replace them there."

I looked down into the valley, where the river showed only a few steely glints in the twilight. The trees down there were stunted, gnarled. Not much chance of finding a straight limb for a cleaning rod. Then I realized the ridiculousness of my objection: why worry about cleaning the shotguns when we had a chance to go after cave bears? We could always use our bootlaces to draw patches and brushes through our gun barrels. My son spent the rest of the evening whittling down the pine rods and fitting the arrowheads, fletching the bolts with grouse feathers, tying down the vanes with monofilament fishing line until it got too dark to bend a knot.

"We'll practice with the crossbow in the morning and then hunt along the ridge, keeping the river in sight," I said as we zipped our sleeping bags. "I'll back you up with the Luger on any bear we come across. You're right: we sure could use some meat and a good, thick bearskin."

It rained during the night—a cold, sheeting rain that felt all the chillier for the ancient granite markers towering over us. I slept uneasily with the shotgun under the edge of my groundcloth, loaded and with the choke wide open. The rain stopped at first light. The sky to the east was lemon yellow, and it sent a sour shiver down my back. We could see the dim shapes of mandiggers flapping along the river far below; their skirling cries reached us on a raw wind. A breakfast of jerky and tea, an hour's practice with the crossbow, and we moved out along the ridge. The crossbow shot flat and hard at thirty paces, punching neatly through an old shirt stuffed with heather. The tightly braided copper wire of its string had not weakened with the centuries. I dug up the Luger and tucked it into my waistband at the small of my back. We walked slowly, stopping short of the skyline whenever the rolling ridge dropped away from us, then easing up to scan the country ahead. The sun was high, but with no warmth to it, when we spotted a small band of vervex scuttling up a draw ahead of us. They were gray-brown, with scrawny horns, and they were in a hurry.

"Keep down and don't move," I told my son. But nothing appeared chasing the sheeplike creatures. We backtracked them down the draw, and my son found what might have been a horseshoe print at the edge of a thicket of dwarf willow. The print disappeared before our eyes as the heather sprang back upright, but it seemed that the horse had been heading north-west, just as we were.

"Are they shadowing us or are we shadowing them?" he asked, laughing.

"It's no joke," I said. "The only animal up here that would consciously stalk us is man. All the tigers have been shot out of here, and the bears are timid unless you've got them cornered." I looked down toward the valley. The Hassayampa was nearly a mile below us, and up ahead it looped to the left, carrying its safety even farther from the open ridges. "Maybe we ought to forget about bears until the return trip, or until we've gotten clear of these horsemen."

"Aw, come on," he said, rolling his eyes. "We haven't nailed anything big on the whole trip. The mastodon was a dink, and so was the marlin. There weren't any aurochs left in the aurochs country. All the caribou seem to have gone north, and you say that the tigers have been shot out. That leaves bear, and I want a bear. Come on, Pop!"

"You might have to kill a man," I said angrily. "How would you like that?"

"I could do it if I had to," he said, but he looked doubtful. "Anyway, maybe they're just trailing us out of curiosity. Probably they just want to go through our garbage for some wornout clothes or tools or something. Or maybe they're looking for a chance to steal our gear while we're away from camp, fishing or hunting."

"Look," I said, "you don't know this country, and I don't know it that well either. I haven't been up this far in more than twelve years—since before you were born. Conditions change. These people have always been quick to kill—an ambush is safer than sneaking into a camp. They want our guns and our knives, our axes, our fishhooks and frying pans, our belt buckles and our boots. And even if we gave them all of those things without a fight, they'd probably still kill us just to see us die. For entertainment. They haven't got any television up here."

We both laughed at that, and then there was a clattering sound up ahead. It came from a brushy draw leading off the vervex run. I drew the Luger and flicked up the safety; my son checked the seating of the bolt on his crossbow. We spread out and walked quietly up into the mouth of the draw. The wind was downhill, strong and gusty in our faces. The clattering continued from time to time, and as we came closer we could hear a throaty grunting sound through the wind, and the clatter of dwarf birch. I caught a whiff of something rank, something warm and musty and sour.

"There's your bear," I whispered as we came together again behind a mossy boulder.

The bear was ripping apart a rockpile, searching for marmots. It was a full-grown gray bear, easily ten feet long from its scoop-faced snout to its burr-clotted tail. It slapped the rocks around as if they were Styrofoam, and it chortled at its work with a kind of rumbling abandon. Its frayed claws, as brown as rusty sabers, rattled as they worked the rock.

"How is he for size?" my son asked.

"Not a record trophy," I said, "but perfectly respectable."

"What do you make the range?"

"About two hundred yards. You'll have to work in a lot closer."

We studied the draw ahead of us. A lip of fractured granite, from which our boulder had splintered, angled to the left up the draw, terminating in a pocket grown with birch. Beyond that, a sheer granite face mottled with lichens. But the birch pocket was still a good fifty yards from the bear—too far to risk a shot with the crossbow. To the right, across a game trail that originated somewhere up the draw, nothing but dense brush and a few scattered boulders. Assuming that we could cross the trail without the bear catching sound, sight, or scent of us (the wind was eddying, and it would be only minutes before our scent pool spread enough to grant him that warning), we would still have a full fifty yards and ten minutes (at best) of stalking through heavy, noisy brush before my son would be within range.

"The left," my son whispered. "It has to be the left."

"What do you do when you get there?"

"Stand up and charge him. Run up as close as I can and put a bolt through his noggin. Or up his ass if he

takes off, which he probably will. The old Texas brain
shot—right up the dirt track."

"What if he comes at you rather than run?"

"You've got the Luger."

We slipped out of our backpacks and began the
stalk on our bellies under cover of the granite lip, up
the left side of the draw. There was no need to raise
our heads to check the bear's actions or position: the
grunts and clattering kept us informed. When we
reached the birch pocket and caught sight of the bear,
he had his head well down into the marmot den. My
son smiled quickly and rose, checked the crossbow
again, and pussyfooted toward the bear. I followed,
angling to his right to keep a clear line of fire.

When we were within ten yards of the bear, my son
raised the crossbow and sighted. The bear was starting to back out of the hole, its chest and shoulders
red with the raw dirt of its diggings. Before the huge
head could emerge, the crossbow snapped—a single,
crisp *splat* of released tension—and the bolt disappeared behind the bear's shoulder.

The bear convulsed—a huge quaking thrust that
bent its back like that of a cat stretching, and a muffled *whuff* sent red dust spewing from the marmot
hole. Then the bear's head exploded from the hole, its
eyes blinking away the dirt. It looked like a great pig
rising from the mud, shaking the red into a halo. One
great, red paw swiped at the wound and the bear
moaned, then galloped lumpily up the draw. I followed it out of sight with the barrel of the Luger.

"Nice shot," I told my son.

"Oh, Christ, were we lucky!" he said, grinning. "To
have him head down like that, and get in that close!
I'm sure I hit him in the heart, and if not, at least in
the lungs. It *hadda* be a heart shot! How long will it
take him to die?"

"We'll wait a few minutes and follow him up," I
said. "I think you got him dead to rights."

Farther up the draw, we found lung blood—bright
in the lemon light, almost incandescent, great ropes of

it on the heather—and at the top of the draw, the bear lay dead against the lichens, its claws hooked over a boulder. The eyes were still wet and bright, the fangs blunt and yellow. We sat a few minutes more, watching, and then poked the bear with a stick. It was finished.

When we dressed it out, we found the crossbow bolt embedded in a far rib. It had pierced both lungs and the heart. We took care with the hide, then wrapped the backstraps and the hams in that warm, limp, slippery blanket and dragged the meat down to our boulder.

Our packs were gone. A few yards from the boulder, a heap of horse manure steamed in the chilly air.

22

It snowed that night, but the bear kept us alive. We slept under its heavy hide—crinkly with dried blood, but still retaining some of the warmth of the living creature. A fire would be too dangerous, so we ate raw bear meat seasoned with gunpowder. We drank our water cold from a rivulet in the gully where we slept. In the morning, our backs against the wet, black walls and our mouths puckered with the taste of smokeless, we tallied our possessions. The Luger and four magazines of 9mm Remington Soft Points. The tiny Svea gas stove, three-quarters full of fuel. The crossbow and three quarrels. A half dozen bronze arrowheads. Two Puma belt knives and two Swiss Army pocketknives. A packet of Mustad fishhooks, ranging in size from 2/0 to No. 14. A nail clipper. Approximately two hundred yards of eight-pound Trilene monofilament fishing line. Six Band-Aid Sheerstrips. A packet of Kleenex (for toilet paper). A six-by-six-foot square of oilskin tarpaulin. Two match safes holding a total of eighty-three Bluetip phosphorus matches, sometimes known as Lucifers. The clothes on our backs. Outrage.

"Enough fire for nearly three months, if we play it conservatively," I said.

"One fire a day?"

"Conservatively."

"It's a good thing we killed the bear. How long will the meat last?"

"If we can get down into good cover tonight and smoke it, we can get back home."

"We're going home?"

"Did you figure on sticking around? On short rations?"

"Well, I'd like to get some of our stuff back from

those crooks. The guns for example, and my fly rod—you only bought it for me last April when the trout season opened. And my Bedford dump truck. I've had that truck since I was a kid."

I knew he liked to keep the toy truck under the head of his sleeping bag at night, the way the Japanese use wooden blocks under their mats, or for some more basic supportive purpose.

"It'll be hard to track them," I said. "They're moving fast, on horseback. They're better armed than we are, now that they have our gear. If we do catch up with them, we'll have to ambush them, and even at that they may kill us."

"I'd really like to get that truck back."

"Look," I said, "we ought to figure that we're damned lucky they didn't just kill us out of hand and *then* steal our gear. We ought to leave well enough alone. If we cut out of here right now, we'll be home in two weeks, none the worse for wear. We can build a raft and catch enough fish . . ."

"How many days could we track them before we'd use up our reserve?" he asked. I could see that the truck was important to him; he was angry at the thieves.

"Maybe three days," I said, "depending on the weather and the direction they take. If they cut away from the river, we're screwed. We can't live off the land out there"—I gestured, a bit melodramatically, toward the brazen hills to the east and west. "And if I were them, I'd cut away from the river right now."

"We ought to track them anyway, just to make sure." He looked up the river to the northwest. Mandiggers were circling in the mist, fluting mournfully in the weak light. The river wound ahead in grand, erratic swoops, up into the crooked heights of the Altyn Tagh.

We tracked them for three days. The added weight of our possessions, along with melting snow, which softened the trail, made their horses' hoofprints much easier to spot. The thieves kept to the river, appar-

ently trusting to their speed and our fear as a safety
factor. On the second day, my son shot a mandigger
out of a tree along the bank. It was a fair-sized representative of its species—fully twelve feet from nose
to tail, with a wingspread even greater. The crossbow
bolt had taken it through the chest, clipping the spine,
and the creature fell flapping but voiceless, its red
eyes flickering out of focus. It lay in the mud of the
riverbank, bearded and trembling, clashing its triple
rows of teeth like a gutted shark.

"I didn't realize they looked so much like us," said
my son, awed by his shot. The mandigger's face was
quite human: a turned-up nose; a supple, sensitive
mouth; tears in its large red eyes.

"The locals claim that they're man-eaters," I told
him, "but Myerson couldn't find any proof of it. He
claims that they're the *Manticora* of legend. I think
they probably eat human corpses, and they may take
a dying man or a baby now and then, but basically
they're harmless. They aren't worth the ammo for
eating, though. They have a lot of bones floating free
along the spine—too much trouble spitting them out.
My grandfather said that if you soaked the backstraps
in milk after filleting them and then fried them fast in
boiling fat, the bones dissolved, but I never tried it."

"Well, I'll dress him out anyway. We need the
meat." My son flopped the mandigger on its back and
cut up from the anus to the sternum, then worked his
knife into the windpipe and cut it free from the inside. He slashed the fascia along the lung cavity and
worked the intestines loose.

"Should I keep the liver?"

"Probably not. It may be poisonous."

He dumped the mandigger on its side, and the innards spilled out onto the dwarf shrubbery. Steam
and a sweet odor rose in the cold air. We hacked
through the wing bones with our belt knives and then
peeled off the thin, scabby hide.

"Let's get rid of the head," my son said. "It's not
only heavy, it's scary."

Dressed out and quartered, the mandigger came to about sixty pounds apiece. We finally peeled off the backstraps and kept one haunch, reducing our load by half. As we walked away from the heap of guts and hide and crumpled wings, other mandiggers were already gathering in the sky overhead. Their pipy voices sounded contrapuntal, Bach-like against the rumble of the nearby river. The dead mandigger's eyes glared at us from beneath the pile of offal, its own dismembered body.

23

Late in the afternoon, it began to rain. We walked awhile through the drizzle, looking for a ridge that might protect us against the weather. The sky to the northwest was growing darker through the trees, the wind peeling the skin of the sky from gray to gunmetal to black, rimmed around with that dirty white that threatens lightning. We saw the first flashes just as we reached a likely outcropping—ancient sediments of red sandstone, hollowed by oceans long ago sucked up by the sky.

The little gas stove hissed at the wind, and our tea was hotter than the wind was cold; the first pellets of sleet bounced against the brazen belly of the stove like spent bird shot. It was at this moment that we once again understood the delight of wool. Small balls of sleet caught in the wool of my son's sweater, grew in the kinky fibers, melted and evaporated in the heat of the pile. Sleet clotted like burrs in my eyebrows; my wool-capped forehead melted it into sour rivulets.

The water running into my eyes, each bead frozen in the glare of the distant lightning, each runnel pronounced aloud like a prayer to the Belly-god Thunder, washed away the dirt of the day's hike.

We rigged the bearskin against the sleet and fried two small trout over the stove. They tasted as spicy as the weather. Then we rolled into the fur and sipped rose-hip tea while the sleet rattled off the rocks overhead and shivered the willows across the Hassayampa. We dozed off, finally, warm . . .

Just before dawn, I awoke to an unaccustomed silence. The sleet had moved on beyond us. A waning moon, slim and callipygous, danced its light on the crusted ground. The trees were caked with sleet and frozen rain, sheaths of silver in the moonlight. Then the first blue line of approaching sunlight eased up over the hills to the east, and the silver turned to steel, and then to copper, finally to gold. I watched the light snow through dozing eyes, listening at the same time to the rising moan and crackle of icy branches as the dawn breeze pushed its way into the willows along the river. . . .

Maybe Ratnose was down there in the bush. Maybe it wasn't just the wind. Maybe he was walking in time with the wind and the rising sun, shaking the branches and peeling the rotten sleet from the razor-sharp blades of the frozen bear grass. Dragging a thumbnail across the shadowed boulders. The hair began to rise on the nape of my neck; my eyes strained at the shadows. I slid the Luger out of its holster and lay there under the tent of bearskin, whiffing the sour hot stink of my fear. I aimed the pistol into the willows, but there was no target, only sound and light. How easy, I thought, to kill in this mood—but what? I tensed the trigger, brought its sear up to the cracking point, fanning the tall blade of the sight through the black-and-gold webwork of willows, searching for flesh, any flesh. The sleet melted from the branches and fell in clumsy, sibilant splatters. The moon grinned sideways, going down. Madmen, all of us.

Something grumbled in the last of the shadows and splashed noisily across the ford immediately below our campsite. It might have been a moose, or it might have been Ratnose. I couldn't be sure, so I never took the shot.

24

The following morning, we began to close on the thieves. By now I could distinguish clearly among the three horses, by the depths of their hoofprints: one horse carried all the gear and walked in short, dainty, probably sore-footed steps; another horse carried a light, human load but stayed just ahead of the pack-horse, its rider probably holding the lead line; the third horse carried a slightly heavier human load and ranged out from the bunch every few hundred yards, probably so that its rider could scout the country ahead. Study of the thieves' campsites revealed further probabilities: One of the two thieves pissed standing up, the other squatting; ergo one was a man, one a woman, or else one was a man and the other a small Mao Mao, male or female. Judging by the heavy molar action on a frayed dragon wing we found among the garbage at one campsite, the smaller of the thieves had no front teeth; alternatively, his or her front teeth had been filed down to points, a dental fashion favored by some of the Mao Mao, especially the witchmen.

"What's a witchman?" my son asked as we studied the wing bone.

"It's a shaman—a sham-man," I said. "A man who has been turned into a witch and who does all the magic for the Mao Mao. They take a young kid who seems to have a bent for mystical stuff—a kid who swoons a lot, and goes off into transports when he sees a particularly beautiful sunset or a particularly scary cloud formation. They stone him on dragon's-tooth, ground up with dried bat blood and the singed beard of a female mandigger. They mix that with peyote pollen, catfish whiskers, the powdered cunt hair of a recently deceased shaman, and then they add just a drop of venom from the spines of a stonefish. They boil all of that in the fat from the thighs of a young girl, sacrificed for the occasion. Then they roll a pill out of the mess as big as a golf ball. The kid drinks it down in a gourdful of mother's milk spiked with brandy, if they have any, or else with white lightning."

"What happens then?"

"The kid falls into a stupor. In fact, he's damn lucky if he ever wakes up—or unlucky, when you consider what they do to him next."

"Like what?"

"They do a sex-change operation on him. The other Mao Mao are chanting madly through all of this, quotations from the Chairman mixed up with phrases from local folk songs—'Be resolute, fear no sacrifice, and surmount every difficulty . . .' Like that. Then they break out the straight razors. They file the kid's teeth down to points with an old iron file, like we use to sharpen our crossbow bolts with. When the kid wakes up a few days later, he has to eat his own remains— what they cut off of him during the operation. Then everyone in the camp balls him to break in his new cunt. Even the women ball him. They use dildoes cut from old mop handles."

"And then?"

"Well, then he's a witchman, a sham-man, a he-she. He learns everything they can teach him about magic, what yarbs to pick, how to mix them with whatever else they use. Chants and curses and necromantic incantations. He has power now, but he must always remain submissive as an individual, use his power only for the group, and be used by the group whenever it needs him."

"Let's go kill the bastards."

"Why?"

"They stole my dump truck."

We caught up to the thieves with an hour of light left in the sky—a dilute light, like watered-down blood from the rainy sandstone cliffs along this stretch

of the Hassayampa. We slid up on our bellies over a
rise in the standstone, grit in our teeth, and saw the
horses drinking daintily at the edge of the stream. Out
in the middle, the Hassayampa was boiling, pellucid
and pelagic, a great chain of rolling ocean fish—
whales perhaps, or broadbill swordfish—rumbling
over its groaning load of rocks. "That dolphin-torn,
that gong-tormented sea!" as Yeats put it.

"Can you make out the taller guy, back there
against the boulders?" I asked my son.

"No . . . Yeah, now I can see him. With the rifle on
his hip."

"It looks more like a shotgun—our pump."

"Yeah, you're right. He has his hand on the slide—
that's what threw me off."

"Okay, I'm going to slip around and get up above
him on that bluff. I should be able to hit him with the
Luger from there. What I want you to do is belly on
down to the river—through this draw, right here,
where we're sitting—and then work your way through
the shallows under cover of those rocks along the
bank, and then nail the smaller guy where he's holding the horses. Shoot for the body; no head shots—I
don't want you to miss him. Then when you've shot,
I'll hit the big guy, and back you up if the small guy's
only wounded."

"Okay."

"But remember, if you miss your man the first shot,
don't get up or show yourself at all. Just lie low and
reload. I'll cover you. If you hear me yell, start working your way back here slowly and quietly and pick
up our gear and split back down the river. Got it?"

"Check-o," he said, and threw me a sickly grin.

25

I watched him start down the draw, the crossbow delicate in his left hand and the bolts tucked securely through his belt. A terrible thing to send a boy to do. His mother would never approve. Ambush. Yet wasn't ambush what it was all about? We had ambushed each other, this boy's mother and I, and the rest of our lives, anyone's life, was a battle back out of the ambush. The trick was to emerge on the far side of the ambush with the enemy your friend. Easy enough to kill, but very tough making friends. I slid up over the rocks and began moving in on the bigger thief, the one with my 12-gauge pump in his hand. I trembled—was it Ratnose? Was this my moment? The rocks were warm and smooth, dead silent, without rubble. I drew the bead on him. . . . I could see . . .

I could see by the profile that this wasn't Ratnose. In a way, I had known all along it wasn't Ratnose. Not this easy—not Ratnose this easy. This man was too clean to be Ratnose; he stood too straight, his shoulder blades holding him out like cantilevers from the warm stone wall. He wore a mackinaw, not fur. His nose was aquiline, not sharp. Disappointment flooded through me, followed instantly by doubt: should we kill them? But it was too late now. Orders given. Where was the kid? I could see the smaller thief standing there by the sucking horses, wearing a high-crowned, wide-brimmed hat and . . . yes, a fur coat! Maybe Ratnose! Maybe . . .

The bolt hit the smaller thief before I heard the slap of the crossbow's string. The horses reared and plunged as the small thief disappeared into the shadows—my eyes were shifting from horses to fallen body to my own man, concentrating on the trigger squeeze from a butt rest on the sandstone—and then the horses were moving, bucking and clattering up over the riverbed rocks so that I feared they would snap their cannon bones, and *spang!* the Luger went off with a ricochet off the rocks below. No hit on my man. *Spang!* Again no hit—my man was now down and swinging the pump gun my way. *Chug-a-pow!*— the buckshot chewing great chunks of sandstone out of the cliff behind me—and *spang-thunk!* I'd hit him. I heard him grunt. The shotgun slid and rattled down through the rocks below where the hit man lay. I looked past my man to where the other thief had been standing. Sure enough, there was a body down on the riverside rocks.

"Okay," I yelled to my son, "we've got 'em. If you're reloaded, come on out, but keep your guy covered."

It was almost dark now—just the red glow from the rocks, the high clouds carrying the knife edge of the dying day. My man lay on his back among the round boulders, still alive and staring at me. My bullet had clipped his spine just above the hips. His hat was couched at the back of his head like a pillow. He looked familiar. It was Johnny Black. My old buddy from trapping days . . .

"Hey!" my son screamed from down at the riverbank. "This isn't any witchman. It's an old woman."

I searched Johnny Black for weapons, took a knife off his hip, picked up the shotgun, and climbed down through the boulders to where my son stood over the small body. It was an old woman, all right, heart- and lung-shot, with blood pooled in her toothless grin. She was unarmed. Her eyes slid out of focus toward the sunset.

"She looks like Grandma," said my son. Then he started crying. Comforting him, I wondered how often she would have to die. As often as Ratnose?

26

I turned the old woman's head sideways to drain the blood from her mouth and then went through her pockets. The blood, already congealing, permeated the sandstone as if it were a blotter. The fur coat was splendid—wolfskin fringed around the hood with wolverine to keep the frost of the wearer's breath from icing up. It was scarcely damaged by the fatal shot: the crossbow bolt had punched through the left breast side, penetrated and killed the old woman, and then stopped without ripping the far side of the coat. An easy repair job with a needle and a length of fishing line. I stripped off the coat, taking care not to bloody it, and then extracted the crossbow bolt. My son was still snuffling, hunkered back on his haunches against the boulders. I told him to take the bolt and wash it off in the river, then go up and cover Johnny Black with the Luger, provided he was still alive.

"Who's Johnny Black?"

"The guy I just shot to get back your dump truck," I said. "I used to know him when I was a kid. He's a Wyandot Indian trapper, an old man—this woman's old man, actually. Years ago, a friend of mine and I saved him from a bandit gang—Ratnose's gang."

"Who's Ratnose?"

"His real name is Ratanous," I said. "Some people say he's French-Canadian—an old *coureur de bois* and roustabout who makes nothing but trouble for the right folks along the Hassayampa. But I don't know for sure. He speaks with a Mexican accent and looks Chinese. When I met him, he was leading a Chinese bandit gang, but I've heard stories about him leading other no-goods, too. He's old and tough and mean. We're damned lucky it was Johnny rather than Ratnose who swiped our stuff. Ratnose would have preferred killing us to any simple thievery. Now get on

up there and keep a watch on the Indian. I think I hit
him in the spine, so he shouldn't cause you much
trouble."

In the old woman's pockets I found a worn but
well-honed K-Bar clasp knife; a packet of heavy steel
needles and a coil of dried gut; a flint-and-steel fire
starter; a set of brass earloops decorated with alternate black and red beads and each bearing a backwards swastika beaten out of what looked like
lowgrade gold but might have been brass. There was
a packet of jerky in one pocket; I was about to taste a
piece and find out what kind of meat it was—dragon,
mandigger, aurochs, mastodon, maybe just plain
deer—when I noticed that the old woman had bled on
top of it. I threw the jerky into the Hassayampa; it
floated for a few seconds, and then a huge fish swirled
and took it. Judging by the scales in that minimal
light, it was either a tarpon or a mahseer, though we
were a little too far upstream for either. . . .

Maybe a huge pike. My uncle told me a story once
about the voracity of the pike on the Upper Hassayampa. He had been fishing with some of his Indian
cronies in midsummer and with little success. They
had taken a few "hatchet handles"—small pike, skinny
and fanged, reeking of that mucilaginous slime that
belies the good taste of the meat within. Heading
downriver in his canoe one evening after fishing all
day with the Indians, my uncle let the current carry
him as he took his ease in the stern, a steering paddle
under his armpit and a fat, fragrant Havana cigar in
his teeth.

"It was a lovely evening," he told me, "with the sunset illuminating the canyon walls ahead of me and a
breeze ghosting upriver against me. Mandiggers
chuckled at me from the cliffs and the trees, and I
could see fish rising in the riffles to suck down the
evening moths. But I'd had enough fishing for the
day, and I just wanted to savor the evening and my
cigar. Puffing and steering, I was really enjoying myself; now and then I'd flick the cigar ash over the side
and watch it dissolve as it broke up and raced the

canoe. Then, out of the corner of my eye, just as I
flicked the cigar tip bright red in the last light of the
day, I saw a gigantic maw rise through the water, angling up so fast from behind the canoe that before I
could react it had broken the water with a mighty
splash and bitten onto my cigar hand. Out of pure re-
flex I flipped it into the canoe. It was a pike—not just
a hatchet handle or an ax handle, but a goddamned
log of a pike, its teeth buried in my hand, thrashing
and slapping its slime and its teeth all over the canoe,
not to mention my lap. I damn near capsized getting
that fish off of my hand—I still don't know how I did
it; but then I smashed the fight out of it with an
empty beer bottle that was lying conveniently to
hand.

"That pike had risen to my cigar coal, must have
seen it as a monster firefly or some strange fiery
bird—they take birds on the wing, you know, low-
flying swallows and nighthawks that work the river at
dawn and dusk. He tore the hell out of my hand, and
it was weeks before the infection cleared up, but he
sure made the fishing trip for me. I have to admire
that kind of voracity, that grand and insatiable appetite that brooks no hesitation. Pike have no problem
with menus: they surge before choosing, or perhaps
choice and consumption are the same act for them.
It's there; I eat. When you think of all the sad people
who flip out over the choice between mustard and
ketchup on their cheeseburgers, it seems a shame
there isn't more of the pike in us."

. . . Staring down at the dead old woman, I consid-
ered our own voracity. We had killed her for a toy
dump truck. Our voracity was sentimental, the curse
of memory and foresight. I rolled the old lady into the
Hassayampa, and as she spun slowly off into the main
current her face remained down, her eyes focused
now on the river bottom rather than the absent sun.

"He doesn't have my truck," said the boy as I
climbed back up the rocks. He had the Indian covered where he lay propped back against the sandstone
cliff. My son had built a small fire of driftwood. Water

was boiling in the teapot. "He says he remembers you from the Ratnose expedition. I don't think he's hit that bad—he moved his legs when he crawled back up against that rock."

The man's eyes shone like rain puddles in the firelight, the rest of his face dark cement.

"I'd offer you a drink," I told him, "if some sneaking yellowbelly hadn't stole all my gear."

"There's most of a bottle in the pack on the pinto," he said. I signaled my son to fetch the horses; we could hear them nickering only a few hundred yards upstream. He handed me the Luger, took the shotgun, and slid up over the rocks.

"How are your legs?" I asked the Indian.

"Not bad," he said. "Numb, but the feeling is coming back. I think your bullet only nicked the small of my back. Not much blood, and I can feel an exit wound, so if there's any lead in there, it's only a little bit, a few pieces at most."

I dragged him by his bootheels closer to the fire and washed the wound with the hot tea water. He was right: it was a minor wound. The mouth of the wound was just at the top of his Mongol spot—a purplish, puckered rip just an inch away from the spinal column. The exit wound was only another inch away—larger, but a clean tear that had not taken much meat or muscle with it.

"I couldn't have stunned you better with a sandbag," I told him. "When the kid gets back, I'll pour on some sulfa and bandage you up."

"No sulfa," he said, "and no bandages either."

"Why not? They were in my first-aid kit."

"I sold most of that stuff."

"The kid's truck too?"

"Yes, and the fishing rods, the lighter shotguns, the tent, and the tools. All I kept was the big shotgun, the ammo and the whiskey."

"Who did you sell it to?"

"Ratanous."

"Well, I guess I'll need the whiskey."

27

The boy returned with the horses, and while he rubbed them down and picketed them, I poured Johnny Black a drink, then one for myself. A wind with the taste of winter on it worked down along the backbone of the riverbank like a fillet knife, but we were beneath its edge, tucked into the rocks with our smoky driftwood fire that coughed and popped now and then—an old man rolling the black phlegm of his fatal illness around on his tongue, enjoying it, hawking up more, making the most of it. Johnny Black spoke of his wife, but there was no dignity in his rambling. Maria Elena. An over-the-hill hooker when he rescued her from one of Ratnose's brothels on the border. Reduced by clap and toothlessness to a blow-job specialist. Before her teeth fell out, she starred in Ratnose's geek show under the stage name of Erogenous Jones, a pun that Johnny Black felt was wasted on the loggers and trappers frequenting Ratnose's establishment.

"Do you know Pecker Point?" Johnny Black asked. "The red-light district across the river from Silenius where Crown-Zellerbach had that big cedar sawmill? They've closed it down now, but back when I met Maria Elena it was booming. They averaged six stompings and two knifings a night, more gougings and nose bitings than you could count. Every other guy seemed to have something missing—an ear or an eye, a few fingers, his nose; one guy even had his lower lip ripped off, in a fight with a fag Nigger piano player whose teeth were filed down cannibal style.

"I tracked in there one spring with a load of furs— otter and caprizond from the Altyn Tagh, mainly— and the first thing I saw was that riffraff lynching the poor Nigger. They had him lashed to a freight-wagon wheel outside Ratnose's cribs, buck naked and bleeding into the mud, those sharp teeth flashing under those frightened eyes. His name was Butch Beck-wourth, and he claimed to be the grandson of Jim Beckwourth, the runaway slave who was later a war chief up with the Absaroka. Nice fellow—or at least, he played the piano nicely—Butch. A bit of a pansy maybe, but in those days in that country, a man would punch anything, including dead otters; I ought to know. After you've been in the woods long enough, there's a kind of sexual democracy develops that you'll never find in the towns—maybe in the cities, but never in the towns.

"And certainly not in any town that Ratnose had a stake in. That bastard hates to see anyone have fun, of any kind. In fact, he gets his own fun out of wrecking other folks' fun. When he bought into the fuck busi-ness in Pecker Point, he changed the name of his whorehouse to 'The Pecker Wrecker,' and he stocked it with the most clapped-up, syph-ridden, blue-balls-breeding collection of rotten ginch you've ever sniffed —Christ, you could get boils on your ass just walk-ing through the door. They say he spiked his booze with his own drippings, but even if he did, it couldn't have hurt the flavor. The only music they played in there was that stuff that wrecked your ears—Stravin-sky, Pollack, Robbe-Grillet.

"Butch Beckwourth played in the Pecker Wrecker, which made it all the worse what Ratnose did to him. Butch played country blues, and he sang it through those filed teeth of his so that you could hear the den-tist's saw on every nerve. He sang about bridges and crappers and thin possum gruel like only a file-tooth spade sissy could sing it—broke your heart after a winter in the woods.

"When Ratnose took over the place, he made Butch play Debussy, just to wreck Butch's style. He put Maria Elena into the geek show, as Erogenous Jones. Butch would be playing Debussy or Ravel or Carl Orff, sometimes *The Rite of Spring*, on a good week-end, and Maria Elena would appear on the stage leading a donkey. The donkey's name was Herbie;

he'd been the asshole buddy of a prospector named Herb Petrov. The donkey would hump Maria Elena for openers. Then Maria Elena would drag out a leather mail pouch and open it up on a card table. In it she had a bag of burnt-out flashbulbs, a cage of baby chickens, a loaf of bread, and a butcher's knife. While Butch played that crazy music, she pranced around, dunking the flashbulbs in her cunt, then eating them as if they were artichoke hearts. Very elegant. Then she took the chicks, one by one, petted them and cooed over them, dancing all the while, and when they were clucking, cheeping, all worked up, she would bite off their heads, one by one, and suck them dry—guts and all; just a wrinkled yellow sack left. Finally, remember it's Debussy or Stravinsky and those wicked pointed teeth flickering over there at the piano, she would slice two pieces of bread, crap on them, and eat the sandwich. Ratnose's idea."

The fire was dying, so I threw on some more driftwood. Johnny held out his cup for whiskey. I refilled both of our cups. My son sat back against the rocks, whittling a piece of driftwood into the shape of a rocket. I told him to take the crossbow and hunt up some breakfast in the swamp just a short distance downriver. Grudgingly, he went.

"Where was I?" Johnny Black asked.

"They were lynching Butch Beckwourth."

"Sure they were. He'd bitten off a logger's lip. The logger was sitting there on the seat of the wagon, trying to glue the bitten-off chunk back onto the place where it belonged, but the blood was too slippery; he was whimpering there; it looked like he was trying to eat a piece of raw liver. Butch was lashed up against the wheel of the freight wagon. Ratnose was in charge. He had all of his girls out there, trying to give Butch a hard-on and not doing too well. They tweaked his balls and went down on him, they poked their fingers up his ass. But Butch was too scared to get it up.

"Finally Ratnose brought in the two grungiest log-

gers in camp and promised them free tickets to the
geek show if they'd jerk each other off in front of
Butch. While they were flailing away, that purple
hose of his started to get stiff—against his own will,
you could see, from the way he gritted his pointy
teeth. Finally, when it was up and straining, Ratnose
chopped it off with a brush hook and stuffed it in
Butch's mouth. It was strange to see—Butch didn't
know whether to be happy or sad; he sniveled a bit
with the blood running off of his chin, but his eyes
were happy even while his teeth did their dirty work
and his life drained away into the mud. He never
resolved the problem, the poor son-of-a-bitch; he died
with his eyes happy and his mouth sad.

"Later that month, when Maria Elena's teeth fell
out, I swapped my peltry to Ratnose in exchange for
her freedom. She turned a trick or two for him during
the off months in later years, but generally she was
content with the trappers' life."

I found it hard to believe Johnny Black's story. In
the first place, I was sure that Ratnose had never
owned a whorehouse in Silenius. He was a woodsman,
not a townie. In the second place, I was by now rea-
sonably certain that Ratnose was the German poet
Horst-Dieter Rotznase, a homosexual militant whose
1927 epic, *Smegma*, had only recently been translated
from the Silesian. . . .

Why had Johnny Black helped Ratnose? Why did
Ratnose have my son's dump truck? Where was the
bastard? Johnny wouldn't say—he was now sound
asleep.

I drank for an hour, eating my grievances as Butch
Beckwourth had his own prick, and then I awakened
Johnny Black to face his reward.

28

"You tried to hurt me," I said. "Us."

"But not personally," he answered. "I had no idea I was stealing from you. If I'd known . . ."

"That doesn't matter. The point is, the person you tried to hurt was me, and since my son was with me, you tried to hurt us—whether you knew it was me, and thus us, or not. Let's not get caught up in semantics."

"Look," he said, "if I had known it was you—that moustache, all those years, you're much heavier than you were; sure I watched you while I tracked you, but with that heavy clothing . . . maybe if the weather had been warmer . . . I didn't want to hurt *you*."

"That's tough, Johnny. You did, and now I'm going to hurt you back."

I had him sweating now, the sweat gleaming in the firelight on his lined, sagging face. His eyes were sick. I remembered how tough he had looked when he cut down the Chinks back there when he was younger. A man bent on revenge is tougher than a man bent on thievery—or was it just the years? I could feel myself softening, the humanism creeping in again. Why are there so many sides to an action?

"Why don't you just leave it where it is?" he asked, sensing my indecision. "You already killed my old lady. You have my horses and my weapons, and the money Ratanous gave me for your gear. Just let me crawl out of here—it'll be tough enough. I'm eighty-six years old, and you've already kicked the hell out of me, and it's almost winter. I probably won't make it out of these hills alive anyway."

His eyes watered within the dark wrinkles of his sickness and his age. I might look that way one day. . . .

But wait a minute: this was a rugged old scoundrel, a killer, a mountain man, a sneak thief. He'd done me dirt. He could certainly do me no good. . . .

Still, I might tie him up and see how I felt in the morning. If I shot him, I'd have to watch him die and then drag him out of here, and then look aside when we rode away. . . .

But if I tied him up, he might get loose and kill us while we slept—a knife, a couple of bullets . . .

No, I wasn't really afraid of that. He wasn't strong enough for murder anymore. Age had reduced him to petty thievery. If he got loose, he'd simply steal our gear and ease away into the night. And anyway, I could stay awake and watch him; the boy and I could take alternate watches. . . .

God, I was tired of this place—this river and this bleak country. I wanted nothing more than to get out of it. Back home, where it was warm and complicated, where the complexities themselves were excuse enough to justify inaction. Down there, if someone robbed you, you called the cops and the insurance man. The cops did nothing and the insurance man sent you a check. If you saw the thief on the street, you looked the other way: it was taken care of, you had your check, it was police business. Up here . . .

"All right," I said finally. "I won't kill you, then. We've got our gear back, or some of it, anyhow, and I guess you've paid with your suffering."

With that, a sudden transformation hit him: the suffering left his eyes, replaced by a flicker of triumph.

"You shouldn't have come this far up the river," he scolded. "Not with a youngster in tow, and so lightly armed. This is strong country. It's not for you lowlanders." He shifted his position, flexing his legs, and I could see that the paralysis caused by the bullet wound had been only temporary. A strident tone entered his voice, something between a sneer and a snivel. "If you'd stayed where you belong, none of this would have happened. My woman would be alive; I would be warm and happy—not as I am now, facing the prospect of a long, dangerous, and painful journey, unarmed and on my knees. . . . Give me a horse, at least, and a knife. You owe it to me . . ."

Rage flushed through me—the sneering, imperious old sneak thief! His mouth was curled with righteousness and self-pity. His eyes flashed like a cash register totting up the amount of my moral indebtedness to him. . . .

"This is all I owe you," I said. The Luger banged like a slamming door. His chest caved in, and the wheedling outrage in his eyes faded into an instant of surprise, which in turn faded to nothingness.

When he was quiet, I caught him by the hair—he still had a thick, strong mop of it, streaked with gray—and dragged him out beyond the firelight. I rolled him into a gully and kicked some dirt and leaves over him. My knees were shaking. The man-diggers would find him soon enough. I could hear the river grumbling off in the night, down below.

"Well," I said, my voice as shaky as my knees, "serves you right for stealing."

Walking back to the fire, I passed the horses. They snuffled wetly in the dark. I cut their hobbles and slapped their rumps, then watched them gallop away downriver. I wanted nothing of the old man's—nothing.

The boy came back a short time later, empty-handed.

"Where's Johnny?"

"Gone," I said. "The horses are gone too."

"What do we do now?"

"First thing in the morning, we're getting out of here. We're heading for home."

He was silent, staring into the fire.

"Couldn't we go on to Ratnose's camp?" he asked finally. "See if we couldn't buy back the rest of our things?"

"Ratnose would string us up by our own guts," I said. "He'd skin us out for glove leather. We're going home while the going's good."

He fed sticks into the fire, chewed on a chunk of jerky, whistled a random tune.

"I think I spotted a salt lick up the river a ways," he said. "Why don't I take the shotgun and belly on up there? Maybe I can knock over a deer. We'll need meat for the return trip."

"You ought to get some sleep," I said. "We'll be taking off at first light."

"I'm not tired," he said. "I'm still all wound up about the old lady; I don't think I could sleep."

"Don't worry about her," I said. "She was just an old whore—crowbait. She'd have cut your throat as soon as look at you, if the positions were reversed."

Yes, I thought, it's time to leave. We're getting too hard. Some Boy Scout—he helped that old lady across the street, all right . . .

The boy stood at the edge of the firelight with the shotgun in the crook of his arm. He stared at me; his face was solemn. For a moment I thought he intended to shoot me, but it was only the flickering shadows. He turned without a farewell and padded up into the rocks.

The next morning, when I awoke, he was still not back. I waited until the sun had cleared the horizon, fear knotting my gut. Ratnose, I thought, finally. I had been afraid even to pronounce the name silently. I ran up to the top of the ridge and looked out over the country. It rolled away in all directions—empty, cold, vast, and impartial.

"Ratnose!" I yelled. "Ratnose! Ratnose! Ratnose!"

Part 2

29

I'd like to tell you how when I went out wandering in
the woods that night with the shotgun, looking maybe
to drop a deer at the salt lick, I was instead surprised
and captured by Ratnose and his gang—not without a
fight, though—and then, with my hands lashed to the
wooden stirrup of Ratnose's horse, a stinky little mare
who kept farting all the while, they yanked me up the
first long hill with her belly gurgling like a sewer and
the smell of sour grass in my nose mixed with the
taste of my own blood, like when you've been
creamed playing football; stunned, the cut of leather
on my wrists, rocks buckling my ankles, and Ratnose's
sjambok slashing my face whenever my weeping rose
too loud over the clatter of hoofs and the creak of saddles and the horse's endless cannonade of farts, his
harsh curses and raucous laughter at my plight, poor
little boy, and how we stopped finally at first light and
the horsemen in their greasy jerkins slipped from their
high, wood-and-fur saddles like so many two-legged
oysters, lighting a small fire of birch bark first and
then hickory twigs to keep the smoke down in case of
pursuit, the teakettle steaming over the white flames
as if to thicken the night fog in its last few minutes of
life, Ratnose leaning there against the lathered leg of
his rumble-gutted mare, his plug hat back on his forehead, picking his nose and then flicking the boogers
into the little fire, fuel for our tea, Ratnose with his
one good eye bright and the other an empty cave that
led down to a world of twitching black wires, questioning me, the *scritch* of his fingernails in the armpit
of his ratskin shirt as loud as the scrape of steel on the
oily whetstone where he sharpened his toad stabber,
and chortling at the thought of my death by slow torture, yuckety-yuk . . . I'd like to tell you all of that,
but it would be a lie.

What actually happened, I ran away and joined up with Ratnose's band out there in the mountains. And what's worse, I don't regret it one little bit.

I was plugged at my old man. Here we'd been hiking up this rotten river for what seemed like years without any teevee since we'd left old Otto's jerkwater town—no Cokes or hotdogs or fruit rolls in all that time; not that I really needed any of that junk—any kid who just has to have junk like that is really gross—but still, you kind of miss it . . . No food other than what we shot or snagged out of the river, no game of any decent size except that dwarf elephant and the bear; what the hell were we doing up here? We could have killed more game and in greater comfort down home. And then that Indian comes and clips our goods—my books, my dump truck. And then my dad makes me kill the old lady while he chickens out and lets the Indian go without getting our stuff back. Not that I really needed that dump truck, but it was the principle of the thing. Being up here bored, and they take away the one thing that makes me feel like I'm back home, or anyway stand a chance of getting back there. The thing is, I knew Ratnose had that truck and that Ratnose was around here somewhere, and I wanted to meet him. I knew my old man would head back down the river without chasing Ratnose or getting our stuff back from him, and even if he tried to, Ratnose was too clever for my old man ever to catch up with him.

And then too, I was really fascinated with Ratnose. He was mean, he was ugly, he took what he wanted when he wanted it—not one of those mealy-mouthed grown-ups who's always telling you that self-denial is good for your soul. He was rotten to the core, and frankly I'd always suspected that I was that way too. Or maybe it's only now, looking back, that I suspect it. I changed a lot during the time I spent with Ratnose and his people. They say that drinking the water of the Hassayampa makes a liar out of you, but I don't think it's quite that simple. More likely what happens is that the weird things you see and do on the Hassayampa confuse the hell out of you, so that what seemed to be true when you started out at the mouth of the river gets all kind of flip-flopped by the time you reach its head, and then when you get back home again, if you ever do, and tell people what you saw and heard and did up there, and they remember what kind of a person you were when you left, there's no way they're going to believe you. Nobody changes that much, they think.

Oh yeah?

It was easy enough to find Ratnose's hideout. When I split from my father's camp that night, I hiked northeast away from the river toward a bald-topped knoll I'd noticed the previous afternoon, taking care to walk bare rock as much as possible to leave no trail. By dawn I was at the top of the ridge. I ate a chunk of jerky while I looked down on the country ahead. Low gray hills bumping away toward a tall blue-black horizon splashed with white as if some huge bird had crapped all over it, except I knew it was snow on the Altyn Tagh.

After a while, I noticed that some of the hills in the foreground formed two low ridges like an upside-down V, a tributary of the Hassayampa flowing between them. There were three smokes in the middle distance. One of them was too big to be the smoke from a camp—probably it was a muskeg swamp burning—and the other was so small that it burned out while I was finishing my tea. The third smoke was up near the crotch of the V and looked steady enough to be a campfire or a group of campfires. I took a compass bearing on it and then picked my way down the ridge, heading toward the smoke for as long as I could see it, then checking my compass every half mile or so, like my dad had taught me.

The stream, when I came to it, was fast and cold, with kingfishers, dive-bombing the shallows, spearing what looked like baby Dolly Vardens. I could see bigger trout hanging in the brown bulges of water be-

hind the rocks and finning under the roots of trees
along the bank, but I had left all the fishing gear back
with my father, and anyway, I was in a hurry.

In the late afternoon I spooked a big animal away
from one of the pools—a bear most likely. I heard it
crash away through the devil's club for a short distance when it stopped and began to moan. None of
that *chuff-chuff* and clacking of teeth that you read
about in the boys' adventure books, but instead a low,
sorrowful moaning, up and down, like my father
sometimes makes in his sleep when he isn't snoring. I
thought I could see its eyes glittering through the
spiky devil's club.

I backtracked slowly for a ways and then shucked
out the shells I had in the pump gun—they were 6s,
since I'd been hoping to maybe puddle-jump a few
ducks—and replaced them with slugs: not that even a
12-gauge slug could stop an angry bear for sure, but
at least it gave me a chance. Then I crossed the
stream to the opposite side from the bear and pussyfooted my way around him, not stopping until well after dark.

I built a big fire in the lee of an uprooted fir tree,
and the popping of the logs drowned out any sounds
that might have scared me. Before dawn I woke up
with the fire burned down to a bed of coals. I thought
I heard singing way off in the distance, but it was
probably just the stream running over the rocks. I
made an early start.

About noon the next day, I cut a horse trail that
came in from the west and then ran parallel to the
stream I was following. I kicked a few road apples
open and saw that the horses had been well fed. Ratnose's ponies? In the edges along the horse trail I
jumped a few partridges, but I didn't dare shoot for
fear that someone would hear me. Or maybe I should
say that the partridges jumped me. I've always been
edgy in good bird cover—"grouse-shy," my dad calls
it: they go off with such a sudden roar, any which
way, and you have to get up on them so fast, it gives

me the same tight feeling in the balls that you feel when you're playing hide-and-seek or kick-the-can and you're "it." Still, I wish I could have taken a poke at a couple. It's such a great feeling when they explode to the shot all broken-winged and loose and you hear that *thump* when they hit the ground. I killed one once that flew out of the briers across a stone wall directly into the setting sun, and after the recoil all I could see past the end of the muzzle was a perfect halo of grouse feathers, bronze and blue and buff against the light, drifting downward with the sun. Ratnose says there is beauty in killing, and of course he's right.

Now it started to rain—one of those cold, quiet soaking drizzles that seems to drain into your ear holes and run down your spine just under the skin and fills your boots in a hurry. Toward dark I came to a rusty barbed-wire fence strung through the open woods along the horse trail. There was a dead coyote hanging upside down from the wire. The rain had soaked his dirty blond hair and dripped from his nose. His teeth were so white that they looked luminous in the gloom. One of his eyes stared at me almost cynically, I thought, like a pale blue marble. The other had already been pecked out by the whiskey-jacks.

In those days I still thought that disfigurement was worse even than death, and the sight of a legless man or a kid with a withered arm would give me nightmares for weeks. One of my friends had a dog named Harry that had lost one of its legs in a trap, but even though old Harry could still get around well enough on three legs to catch a woodchuck now and then, I was very relieved when he finally got run over by a cement mixer. As for myself, I knew I would rather be dead than maimed, so the sight of the coyote, who was both and getting worse all the time, really spooked me.

I remember leaning there on the shotgun, wet and miserable in the rainy dusk, staring into the marbled eye of the coyote and thinking that I could turn around right now, I could walk all night and all the next day and be back at my dad's campsite on the Hassayampa by sunset. A friendly fire. Tea and talk. Caution and good sense. We would build a raft and get the hell out of there—home in two weeks if we were lucky. When we got home, Mom would be baking bread and the kitchen would smell all sweet and nutty, and I'd turn on the teevee—something really gentle like the *NFL Game of the Week*—and I'd just lie there on the new carpeting in the den, wrestling with the dog maybe, or building a model rocket, and nibble on an apricot-flavored fruit roll while it rained outside, getting darker and darker while the house got brighter and warmer . . .

A horse coughed in the distance over the next hill, and another horse answered it with a whinny. The wind had shifted, carrying both the sound and the rain into my face on a chilling slant. I could hear a hollow clatter like that of cooking pans, and the thin yelp of dogs and children. After checking the shotgun to be sure I had a round of Double-O-Buck in the breech and the Polychoke at open cylinder, I started slowly and quietly up the rise. I wondered if Ratnose would like me.

30

At first glance, the camp was a mess. Tarpaper shacks and tepees stood jumbled in the bare valley bottom, while from the hillside gaped the wooden-lipped mouths of dwelling caves. Three or four huge fires sputtered redly under the rain. In front of some of the dwellings stood cranky poles of peeled saplings with skulls on the top, not all of them human. A great mottled, tangled heap of something or other lay at the far edge of the encampment—bones, I later learned, of all kinds from trout through men to mastodons. Even the big vegetable garden at the far end of the camp looked untidy, what with its straggly bean and tomato poles and the mounds of rotting compost that studded it. Wisps of rancid steam rose from the piles and drifted my way.

A herd of perhaps fifty ponies and mules stood drenching in the cockeyed corral, looking as dull and miserable as the weather. Dogs of all shapes and colors and sizes lay curled within their tails under the protection of the eaves. Mastiffs and mournful hounds, bluetick and Walker and black-and-tan. Snipy shepherds and burly, sausage-bodied Labradors. Palsy-walsy beagles and some big stud bassets with balls on them the size of apples. Chows, huskies, malamutes, Dobermans, boxers, spaniels, setters, pointers, poodles, terriers, collies, shelties—every race, along with some monstrous mixes. It occurred to me that either this must be Doggy Heaven or else Ratnose was the world's top dognapper. Which he was.

As I walked toward the fires, the dogs winded me and set up a hell of a racket. Some of the guard-dog types came trotting out to sniff me over, stiff-legged and growling and with their ruffs all bristling and scary, but my dad always said that if you kept right

on walking and didn't shy away from them they'd
usually leave you alone. In fact, he believed that a human being could face down nearly any animal just by
heading straight toward it and looking it in the eye.
The only creatures it didn't work on, he said, were
sharks, grizzly bears, Cape buffalo, and yellow-bellied
cowards carrying guns. It worked all right on these
dogs, although some of them kept swirling around me
and muttering so fiercely that I had to laugh—they
got such a kick out of acting mean and nasty so as to
impress the other dogs, just like kids on a playground.

But then when I came near the tepees, one of the
flaps opened and a toothless old woman with long yellow braids and a leather shirt looked out at me and
then ducked back in. She was back out in a second
with a poncho over her head and a butcher's cleaver
in her hand. She looked at me again and I smiled, carrying the shotgun now over my shoulder by the muzzle. She ran through the rain up to one of the caves. I
stood by the fire, warming my hands in the sweet,
steamy smoke.

The old woman came back in a minute with a man
who wasn't Ratnose. The man was about my father's
age, flat-faced and dark, a short guy but with wide
shoulders and thick arms under his ratty mackinaw.
He was wearing a beat-up old bottle-green derby, and
he had a long-barreled revolver strapped on his hip.
He said something in a language I couldn't understand, so I smiled at him and shook my head.

"Hokay," he said then in a thick, gurgly voice,
"Hinglish then. Who you are and what you want?"

"I'm a runaway," I said, "and I'm looking for Ratanous. I was told that he takes in runaways provided
they're armed and can ride."

"Not always so," said Flat-face with a nasty grin.
"Sometime de Ratnose he—" and the man ran his finger across his throat with a wicked *squitch*-ing sound.
"Den he cook'um an' we eat'um." He pointed to one of
the poles with a skull on top. The old woman laughed
a dirty laugh, and I could see her tongue writhing
beyond her naked gums.

"Well," I said, "I wouldn't taste too good. My mother was scared by a bottle of ipecac. Where's Ratnose?" I figured it was safe to use the nickname, since old Flat-face had used it.

"De Ratnose, he out hunting. Mebbe back tonight, mebbe tomorrow." Flat-face stopped and looked out into the mist. "Mebbe never come back; mebbe de Ratnose go under"—and he laughed uproariously at the silliness of the idea. Then he turned to me and made a horrible face. "You give me dat shotgun, hear?"

I just stood there and stared at him as steadily as I could, not saying anything. He put his hand on the revolver butt and glowered some more. Rain dripped from the brim of his derby. A few drops splattered on his broad, splayed nose. His eyes were locked on mine, and neither of us blinked. We eye-wrestled for what seemed like half an hour, each of us looking as mean and deadly and serious as we could. Then I slowly crossed my eyes and stuck out my tongue. Flat-face broke up.

"Haw!" he yelled, scratching his wet nose. "Hokay, kid, you keep shotgun for now. I only want clean him up for you, oil him so he no rust. Nice piece—no like see him get all shitty."

"Hell," I said, "why didn't you say so?" I shucked the shells out and handed him the gun. He spun it neatly, thumbed the breech closed, and swung the gun to his shoulder, dropping a nifty imaginary double—*pow, kapow!* Then he grinned and gestured for me to follow him up the hill to the caves. Faces filled all the doorways, staring at me as we climbed—mainly kids' faces and women's faces, some of them quite pretty, most of them seamed and smoky-colored; a few faces of old men, scarred and hard-eyed. I noticed for the first time that Flat-face was limping. A dirty bandage showed at the top of his rawhide boot.

Flat-face's cave was warm and smoky, with a floor of hand-hewn planks and walls shored up with heavy, smoke-blackened beams. A cast-iron stove glowed apple-red in one corner, its pipe disappearing up into

the clay roof. Flat-face put a coffeepot on to boil and
gestured for me to sit down in a hide-covered chair
near the fire. I slipped out of my shirt and peeled off
my boots; I was wet to my soles—to my soul, if the
truth be told. The heat felt good, and I suddenly took
a great liking to Flat-face, who was pulling his own
boots off and looking worriedly at the bandage on his
calf. He unwrapped it and revealed a nasty puncture
wound, black around the edges, oozing pus.

"Dart shot," he explained, smiling a bit shame-
facedly. "Dayak poison dart. Damn near rub me
out"—and he grasped his throat, extruding his tongue
and rolling his eyes in accompaniment to a hideous
gurgle. "No breathe, all numb, much strong poison.
But de Ratnose, he fix with yarbs. Now just left de rot
aroun' de hole." I rummaged through my pack until I
found the first-aid kit. I pulled out a tube of antibiotic
paste and handed it to Flat-face.

"This ought to clear it up," I said. "Just squeeze out
the pus and squeeze in the goop."

"Goop?" he said, and laughed. By the time he'd
dressed the wound and rebandaged it, the coffee was
done—a strong, green-tasting, pungent coffee that
soon had my head expanding like a balloon. Wait a
minute, I thought with a surge of fright, he's doping
me! But the worry faded quickly into a warm, grainy
feeling, as if my body had suddenly slipped into a
broader focus, the molecules moving away from one
another to let the warmth and the smoke filter
through my hide and circulate around my shivering
liver and my goose-pimply heart. Flat-face was cleaning the shotgun: the rasp of the wire brush, the
banana smell of nitro solvent, the clean gleam of 3-in-
1 oil on the blue barrel; the occasional creak of the
stove coupled with the rattle of rain against the door
. . . I was drowsy. Flat-face was talking—sometimes
in a tongue I could not understand, sometimes in his
easy broken English, sometimes singing as he limped
around the cave, showing me his trophies: jawbones
and fangs, skulls, hides, bits of bent metal from old

battles, knives he had picked up here and there, a kukri, a kris, a Green River butcher's blade ground almost hollow with the years, the metal warm and slick with oil . . . I dozed off.

It was dark when I woke up to distant cheers and muffled gunshots. Flat-face was gone, and outside the oilskin window of the cave I could see the glare of fires and the figures of people capering in the red light. I was very hungry. There was a stone lamp on the table that sputtered with blazing fat, and beside it a loaf of bread and a crumbling wedge of cheese. I hacked off a hunk of each with my pocketknife and, chewing them down in a hurry, the cheese so sharp that my sinuses ached, I looked for something to drink. There was a bulging possumskin dangling by its looped and knotted tail from one of the wall beams, and I uncorked the snout and sniffed. Wine. I gulped a few swallows, sour and resinous, then filched an apple from the barrel beside the door. Worm-eaten but crisp and sweet, it eased the bite of the wine, which I could feel now spreading warm and strong in my belly. I looked at my shotgun, leaning against the wall, but left it there. No sense in antagonizing anyone this early in the game. I went out and ambled down the hill toward the firelit action, munching my apple.

Half a dozen men on horseback capered around the fires, whooping and posturing and blasting off their guns into the night. The rain had stopped, but a fine fog still filled the sky, blooming like yellow dandelion pollen around the flash of the gunshots. A string of mules stood to their tethers, sullen and heavily laden with quarters of meat, some of it already glazed a greenish black. Ratnose was back, sure enough, and he had scored. I looked for him among the horsemen, but for the longest time I couldn't spot him: all of them looked ratty and mean, but none of them was big enough, it seemed to me, to be Ratnose.

Two of the riders were just kids, with wispy beards and snotty, self-serving grins and all their teeth, wearing colorful wool serapes over their leather shirts and wide-brimmed cowboy hats with snakeskin bands flashed with cheap brass coins, and big handguns in their mitts. *Blam, blam!* Show-offs. The other riders were older, slump-shouldered on their mounts and wearing the same shy grin that Flat-face favored after I whipped him at eye wrestling. They were dressed in wool and leather that had gone black with sweat and grease, high moccasins with no spurs, heavy hide gloves to protect against the briers while riding through underbrush, and scruffy fur caps. You weren't aware of their weaponry—like, the younger riders, I mean they were positively bright with cartridges and foot-long bowie knives, while these older men carried quiet little clasp knives tucked into leather sheaths on their belts, and short-barreled cavalry carbines whose butts barely peeked out of their saddle scabbards. They sat their horses, lumpy little pintos, with a kind of, well, *quiet*—no jerking around and sawing at the reins; kind of like the riders grew out of the saddles like mushrooms, but with a sense of poison like a mushroom has until you study it closely and discover its real nature.

Finally, one of the older horsemen held his pony in check, and Flat-face ran up to him, grabbing at the stirrup. He whispered into the rider's ear, and the rider looked over at me. Then I knew he was Ratnose. He only had that one eye, a bright black eye that blazed like a match head under the brim of his ratty cap, while the other eye was out, a socket full of black worms—muscles, I guess; but the good eye was more than twice as bright as any eye I've ever seen: a real purie. Ratnose looked at me for a while, his mouth limp, deadpan, and then he pounced off his horse. Usually you think of pouncing being an upward movement, but Ratnose made it a movement in any direction. He flexed his thick wrists, and then his body just kind of peeled off of the pony and Ratnose was walking towards me, leading the pony. I couldn't help thinking that he was a dink of a guy, not much

taller than I was, with a bit of a gimp to his walk as if
his hip had been broken some time ago; a pointy kind
of face, the nose leading the man, unbalanced with
that eye gleaming out at you from the side of his head
and nothing but blankness on the other side. As he
came closer, I noticed that he smelled bad, but then
we all did.

"You're the runaway?" he said. His voice was deep,
grating, and I noticed a puckered scar beside his
windpipe.

"Yeah."

"Well, Hunk here says you're okay." He gestured
toward Flat-face, who smiled his sheepish smile.
"Normally I wouldn't take anybody into the tribe at
this time of year, but we made a lot of meat on this
hunt and we lost one of our riders. Can you ride and
shoot?"

"Yeah," I said. "Maybe in the morning . . ."

"Sure," Ratnose said. "We'll take a look at you in the
morning. Meanwhile, you can help out by unloading
some of this meat and hanging it in the springhouse,
down there by the creek." He pointed to the stream,
toward which a number of men and women were already lugging quarters of meat, bent and dog-trotting
under the weight. He flicked me a quick little smile,
his goat's beard waggling playfully, his one eye fixed
square between my two. "Welcome to Shit City," he
said.

31

That night, after we had hung most of the fresh meat in the springhouse, Ratnose gave permission for a feast. The women held out one side of an aurochs, which was quickly spitted and set to turning over the big cook fire. The older men grunted and farted under the weight of a huge black cast-iron caldron which they hung by means of a chain and an iron dingle stick over another fire. Soon the caldron was seething: a thick, almost viscous green liquid that smelled like the "coffee" Flat-face had given me. This was the "hempen gruel" my father had always puzzled over when he read about it in Myerson's book on the Hassayampa: nothing more than liquefied pot, but to take the sleepy-bye out of it, the old men were spiking the broth with white powder—dragon's-tooth meth, I later learned. A few belts of that stuff and you were strung out like a dancing puppet somewhere between Betelgeuse and Erewhon.

The two young dudes who had ridden with the hunting party stayed away from the liquid grass; they preferred to smoke theirs, in the form of banana-sized "bombers" rolled in tobacco leaves. Apparently there was no shortage of weed in Ratnose's camp. Later I saw a whole shed packed with the stuff—good-quality smoke, on the order of the best Colombian shit that had been available back home. Another shed was packed with bricks of hash that Ratnose had captured along with an Afghan camel train; the camels had all died of catarrh that winter—victims of the Upper Hassayampa's hellacious climate—but Ratnose still hoped to deal the hash to some people he knew downriver, so no one was permitted to smoke it, eat it, or even touch it. "Mess with my shit," Ratnose croaked, "and I'll smoke you—over a slow fire."

After everyone had gotten mildly lit, the two young dudes broke out their "axes"—an acoustic guitar and an alto recorder—and got it on with *la musica*. I had to admit that, snotty and smirky as they looked, Fric and Frac were plenty good. Their repertoire ran from medieval *chansons* through Elizabethan ballads, show tunes, Sousa marches set to a rock beat, patriotic songs, Merle Haggard, Buck Owens, and all the way up to Dylan, Joplin, and Kristofferson. Now and then, one or another of the old women sat in with them, with a jew's harp or a dulcimer or something that looked like a dwarf sitar. Some of the people joined in with the singing—those who weren't otherwise occupied with wolfing down seared but bloody strips of aurochs meat that they'd broiled at knifepoint over the fire, or scarfing down mugs of *crait* (as the hempen gruel was called), or fucking in the firelight. Yes, fucking right there in the open. It shocked me at first—I'd never seen it done before—but Ratnose's people had no shame. To them it was part of eating and singing and killing and burning and sleeping and waking and shitting.

I first tumbled to what was going on in that regard when I heard a horrendous yelp, a female yelp, coming from the direction of the crait pot. At first I thought one of the women had spilled some of that boiling head medicine on herself, but the yelping continued, mixed in with grunts and yodels and heart-rending moans. Murder, I thought, and edged a bit closer to see what was happening, maybe even to catch a glimpse of some gore. What I saw—well, I sure don't want to sound like some simp, but then again I *was* a simp when it came to sex back then (I make it sound like it was years ago, and in a way it was). I could see this double-assed animal writhing around on a moth-eaten old horse blanket, its two pairs of legs—one set hairy and the other set smooth—going off in opposite directions, the smooth set flailing at the sky like they wanted to take a running broad jump at the moon, while from the tangle of hair that made up the animal's gigantic, lumpy head (see? I figured it was one head, not two) came this piteous, horrifying nonstop outpouring of sound. Pain? Complaint? Warning? Glee? I'd never heard noise like that before. Then half of the shaggy head pulled away and turned, and I saw my pal Hunk's flat, grinning face looking up at me even as he humped away, a pleased and foolish kisser it was, and he said by way of apology tinged with pride, "A real whooper iss dis one—what de Rat-nose call a leg-flailing lay."

I turned away, stunned and blushing, and some-body handed me a cup of crait, which I gulped down without even tasting it, and then I became aware that all around me people were doing it. Old folks and young folks. Old folks and old folks. Young folks and young folks. And over by the corral, old folks and young folks and horses even. Blondie, the toothless old hag with the long yellow braids who had been the first person in camp to spot me, was avidly blowing Frac the recorder player, who scarcely missed a note in the number—I think it was a rock version of the *Horst Wessel Lied*—until he came. Then he let fly with an exultant wooden bleat.

The crait was hitting me now, and I couldn't quite handle it all. The fires, guttering and popping. The red, white, and black of the scorched and sizzling au-rochs' carcass turning stiffly on its counterweighted spit, while the coals beneath flared up from time to time with gobs of burning fat. The crait caldron bub-bling and belching, its skull-popping steam snaking off through the wet night air toward the corral, where the horses—high on crait steam and bestiality—shrieked and nickered like Hunk's woman. I dipped another mug of crait from the caldron, determined to get with it, and then tightroped my way through the humping horde toward the edge of the light to wait for the dope to take effect.

At the edge of the dancing shadows, I caught the gleam of metal. A small figure bent and alone. As I angled closer, the metal object sharpened in focus: it

was my dump truck! Somebody was fiddling with my
dump truck while Rome burned? Suddenly I felt full
of rage, pulsing with a fury compounded of crait and
confusion, the day's anxiety tamped down like prim-
ing powder into the frizzen of my fist, the charge
rammed home by all those pounding peckers and ig-
nited by that flash of familiar metal. I jumped forward,
grabbed a handful of hair, and started slugging: a
small kid, no bigger than myself, easy pickings. But
I'd thumped away for no more than a dozen good
shots when something fiery and fast lashed around my
punching arm and yanked me off my victim and over
onto my back. Another slash hit my cheek, and I felt
it split. I tasted blood.

"Goddammit, Runaway! Fucking and fighting don't
mix—not in my camp they don't. They're not the same
thing!" Ratnose was standing over me, croaking madly
and whistling his sjambok through the air—his cattle-
driving quirt, made of raw rhinoceros hide; the kind
of whip the South African Boers use for keeping their
kaffirs in line. Ratnose enraged was something to see.
His good eye bulged and sparkled in the firelight like
an electric zircon, while the empty socket seemed to
spit little bits of barbed wire. His lips were drawn
back from his broken brown teeth; his grizzly goatee
shot sparks of ire and sputum. Without his ratskin cap
to hold it down, his stiff black hair stood up like the
roach of a kingfisher, ragged and slightly mad, and his
bent pointy dark beak only added to the likeness. A
kingfisher ready to swoop and spear me, poor baby
trout! Hold me helpless in his beak and then bat me
against a tree limb until I stopped wriggling and he
could gulp me down headfirst into his fishy-foul, primitive gut.

Indignant now and with tears in my eyes, as much
from hurt feelings as the whip cut on my face, I was
about to yell out, But it's *my* truck, you filthy thief!
Until I realized where that would lead. Ratnose
thought I was just another hippie-dippie runaway,
come to join his merry band. If he connected me with

the truck, and thus with the loot that Johnny Black had sold him, he'd know I was from a party that had been ripped off on the upper river, a party plotting revenge. He'd probably send off a bunch of his killers to do in my dad. He'd certainly serve me up for tomorrow night's supper. So I kept my mouth shut and just stared back at him, in neutral.

"Okay," he said finally, his kingfisher's roach relaxing. "It was probably just the crait. But goddammit, kid, you shouldn't beat up on girls."

Girls? I turned and looked at my little punching bag, and sure enough it was a girl. A woman, actually. I hadn't noticed the tits, small but definitely there, when I was flailing away at her head. She had the typical Upper Hassayampan features: wide cheekbones; a straight, thin nose; almond eyes; the mouth wide and thin-lipped, rather slack but smiling shyly at me now; and all of it framed in a coarse, lank mop of shiny black hair. Like most of Ratnose's people, she was dressed in a loose shirt of smoked leather, which she wore over a thick vest of quilted cotton that helped disguise her superstructure, frail as it was. She wore the high Mountain Wyandot moccasins with a pair of worn wool pants tucked in, and around her waist was a heavy, brass-studded belt that carried a knife, a set of pliers, and a gut bag of junk like needles, thread, a waterproof match safe, an awl, a lid of grass, and suchlike staples. She also wore a headband of very fine hide that was marked in black with intricate geometric designs—a strip of human skin, I later learned, from the thigh of a tattooed Iban warrior whom the gang had rubbed out the previous winter during a foray down South. She also had a wolf's tooth dangling from a piece of 20-pound-test monofilament. She kept the fang warm between her tits and used it to clean her ears.

Her name was Twigan, which I learned when Ratnose invited us over to his fire to eat. He had calmed down now and was playing the genial host.

"You two should make up," he said, leading the way

through the still-active bodies toward his bearskin. "The Runaway here will probably stay with us. I need him to replace Chipper. Poor old Chipper. A big bull knelt on him and then bit his nose off—blood and snot all over the snow. That wasn't so bad—we probably could have saved him—but one of his broken ribs went through his lungs and he was dead before we had the bull gutted. Tell me, Runaway my boy, what do you make of our little Twigan here? Cuddly little number, isn't she?" He patted Twigan's round little butt, and she smiled happily up at him. She still had my cuddly little truck in her cute little paws, so I only muttered something polite.

We dined on a dish that Ratnose called "shag-worp," or words to that effect. It was his favorite dish, he said: a rarity—something he had learned from the Chinese during his days of banditry on the lower river. "Like everything in the Chinese kitchen," he said, "it has philosophical meaning as well as the culinary." One of Ratnose's women served it up hot from a sizzling wok, along with small cups of hot rice liquor and steaming bean sprouts. It was a thin, crisp cutlet: white meat, smooth and sweet with just a tang—the merest taste—of something wild and willful. Ratnose took a bite, made a slight face (his long nose wrinkling like a mildly irate rodent's), and then splashed a dash of soy sauce on his portion.

"Not the very best," he said apologetically. "How do you like it, Runaway?"

"Fine," I mumbled through a mouthful. Then, swallowing: "What is it?"

"I don't usually give away recipes," Ratnose said, smiling playfully, "but in this case I'll make an exception. To understand shag-worp—indeed, to appreciate it—you must first understand and appreciate the interplay of life and death, that interplay catalyzed by hunger, lust, desire, demand, competition, call it what you will. You must understand that death is only the acting out of the Second Law of Thermodynamics: i.e., energy in a high state tends to become energy in

a lower state, all the way down to the inert. Contrariwise—would you like another sip of rice wine? A mug
of crait? No?—all right, contrariwise, life is a battle
against the inevitable downstream flow of the Second
Law. Living creatures take other living creatures in
their jaws and consume their high-state energy, thus
delaying the tendency, the inevitable tendency,
toward inertia on their own part. If the living creature
can forestall inertia long enough to reproduce itself,
then the Second Law is violated. Not of course for the
individual, who dies eventually anyway, but for those
countless outlaws who are struggling upstream
against the flow of the Second Law, and their off-
spring, etcetera. Get it? Like salmon, right? We're all
outlaws against nature—anything that procreates:
wolves, lambs, salmon, spearmen, minnows, kingfishers, serfs, kings, crooks, cops, flies, falcons, fuck-offs,
all of us—outlaws!"

"Fine," I said, "but how do you make shag-worp?"

"First off," Ratnose said, "you kill something—a
dog, maybe, or a man if you have to. You let the
corpse lie out in the weather, on the earth, until it's
infested with maggots. You wait until the grubs are
squirming around the eyes, the nostrils, the lips, the
ass hole. Then you put the infested meat into a container. A twenty-gallon gas can will do for a dog, anyway, or a small child. The maggots, hungry on their
upstream journey against the Second Law, consume
the corpse in its entirety. Then, hungry still, they turn
on one another. The strong consume the weak, until
finally there is only one maggot left. A giant maggot
that fills the entire container.

"At that point"—and Ratnose leaned forward, ges-
turing with his knife—"you dig up the can, pull out
the maggot, slice it neatly, and fry it in vegetable oil.
You serve it up with bean sprouts and rice wine." He
leaned back to see how I would take it. Thanks to the
crait, I kept it down.

"The only tricky part is making sure the gas can is
clean," Ratnose added finally. "That and knowing

when to dig it up, but you learn that with time." He looked at me expectantly, as if he wanted some comment or question.

"It tastes pretty good," I said at last. "That's a neat idea about all the outlaws swimming upstream against death. Where did you pick that up?"

"I didn't 'pick it up.' I figured it out. Don't let the way I look or act deceive you. I'm not a dummy. I read a lot. I have all kinds of books up in my cave—not just books I've taken in raids, but books I brought with me when I first came up here: physics and chemistry texts, law books, the works of Heidegger and Buber and Sartre, of Conrad and Proust and Joyce, poetry from Donne to Dickey, Sufistic texts in the Arabic . . . I look this way because of the life I lead, that I've *chosen* to lead, and that kind of a life leaves scars on a man. It makes him act, finally, the way he looks. To paraphrase Sartre, a man is the sum of his scars—don't you think?"

By that time, I didn't think anything. I *couldn't* think anything. I was stunned to the eyeballs on crait and fried maggot and an overload of impressions. Besides, I had to take a leak, so I excused myself and wandered down to the river. Walking, I felt wide and light, as if each atom of my body was separated from the next by an inch of clear, cold darkness. The music splashed against the atoms of my body like surf against a string pier, surging through and around them, creating momentary whirlpools of sound and light and then receding again to let the darkness take over. Looking back at the campfires, wincing at the pain of the light, I realized that Fric and Frac were no longer serenading us. The music came from somewhere else, or perhaps from my head, from my very molecules. I found that I could orchestrate it however I wished, so as I tripped along through the darkness I experimented with various time signatures—three-four, four-four, five-four, eleven-eight. My heart was the obvious timpani, my liver a clarinet, my lungs an oboe, my toes a slow guitar, my nose—a nose flute, of

course. And when I unzipped to pee in the river, my
bladder issued forth the entire Vienna Boys Choir, all
rills and trills and chirrups.

Void now, I sat back against a deadfall and listened
to the music as I studied the sky. The rain clouds of
the day had blown through. Bats hunted against the
stars, flying their intricate, random zigzag routes. No
way you could diagram that in a playbook, not even
with a computer. The only way the random manue-
vers of bat and bug made sense was as a death dance.
Or a life dance, as Ratnose would think of it, taking
the predator's point of view. I thought about that for
a while: all life as outlawry. It excited me. My mind
started leaping ahead with the idea to a great clash of
cymbals (I was belching the essence of fried maggot
by now): Ratnose's Law of the Outlaw put the skids
to everything my parents and teachers were trying to
lay on me. An orderly universe. The higher forms of
life as the logical rulers of that universe. The highest
ruling form, mankind—ruled itself by wise, benign,
and thoughtful predators who justly took advantage
of the low-lifes beneath them, whether cow or cowherd
(or coward?), though not so crudely or cruelly as to
incite rebellion . . .

A bat swooped low to suck in a moth that was mill-
ing with its pals just inches above the water. At the
same moment, a huge pikelike fish vaulted off the bottom, broke water with a roar of fins and gill plates,
and gulped down the bat. I could see the broken wing
tips of the tiny, warm mammal protruding from the
jaws of the fish as it plunged back into the stream.
Then a dark streak as the fish turned, like a log bend-
ing back on itself, to take position once again in ambush for another bat . . .

The way Ratnose saw the world, everything in it
was hungry. Everything bit and ate to the best of its
ability. If it wasn't bitten and eaten itself before it
could reproduce, all the better. There were no supe-
rior or inferior forms of life, except in the sense that
some individuals let themselves be put down—went

weakly and meekly to the chopping block. That was what man's law was all about: a con job aimed at making people lie down and take it, accept the bloodless life of rules and restrictions, their tongues coated with the sour fuzz of guilt, their bellies griping with anxiety over whether they were dressed properly, talked properly, carried the proper piece of paper with the proper signature to permit them to do the proper thing. Ratnose said to hell with all of that. He ate his meat fried, all right, and spiced with gunpowder.

I puked up the fried maggot, watched its greasy swirl drift out of sight down the dark water, and then walked back toward the campfires. The music had died. My body was back to its normal size, rather small but very dense, the molecules rubbing happily against each other as if to say, Hi, buddy, long time no feel. The scene around the campfire looked like those photographs you see of places like Wounded Knee or Auschwitz or My Lai. Limp bodies sprawled all around, most of them half in and half out of their clothes. Tits lolling this way, tongues that way, limp peckers drooping towards the earth like night crawlers that hadn't quite made it all the way home. The fires had burned down to beds of red coals, dusted over with that grainy gray ash that flakes from time to time like lava cooling. Dead silence except for the snores and a few throaty moans. The crait caldron had cooled as well, and now its surface was a thick, slack green skin, pimpled in places by iridescent bubbles.

Off in the darkness, I heard a livelier sound, the steady *slip-slop* of people fucking. I moved in for a closer look. It was Ratnose, up on his knees, a dense and beaky blackness against the thinner dark of the night, pumping away in dog fashion against a pale ass that glowed in the dying firelight like an opal. Ratnose was enjoying every millimeter of it, the old push-you—pull-me in slow motion, with half-twists thrown in there now and then as if he were pulling the cork of a wine bottle. His lone eye rolled at the stars like a searchlight. His balls slapped against the girl's thighs with a sweaty, sodden thwacking sound, like bell clappers that had been turned to raw clay. When he came, only his pecker moved; his face stayed still. The girl disimpaled herself and rolled over on her back. Of course it was Twigan. Ratnose leaned over to kiss her and then turned towards me.

"You better get some sleep, Runaway," he said. "In the morning, we have to see how good you can shoot and ride. And it better be damned good—otherwise, into the stew pot." He uttered what seemed to be a laugh with his hoarse, kingfisher croak, and I heard Twigan laughing with him.

32

Hunk shook me awake at first light. The cave was dark and warm, smelling of mushrooms. A heavy frost had laid strange figures on the oilskin window, and while Hunk fried up some thick slabs of aurochs heart and onions for our breakfast, I walked outside to see the day break. Fragments of a nightmare blew through my skull, a broken cobweb in the wind, leaving me weak and on the edge of tears. A giant bat with Ratnose's face had carried me above the Hassayampa, then dropped me. "Learn to fly!" My wings could barely hold the air. I slid down the sky with that helpless, gut-knotted feeling that comes with an uncontrollable skid on ice, cupping my wings and kicking my feet, falling, falling straight for the river, where a dark shape waited underwater, a dark shape that resolved itself finally at the last panic-jerking moment into a water dragon . . .

It was clear and cold that morning, with the underbrush coated in hoarfrost, so I trotted a bit to kick off the shakes. My run took me past the storage sheds near the corral, and while I stood there huffing and puffing the horsy-sweet air, I saw a motorcycle parked in the back of one of the sheds. I choked up a bit, flashing on my lovely little Honda SL-100 trail bike waiting for me back home, all blue and lonely and shiny and ready to race. This bike, on closer inspection, proved to be a Husqvarna 450—a bit bent and dirty, but seemingly in running condition. I rocked the bike on its stand and heard gasoline sloshing in the tank. For a moment I felt a surge of elation. I could escape from here right now if I wanted to: everyone was still asleep or else shaking with hangover from last night's orgy; I could kick this Husky to life and pop a wheelie through those dead fires and with my elbows out in the most impeccable motocross style I'd fishtail down through the camp, farting a contemptuous farewell to Ratnose on the way, bounce down that horse trail in fifth, vaulting the ditches and drifting through the corners, and when I reached the Hassayampa I'd take my dad on the pillion and we'd split for home . . .

But the key wasn't in the ignition.

"I've got it," said Ratnose with a smirk. He walked into the shed and kicked a tire. "You know how to ride this thing?"

"Sure," I said. "I've never ridden one with quite this much power, but I've got my own bike back home, a dirt bike, and I've raced it a bit."

"We killed the guy who had this one," Ratnose said with an air of detached nostalgia. "He was coming down the valley over there to the west, must have been doing about sixty miles an hour. He was a good quarter of a mile away from us. Hunk just couldn't resist the challenge—a fast-moving target at that kind of range. Old Hunky just took a rest on a convenient boulder and swung that little two-forty-three of his, and crack! Broke the guy's neck on the first shot. The motorcycle went about two hundred yards farther than the guy. That's how it got all scuffed up like that. I tried to ride it, but the bastard threw me. We wheeled it back here, though, just in case we could trade it sometime."

"I'll take it off your hands," I said. Ratnose smirked again.

"We'll see about that," he said. "After all, *we* may be taking *you* off our hands before the day is out." He licked his fingers as if they were covered with gravy. "You'd better get your breakfast, because I want to start the test right quick now."

After I'd eaten—if you can call it that; I wasn't exactly ravenous—I took the shotgun and a bandolier filled with various loads and walked out with Hunk to where Ratnose and the others were waiting. It was warmer now, and the frost was flaking from the trees.

Hunk was slab-faced and solemn. He had his rifle slung over his shoulder—a pretty little .243 Browning lever-action with a four-power Weaver scope. Fric and Frac were lying on the hillside, playing grab-ass and yukking it up, now and then taking a squirt from a wineskin. A noseless old man in horsehides, whose name was Beppo and who was reputed to be an excellent trapper, stood next to Ratnose with a pair of skulls in his hands. Some of the women were dragging in wood for a fire. Twigan was among them, and she threw me a friendly smile—the only one I'd seen so far today.

"All right," said Ratnose cheerfully, "before we see how well you can shoot, we want to see how well you can take being shot at. Give him those skulls, Beppo. Now, Runaway, you hike on out there towards the woods about a hundred paces and put those skulls on your shoulders, one on a side, and face us. Hunk here will get rid of them for you, won't you, Hunky?" My roommate nodded gloomily.

"Okay," I said. "I trust Hunk's shooting, after that story you told me this morning. But what about ricochets? I mean, those skulls are hard, and bullets have been known to follow the curve of the skull. . . ."

"Iss hokay," said Hunk. "I got solids in here"—and he slapped the magazine. The steel-jacketed bullets ought to pop right straight through the bone, I knew, but still . . . I walked out the hundred paces, my throat jerking spasmodically, and lifted the skulls to my shoulders. The others looked distant and tiny. Fric and Frac made exaggerated soup-eating motions and laughed uproariously. If I could make it to the woods . . . But Hunk would drop me before I covered ten yards. I tried to swallow and stood as still as possible. Hunk was sitting, his elbows on his knees, and the end of the scope stared at me like a monocle.

The skull on my right shoulder exploded like a grenade, fragments flying every which way, one of them clipping my nose, and I never heard Hunk's shot. With my ears still ringing and my mind racing like a squirrel cage, my knees started to buckle and then, *splat!*, the second skull exploded, louder than the first. I reeled away to my right, but caught myself from falling. Hunk was standing up, grinning proudly as he snapped the bright brass out of the receiver. I took a deep breath and tasted blood in the back of my throat. A bloody nose from that first bone fragment. I stooped to pick it up. It was a chunk of cheekbone, and I pocketed it for a souvenir. I wiped my nose on a shirt sleeve and walked back slowly. At least I hadn't peed my pants. Twigan and some of the other women applauded.

"Fine," I said to Ratnose. "Now let me do the same for you." Everyone laughed. Ratnose took the .243 from Hunk and handed it to me.

"Not just yet," he said. "First let's see you hit that skull on the pole above my cave."

The rifle felt light but well balanced, and I knew it shot flat. I wrapped the sling around my forearm and took a squint through the scope. A cinch. The skull looked as big as a medicine ball at this range. I thumbed back the hammer and squeezed off. Very little recoil. The top of the pole quivered as the skull flew apart. The lower jawbone was all that remained, spinning crazily until I levered in another round and smashed it to bits, the few remaining teeth spattering down like hail. A surge of confidence: I couldn't miss with this piece. Spinning around, I worked the lever again and zeroed in on a flock of chickens that were working over the horse manure at the edge of the corral—nearly a 200-yard shot. I headed one chicken—*pow!*—then another before Ratnose could grab the rifle barrel.

"Goddammit," he roared, "don't show off on the livestock!" Great gusts of laughter. Only Fric and Frac looked glum.

"There's one round left," I said as Ratnose let go of the muzzle. Before he could object, I zapped the wineskin that lay on the ground between Fric and Frac. A spurt of wine hit Frac in the eye while Fric did a backflip getting away. After a moment of stunned silence, everyone descended on the ruptured wineskin, laughing and scratching and guzzling to see that none of it went to waste. Then the men raced to get their own weapons.

One thing about Ratnose's people, a whiff of gunpowder or a drop of blood always put them in a festive mood. For the next hour, the camp sounded like a battlefield. Hunk blasted a couple more chickens so as not to be topped by my shooting—"Need a few more for the chicken soup anyway," Ratnose rationalized. Then Beppo broke out a rusty old foot trap from the storage shed and began throwing targets for the wing shooters. Empty beer and bully-beef cans, pie tins, pot lids, whiskey bottles, even an old wooden clog—we shredded or shattered or ventilated all of them. Fric and Frac, the pistoleros, recovered from their bruised egos and skipped a bottle cap across the stream with their six-guns. Finally, Ratnose called a halt.

"It's always good to burn a little powder," he said, "but we haven't got an unlimited supply of ammunition. And anyway, Runaway here still has to show us how well he can ride."

I had been hoping that they might have forgotten about the riding part. Like most kids growing up in the countryside, I'd snitched rides on old farm plugs from time to time, galloping them to a froth while we played Cowboys-and-Indians, but I knew I was not a real horseman. Not like these people were. They practically lived on horseback, and when I recalled how Ratnose had vaulted from the saddle the other day as easily as I'd step off the front porch, I knew I'd make a bad showing. But not as bad as it turned out.

The horse they led forth from the corral was a raunchy, hammerheaded buckskin. Old and galled, with a rib cage like a tank truck. I'd never get my knees around those withers. And I was expected to ride him bareback, with only a cinch around his belly and a string of rawhide in his mouth. No bit, no snaffle, no nothing.

"Shit, I won't even be able to mount up," I complained. "I'm too short for this damned giraffe."

"I'll give you a leg up," said Ratnose with a wicked grin.

"What do I have to do with him?"

"Nothing much. Just ride him down to the edge of the woods there and back. Take him at whatever speed you want—walk, trot, canter, or gallop."

I looked more closely at Ratnose. It sounded too easy, and he had that slick sound of menace in his voice that I was beginning to recognize as a signal that Ratnose was in a mood to teach lessons.

Suddenly he grabbed me by the leg and threw me onto the horse's back. I had the reins in my hand, but before I could even take up the slack I was upside down in the air, staring down at the crowd that looked at least a hundred yards below me, and then I was back in the nightmare—"Learn to fly!" Skidding, slipping through the air. A splat of white light. The horse rearing over me with rolling eyes and mucky hoofs. A roar of shock and horse laughter in my ears. Somehow I scuttled clear of the hooves and staggered to my feet up against the rails of the corral. I felt clearheaded but numb, and I could see that they were all laughing at me. I was walking over to Ratnose, who held the bridle, and saying "Gimme that!"

Then I was up in the air again—longer this time, it seemed, but the shock of the landing seemed less. I remember thinking: If only I can figure out when he's starting to throw me, then maybe I can correct for it. But I couldn't even tell if I was ever on the horse's back. All I could feel was the flight through the air and then the dirt under my cheek. I could see the people watching me—some gleeful; others neutral; a few, like Twigan and Hunk, looking embarrassed, or maybe sad. I don't know how many times I took that trip, but finally Ratnose grabbed me by the neck and pulled me away from the horse.

"I think we can safely say that you're not a horseman," he said. "You've failed the test." Fric and Frac applauded, and Frac—that rotten bastard—started beating on his mess tin. A few others cheered, too. I tried to focus on them and remember their faces, but my eyeballs were still spinning, and bits of dirt and horseshit kept clouding my vision.

"Wait a goddam minute," I said finally. "I passed two thirds of the test, and I'm willing to keep trying on this part until I can make it. And you told me yourself, this morning, that you got thrown by that Husky over there in the shed. Nobody ate you up because you couldn't ride a simple little dirt bike. I know kids only ten years old who can ride a dirt bike. Let me show you what I can do on the Husky and then give me some time to learn about horses."

They pondered that for a few minutes, the older men talking back and forth in their nasal, hissing language that I couldn't understand.

"Iss good point," Hunk said finally, in English. "I say give kid another chance." Most of the others nodded agreement.

"Okay, Runaway," Ratnose said, "you've gained a reprieve from the charcoal broiler."

By now the numbness that had come with being thrown was wearing off. My left shoulder ached, and I noticed that both of my elbows were skinned raw, my shirt shredded and sticking to the blood with clots of grass and rubbed-in dirt. My nose throbbed; it was thick enough now with swelling that it restricted some of my vision up close. Yesterday's whip cut across my cheek had reopened, though the dirt in it kept the bleeding to a minimum. I asked Ratnose if I couldn't clean up before riding the bike.

"Come on, Runaway, I didn't figure you for a femme. Next thing you know, you'll want to go to the pediatrician—or maybe the gynecologist."

I took a swig from Fric and Frac's half-empty wineskin to clear my throat and then wheeled the Husky out into the sun. Ratnose tossed me the key. I switched on the gas and closed the choke lever, then checked the oil sump: full, though slightly dirty. It took three kicks to get the bike lit off, but once she was running, she sounded smooth and hungry. My father used to laugh at the way I attributed human characteristics to my bike—"anthropomorphism," he called it—but I figured that if men in the olden days could give human names to their horses and mules, and even make love to them, then why couldn't my generation do the same? I mean, they're both transportation, and if anything deserves to be treated like folks, it's the thing that gets you away from them. I didn't believe in going so far as to ball a bike, though. I'd heard of a kid who tried it and got stuck. *Coitus captivitis* of the exhaust pipe.

The big 450-cc motor was warm now, blipping nicely under my left hand, so I pushed the choke lever all the way open and clutched her into bottom gear. She jerked forward a bit—strong, eager to ride. The gang was gathered all around me, goggling like a bunch of Stone Age savages who'd never seen a machine before. Well, I'd give them a magic show, all right. Ratnose was yelling something at me through the engine noise, pointing to his head. Twigan came running up with a crash helmet in her hand, one of those fancy American-flag numbers out of Easy Ridersville. It must have belonged to the Husky's dead owner. I shook my head "no," even though I knew I should take it.

"That's for pussies!" I yelled to Ratnose. He was standing nearly in front of me, and as he started to grin his approval, I brought her up to revs and popped the clutch. The torque came on like the Light Brigade and the front wheel leaped into the air, knocking Ratnose on his butt as the bike took off in a classic wheelstand. The crowd in front of me scrambled and split as I held the wheelie right through them, spewing dirt and sticks and assorted crud behind me like a machine gun. Ahead of me was the big bonfire, but I wasn't ready for that yet—not until I'd gotten the bike sorted out. I backed off on the throttle, the engine torque serving as my brake, and slid around the fire in a sharp series of S-shaped slides, then hit it again and lined out towards the end of the clearing, changing up through the gearbox to top before I got there.

The Husky had more power than anything I'd ever ridden before, but it was a smooth machine, totally responsive. It felt great to be back on a bike, up on the pegs, leaning and swinging my body like a small, upside-down pendulum that controlled the great vibrating steel time machine under me. I had plenty of room to work in, so I cut a few tight doughnuts and figure-8s, then lofted the bike over logs and potholes, getting the feel of her for my big act. I'd noticed that the bonfire was built on the backside of a shallow slope, so as to mask it from the prevailing winds. The rim of the slope was between me and the gang, offering a perfect takeoff ramp for a jump over the fire. I'd give them a touch of Evel. Knievel, that is. Right now I was Awful Knaufel.

Wheeling to the far edge of the clearing, I stopped the bike and lined up for the run. Just the top of the fire was visible from here, owing to the rise in the ground, and I could see the faces of the gang through the flames, warped and goggling and wraithlike. I charged at the fire, the throttle screwed down tight, full revs, belly-tight against the tank, and then as I hit the top of the slope I stood on the pegs, leaning backward to bring the front wheel up and keep it there throughout the trajectory. At the top of the jump, I could see them all ahead of me: hands at their throats and mouths; even Ratnose agog, with his big midnight eye fixed on me in unblinking horror. I almost lost it when I touched down—later, when I paced off the jump, it measured a full twenty strides—but that only made it look more spectacular. Brakes and a sharp downshift, and I was skidding to a sideways stop in front of them, once again lashing everyone with dirt. Dogs and chickens scattered, women screamed, and even Ratnose flinched. I blatted the throttle loud and high, then hit the kill switch.

"Do I pass?"

Everyone blinked their eyes and then started cheering. Ratnose, too. I'd joined the gang.

As we walked away towards the fire for the customary crait celebration—these people celebrated everything, sometimes even the sunrise—Ratnose put his arm around my shoulder. "Ah," he said, "there's an old saying that applies here. 'To ride, shoot straight, and tell a lie is all you need to teach a guy.'"

Yeah, I thought, The Song of the Hassayampa.

33

My first few days with Ratnose's gang had made it seem that they led a pretty easy life. I mean, plenty of fresh red meat, plenty of dope and wine, no restrictions on screwing, or shooting off guns at any time of the day or night. People just jumped up whenever they felt like it to go galloping off on a horse, say, letting it run wherever it wanted. I had free access to the bike, after my initiation, just as the rest of the band had to the horses. We ate when we pleased, drank when we pleased, played when we pleased, worked when we pleased, and slept when we pleased, with whomsoever was pleased to sleep with us. Or alone, if we pleased. But it only *seemed* that way. Actually, we worked pretty hard.

The rumors that drift down the Hassayampa with the skulls and flotsam of the spring runoff would lead you to believe that Ratnose spends all his time raiding and raping and burning. In point of fact, we only raided when we were really hard up, like when we needed more ammunition, or horses, or a new lot of women. Ratnose had a good trading relationship with many of the villages on the outskirts of his territory, and whenever we needed the staples like salt or sugar, the cheap things, we would ride on over to one or another of them and swap hides for what we needed. We rarely raided a settlement, since Ratnose figured that settlements were serious things that could call for reinforcements, and at any rate the people in them had long memories. Instead, he preferred to raid the few caravans or wagon trains that crossed his country. That way he could pick his own time and place, and usually wipe out the party to the last man. Also, caravans were "concentrated riches," as he liked to say, while villages were "concentrated poverty."

Not that Ratnose was any Robin Hood. He had nothing but contempt for such romantic notions as robbing from the rich to give to the poor. You robbed from the rich because they had stuff, and yet let the poor alone because they were a waste of time. Unless you wanted skulls. ("A poor man's head skins out easier and cures quicker than a rich man's because he has less fat on his skull," Ratnose always said.)

No, a raid was a big thing to Ratnose and his people, kind of like a Christmas shopping expedition would be to city folks, except that you did it with guns, though with no less anticipation. We actually went into training for the raids. Men who had grown soft and sloppy on too much crait or eating, too much lying around camp, would hie themselves off into the mountains for a few days of climbing, hunting, and loneliness. Dried meat, raw roots, ice water and solitude would shape them up quick. But few of the men—and very few of the women, for that matter—ever let themselves slide that far into slobhood. We all had work to do, though we never called it that. We got a kick out of providing.

Like on the morning after my Initiation Orgy, when I was lying there in Hunk's cave feeling completely frazzled from pituitary to pecker (more about that later), and old Beppo walked in wondering if Hunk would help him out on the trapline that day. Hunk's dart wound was still kind of septic, he said, but maybe . . .

"How about you, Runner?" Beppo asked. My bones still ached, and the cuts on my face and arms had that stiff feeling that warns against motion, but I said, Sure, just give me a minute to get dressed and eat. I pulled on my boots, stuffed a handful of sarvisberry pemmican into my mouth, grabbed my shotgun, and followed noseless old Beppo out into the trapper's world.

We pounded those wooded draws all day, wading the ice-cold streams and clambering up sheer granite faces to investigate Beppo's sets. He must have had a hundred of them, and he knew each one more intimately than my tongue knew the creases between my molars. He seemed to see the flow of the country through a shrew's eyes, or better yet, feel it through a mole's toes; he knew how various furbearers and predators would use the wrinkles of the earth, where they would step to avoid getting their feet wet, which ones would take to the water rather than continue on land, what patches of berry bush would draw which birds and thus which foxes, weasels or reptiles. He knew the otter slides and the beaver houses, the wolf runs and the bear dens, and he could build a perfect set for each one. Mainly he used deadfalls, snares, and cage traps, though when he had to make a set underwater, like for beaver or otter, he used steel traps. For pine marten and fisher, he used small steel traps which he set inside of little doll-sized log cabins, whose doorways he anointed with an evil-smelling goo that he carried around with him in a milk bottle. The first time I smelled it, I nearly puked.

"What the hell's in that stuff?"

"Fish guts, chicken heads, the eyeballs of codfish, rat brains, the bodies of mice that died in the grain bin—things like that. After a while it turns to liquid. The marten thinks he's found himself a feast, and *snap*, I've got him."

I admired Beppo's skill in reading the wilderness, and I was fascinated with what he taught me about the daily rounds of animal life, the ease with which these creatures were taken by anyone who took the time to study their habits. But I was repelled as well. Beppo was a phlegmatic killer. He carried a cudgel with him on these excursions, and with it he merely tapped the trapped animal over the snout, knocking it cold. Then he jumped on its chest, rupturing the heart. I saw him do it to wolves as well as weasels— standing there expressionless within inches of a set of teeth that could have taken his hand off at the wrist. *Clank! Stomp!* Then the skinning knife. I began to wonder if perhaps he hadn't lost his nose to a wolf bite. No, he told me, nothing so glamorous. A crazy whore he knew in Hymarind had clipped it off one night with a garden shears while he was cooling out from a crait high. It wasn't so bad after he got over the shock of being ugly, he said. At least, he didn't snore anymore.

That was the unnerving thing about Beppo—he was so goddam matter-of-fact about death and mutilation. But so were the rest of them in Ratnose's camp. I had been taught that the inflicting of pain and death was justifiable only in the best of causes—defense of home and hearth, a righteous war, perhaps for a trophy head. We didn't have to witness the deaths of the animals we ate, and if we thought of it at all, we quickly reassured ourselves that it was painless. These people tortured and killed for entertainment; it was their equivalent of teevee. But at least they were honest enough to accept pain and death when it came their way without whimpering or sniveling.

"A quick, easy death, like from a bullet through the head, is nothing special," Beppo told me one afternoon. We had just finished skinning out a black sable, whose hide was drying in the feeble winter sunshine against a boulder. The frail body of the animal, sticky and pink except for a large, misshapen purple bruise that covered its chest cavity, lay bent and (to me at least) pitiful in the weeds. "A slow death without complaint is better, like being skinned alive by your enemies and still having enough strength to spit at them when they peel away your lips. I've seen it done—you'll see it too, when Ratnose gets into one of his moods. And I'll remember the man who spat in Ratnose's eye longer than I will the ones who went under quietly, or who whined for mercy. The only afterlife is what other people remember."

I recalled what Ratnose had said: A man is the sum of his scars.

Of course, I didn't really enjoy thinking about those things, and there was plenty of action just in the daily round to keep my mind occupied. Following Beppo on the trapline for a few weeks taught me where all the good bird covers were. One of the pointers in camp, a German shorthair named Max, was a natural gun dog, all nose and no brains, and between us we filled the larder with game birds: ruffed grouse from the bottoms and blue grouse from the slopes; green pigeons and guinea fowl from the bamboo copses downriver; prairie chickens, sage grouse, bustards, and peafowl from the short-grass prairies; Chinese and golden pheasants from the grainlands near Tor and Hymarind, the only towns in our vicinity.

At first I felt tense, hunting near civilization, but gradually my curiosity—and a little bit of homesickness, maybe—overrode the nervousness. Now and then, when the shooting was slow, Max and I would ankle into Hymarind and enjoy a day on the town. In the old Chinese market, with its welter of strange sights and smells, I would buy myself a bowl of noodle soup and a tidbit for Max—maybe a sheep's heart, or a camel's foot—and we would sit there in the shade, slurping and watching. The townies must have known I was one of Ratnose's thugs, because they left me alone, but the local dogs weren't that perceptive: they tried to pick on Max at first, scruffy little yellow dogs with their ribs showing sharper than their teeth, and only after he had killed two or three of them did they wise up. There was no bluster about Max. He would watch an aggressor approaching, all bristly and cocksure, Max staring at him with his flat, amber eyes until the dog was within range, and then Max would uncoil like a cobra and hit the enemy dog in the throat. There was no sound but that of the other dog scrambling to get loose; Max had it by the windpipe and it soon strangled to death.

Sometimes we would stop at the only American bar in town, a place called the Costive Cowpoke Cocktail Lounge, which was run by a fellow named Hal McVeigh who had stayed on after the war and who suffered grievously from constipation. The bar girls were jolly, and Hal's war stories kept me fascinated for hours, and the beer was cold enough to sweat. Hal often asked me what had become of good old America, down there at the end of the river, but when I told him, he shook his head and moaned. "Glad I stayed here," he would say. "Sounds like it turned into a right shitbox." One day when I came out of the bar, Max was dead. Some mean Chink had fed him a chunk of meat with bamboo slivers in it. Revenge, I guess, for the dogs Max had killed. I buried him behind the bar and then rode back to camp on the motorcycle, but I didn't cry, though I felt like it.

After that, I stayed away from Hymarind. Towns were bad news. The people there were sneaky, and anyway, the noodle soup from the Chinese market always gave me diarrhea. What's more, we were now into the meat-gathering time of the year, and the Husky was valuable for big-game drives. Caribou, elk, aurochs, wild camels, even a few mastodons browsed the prairies near our camp, fattening up in anticipation of winter. We fattened up on them. One day Fric, who had been out scouting for game, rode in excitedly to say that a band of steppe wisent was working down through the brushy draws to the south of us. By the time we got to the ridge from which Fric had spotted them, though, the wisent were already straggling out onto the prairie. We watched them from the shelter of the pines: great woolly black critters that looked like the pictures I'd seen of the American buffalo. "How we can surround them?" Hunk asked. He was in charge of the hunting party, now that his leg had healed. "By time we get down there, they'll be scrammed."

I pointed out to him that my bike was much faster than the horses, so why didn't I coast quietly down the ridge the way we'd come up; circle around to the tail of the ridge, which would put me in front of the wisent band; and then rev her up real loud and run across their path, spooking them back into the draw, where Hunk and his hunters would be waiting. We did it—and a wild ride it was for me! Potholes and hidden wallows, the dust from the frantic herd swirling around me so that I had to ride by the tips of my boots, great shaggy heads suddenly appearing ahead

of me, with rolling eyes and flashing horns, the bike
bucking and coughing like Ratnose's damned bronco
. . . But finally I turned them, and then ran in among
the stragglers. Hunk had given me a .30 M-1A carbine
he didn't use anymore, and I carried it in a boot on
the bike. I drew it now and rode in alongside the big
black beasts, choking with dust and my eyes watering,
my head gone crazy with the sound of the bike and
their hooves, blasting them behind the shoulder and
hearing them grunt and crash in the murk behind me,
splattered with lung blood that turned to sour black
muck, flipping an endo into one deep wallow and
luckily getting the bike rolling again before I was
trampled. We killed about twenty out of the band,
and they were the last wisent that I ever saw.

Later I discovered that coming off the bike had cost
me a broken wrist and a few cracked ribs, so it wasn't
all adventure and joy. Or at least, not all the adventure was joyous. Most of the time, the chores were a
lot less exciting. Cutting wood, fixing the roofs of the
caves, skinning out and butchering game, sharpening
knives and axes, cleaning guns, reloading ammunition
from the stockpile of powder and bar lead Ratnose
had liberated from a Cambodia-bound caravan—
things like that. The winter was cold. We cut ice and
skidded it up to camp, packing it in sawdust under a
shed in the shelter of the hillside, surrounded by the
hay we had cut for the horses. While we were storing
the ice, a child from the camp, Blondie's youngest son,
Lump, fell into the hole we had cut and was swept
away under the ice. The ice weevils must have got
him, because we never found him, not even after the
spring runoff had subsided.

I felt bad about Blondie's loss—probably worse
than she did herself. On the night of my initiation,
Blondie had been the first woman to, well, seduce me,
I guess you'd have to say. Like all of Ratnose's
women, she was a bear for balling, couldn't seem to
get enough of it, and despite her toothlessness she
proved to be what they call a charmful armful. A firm,
plump body much younger than her face; muscular

little boobs with tips like new asparagus; and a guz-zling ginch that wouldn't let go. Just as my gun dog Max had seemed to be built entirely to serve his nose—eyes, ears, legs, liver, lungs, all there only to propel that ultrasensitive, double-barreled sniffer around the countryside—so too did the rest of Blondie seem to be there only to get her cunt locked around someone's tent peg.

I don't remember much about the seduction itself (rape is too strong a word, though it came closer to that than anything else). Most guys can recall every detail of their First Time, right on down to what color socks they were wearing that day, but I was too strung out on crait and self-esteem for that. The main impression was that all my nerve ends had migrated to my pecker, where they were subjected to a sensory overload of tonguing, stroking, nibbling, tugging, squeezing, and shlurping. Toward the end there, I felt like I was being drawn dong-first into a hot, wet vac-uum cleaner made out of meat. With my time sense expanded by the crait, it was impossible to describe my orgasm as a "climax"; it seemed to have no clear beginning, only a steady, smooth buildup of surges, like the pulsations of interference that a passing air-plane causes on a television tube, reaching a peak somewhere along in there, I couldn't tell you precisely when—maybe about 10:47, during the Charmin com-mercial—but then tailing off with no diminution of ecstasy, so that even hours later I was still getting pleasant little aftershocks. And the strange thing was, I could isolate the tremors of the first orgasm from the ones that followed that night—five or six of them, Hunk later estimated.

The whole damned gang of thieves and lechers was gathered around, watching us and offering advice while we screwed. I've read that many of the so-called higher animals, like porpoises and whales and elephants and apes, get turned on by watching, and that seemed to be the way with Ratnose's people. Other women in the band took their turns with me that night, the older women mainly, and I can remember being pleasantly surprised to discover that each one of those bearded clams, as my school pals called them, was different both inside and out. One of them had hair on it that must have been three inches long; another one was scalloped around the edges with a flange of slippery skin the color of a dog's lips; a third pussy—belonging to a flat-faced number named Tekla who was always trudging around camp with a bundle of firewood on her back and who looked about as sexy as a pine stump—sprouted a surprising clit the length and thickness of the tip of my little finger, a prehensile tuning fork the tickling of which could produce sustained high notes of a frequency that would shatter glass. I remember thinking with wonderment that a man could spend his whole life studying the infinite variety of snatch—categorizing it, comparing it, characterizing it, writing odes to each one—and never get bored, never reach any conclusions.

Right then I had my eye on Twigan, who was standing in the thick of the crowd with an avid look in her own eye. But she wouldn't come closer, and it occurred to me that, of course, the older women had seniority rights on a newcomer (though I was rapidly waning into a condition that might best be described as "old comer"). Also, she was Ratnose's favorite, and although the band was basically democratic about sex, the leader had certain vaguely defined rights and privileges that no one might properly challenge. Well, I figured as I humped away there in the glow of the firelight with all those sex fiends ogling me and playing with each other, maybe the time will come for me and Twigan, or maybe it won't. At least, I won't be hurting for female companionship in the meantime.

And I didn't. Winter marked the end of the mass outdoor orgies, of course, but there was never any shortage of singles, doubles, or triples, either for an hour, overnight, or for weeks at a time. Only rarely was there any conflict—two women after one guy, or

vice versa—and then it was always quickly resolved
by making it a group thing. There were no really deep
attachments or antagonisms between individuals in
the camp. It was as if everyone shared a common
skin, and in a way a common skull. But within that
skin and that skull there prevailed a powerful loyalty,
an interdependence balanced with individuality on
every level from food gathering to fucking that would
tolerate no threat, from either the inside or the outside of the band. I mentioned that to Ratnose one
night when we were reloading burned brass in his
cave. It was blustery outside, cold and raw, with a
smell of snow on the cutting edge of the wind, but
our fire kept us warm and a pot of tea was chortling
on the hob. Twigan was there, as usual, stitching boot
tops in the circle of light cast by the fat lamp. Ratnose
walked over to his big bookcase and pulled out a
worn, red-jacketed tome. It was *The Myth of the Machine*, Volume I, by Lewis Mumford. Striking a
mock-heroic pose, he read to us:

"Wherever the seasons are marked by holiday fes-
tivals and ceremonies: where the stages of life are
punctuated by family and communal rituals: where
eating and drinking and sexual play constitute the
central core of life: where work, even hard work, is
rarely divorced from rhythm, song, human companionship, and esthetic delight: where vital activity is
counted as great a reward of labor as the product:
where neither power nor profit takes precedence of
life: where the family and the neighbor and the friend
are all part of a visible, tangible, face-to-face commu-
nity: where everyone can perform as a man or woman
any task that anyone else is qualified to do—there the
neolithic culture, in its essentials, is still in existence,
even though iron tools are used or a stuttering motor
truck takes the goods to market."

"Neolithic?" I asked him. "Do you mean we're living in the Stone Age?"

"Why not?" he said. "The New Stone Age. The New
Stoned Age! For me it never ended."

34

Maybe this is as good a place as any to put down the few hard facts I learned about Ratnose during the time I spent with his band. I sat around with him a lot that winter, reading his books and drinking his tea, talking and just listening to his outrageous bullshit. He was a shifty bastard who got his kicks out of pretending to be a lot of different people at different times, or simultaneously. At various moments and in various places while I knew him he was a priest, a mugger, a scholar, a rapist, a fop, an abortionist, a wit and a fool, a butt and a paragon, an ecstatic and an executioner—all of the above, none of the above, but mostly most of the above. Finally, of course, I came to think of Ratnose as a teacher. A rabbi and a roshi and a Sufi all rolled into one, but with dried blood under his fingernails.

Since everything I saw and heard concerning Ratnose was contradictory and came in no particular order, I might just as well list my information kind of one, two, three. It makes as much sense that way as any other. Okay:

27 THINGS I LEARNED
ABOUT RATNOSE

1. He is short, but very strong, and has a lot of scars (more about them below).

2. He likes to wear silk skivvies under his ratskins, particularly during the big Hassayampan holy days, like Fandanay, their combination Christmas and New Year's celebration where they all get stoned on crait, as usual, and eat a whole baked horse stuffed with kasha and wild apples. Most of his silk underwear is green, though some of it is orange.

3. His full name is Jean-Luc Pierre Auguste Ratanous III. Either that, or Jack P. Rotznase. I saw WANTED posters for him under both names. Of course, there were a lot of WANTED posters I didn't see, or perhaps that he didn't want me to see. It's always possible, too, that he had them printed up himself.

4. His one remaining eye is dark brown—so dark a brown that at times it appears as black as boiling tar.

5. His age, according to the stories that he tells, is anywhere from about forty-five to a hundred and twenty-five years old. He may be older, but I doubt that he's any younger. He claims to have known Jesse James quite intimately, and sometimes says that he *is* Jesse James.

6. His favorite lunch is a cup of tomato soup and a peanut-butter-and-onion sandwich on rye toast. He likes that for breakfast, too.

7. He suffers from sinus headaches in cold or damp weather—the result of a war wound.

8. Sometimes he claims to be the ghost of Calvin Coolidge—particularly when we're out fly-fishing for brook trout. He does a splendid imitation of Coolidge and other Presidents.

9. He is a crack pistol shot with either hand, and his preferred weapon is the Walther PPK in 9mm.

10. He lost his left eye either when he was gouged during a bar fight at the Calgary Stampede in 1947 or as the result of mortar fire in the Siege of Sedan, where he may have served as a *poilu*. Some say he lost it while playing with firecrackers.

11. He claims his cock is ten inches long, but only when he's imitating Lyndon Johnson.

12. He snores.

13. Under his right shoulder blade he has an elliptical four-inch scar of which he is quite proud, maintaining that it was caused by a flint-tipped Assiniboin lance that shattered on one of his ribs, and thus that he is the last man still walking around with fragments of the Stone Age inside him.

14. He never learned to drive a car.

15. He denies that he is afraid to ride in elevators, but people who have been in the city with him say otherwise.

16. Though baptized a Roman Catholic, he now professes faith in the Kandiru sect of Hassayampan Buddhism, an off-shoot of the Mahayana branch that first flourished in this region about 900 A.D. and whose main tenet is a belief that the Buddha has returned to earth as the candiru fish—a wicked little creature that enters the urethra of bathers, lodges there permanently with its barbed dorsal spines, and can only be removed surgically. Ratnose has had the operation three times himself, but in his more pessimistic moments admits that he is nonetheless no closer to Enlightenment than he was when his prick was unscarred. He still keeps the last candiru in a goldfish bowl in his cave, and prays to it when he is very drunk.

17. His favorite horse is a walleyed gelding named Blackie.

18. His fondest memories are of the years he spent in New York as a streetcar conductor. That was in the '90s of the last century, when they still had horse-drawn streetcars. He lived in a boardinghouse on the edge of Hell's Kitchen, and he knew all the whores and the saloonkeepers and the prizefighters. He had a good friend named Eddie Toller—"a welterweight of little talent but with plenty of heart"—who got drunk one night and was run over by an ice wagon. He had a girl friend named Dora who changed linen at the Waldorf and turned a few tricks on the side—a big redheaded girl whose folks lived on a dairy farm over in Jersey. One day when Ratnose was driving his streetcar up Broadway—he was known as "Jack" in those days—he noticed a fellow smoking a cigarette in his car. You weren't allowed to smoke on the cars, because the smoldering butts might set fire to the ladies' long skirts, and there was a sign to that effect in the streetcar. Jack stopped his horses and walked back to the guy, who was a dude wearing a

floppy tie and a sailor straw, and told him to stop
smoking. The guy agreed, but when Jack got back up
front he turned and saw that the dude was still
smoking. Jack went back and hit the man in the
mouth and threw him off the car. Sure enough, the
guy he'd pasted turned out to be the son-in-law of
some Tammany Hall big shot, and Jack was fired
from the streetcars. He went over to Jersey with Dora
and spent a few weeks "listening to the moo-cows"
and shooting heath hens, which were still abundant
in those days on the Palisades but became extinct
about 1920. He sold the heath hens to the market in
New York for ninety-five cents a barrel. One day
when he was over there selling his birds to the hotels,
he spotted the dude who had cost him his job. The
dude was cracking a hard-boiled egg at the free-
lunch counter at Delmonico's. Jack went up to him,
stuck the barrel of a nickel-plated .32 in the dude's
nostril, and pulled the trigger. Then he walked back
out to the buckboard and headed West. Or so he tells
it.

19. Ratnose's favorite color is blue, his favorite
flower the nasturtium, and his favorite movie *Treasure
of the Sierra Madre*.

20. Though he occasionally sleeps in the nude, like
when he's up to some sort of hanky-panky with
Twigan or his other "wrenches," as he calls them, he
usually sleeps in a red flannel nightshirt that was
given to him as a Fandanay present many years ago
by one of his old girl friends. On it she embroidered
the word RATTY in big curlicue letters and the figure
of a pert, rascally rat with a turned-up nose.

21. An avid student of Early Americana, Ratnose is
presently at work on a volume of line drawings and
appropriate text that he has tentatively titled *The
Urinals of Lewis & Clark*. "In well-chosen words and
elegant illustrations," he says, "it both depicts and
evokes the various shrubbery, tree stumps, wild
flowers, anthills, snowdrifts, rivulets, trout streams,
waterfalls, ponds, lakes, swamps, gulches, wadis,

canyons, slopes, and crests on and into which the members of the expedition voided their bladders during their epic journey to and from the Pacific Ocean. I see it as a handsomely bound, exquisitely printed monument to the luxury press, the sort of work that one finds on only the best of coffee tables. Perhaps it will attain a certain elitist standing among students of the Early West. I can envision a day not too far in the future when costly expeditions will be organized to retrace the route, with each urohistorophile pausing at every way station to wet down the sacred spot. I think it will be 'must reading' for anyone interested in the American Westering Experience."

22. On his own way West, he worked one summer for an undertaker in a small town on the Illinois prairies. There was a fellow in town named Bobby Farrell—a railroad man, young and romantic, who was engaged to the local librarian. One day Farrell was having a shave in the barbershop when he saw his intended walking by on the arm of a tall, handsome stranger. It was one of those scorching-hot Illinois midsummer days, and the couple paused under the barbershop awning in the shade while the young man solicitously fanned the girl's brow. When Farrell had paid for his shave, he walked out of town into the cornfields and shot himself dead. (Here Ratnose always chuckles ironically.) Farrell needn't have shot himself, for his fiancée's escort was only her favorite cousin, on his first visit to the town. The girl, of course, was beside herself with grief and self-reproach. Ratnose arranged to short-circuit her tragedy, though. When the girl came into the mortuary alone one night to continue her morbid vigil, she noticed a strange, throbbing bulge in the corpse's trousers. It was the same sort of bulge she'd noticed before when she and Farrell were sparking back in the library stacks on quiet days. She looked quickly at her loved one's face, but it was as dead as it had been before, and the undertaker's sloppy patchwork on his

broken temple had not improved any in the meantime. But the bulge persisted, and finally she could resist her curiosity no longer. She unbuttoned Farrell's fly. Surprise! His pecker leaped out and began waving in the air. The girl screamed and fled—ultimately as far as Danville, where she married a man in the meat-packing business and had five lovely children. Of course, Ratnose had stuck a wire through poor Farrell's paraphernalia and was waggling it from a hiding spot under the bier. "If I hadn't done that," Ratnose liked to say, "the poor girl might have gone to her grave a spinster. As it was, when she finally collected herself, she probably reckoned that anyone who could be horny in his own casket would never have made a faithful husband." Ratnose the Humanist!

23. The reason he likes nasturtiums best is not because they sound "nasty," but because the leaves and the unripe flowers have a sharp, peppery taste that goes well in salads.

24. He once saw a man struck and killed on a city street by a runaway pie wagon. The pies flew all over the place, cracking on the cobblestones and leaking their goodies into the gutter. When someone in the band is killed, out hunting or on a raid, Ratnose says, "Yep, he was hit by the pie wagon."

25. In *Treasure of the Sierra Madre*, he identifies most closely with the old man, Howard, though he feels he is personally more like Fred C. Dobbs.

26. Ratnose was married at one time to a woman named Evelyn Marie Oates, who didn't know he was in the highwayman business. She thought he was a drummer for a Kansas City shoe company. From what Ratnose says about her, she was a thrifty, hardworking, churchgoing woman, big of bone and bosom, and pretty good in bed, too.

At that time Ratnose and his pals were knocking over the small country banks and post offices that had sprung up on the plains in the wake of the buffalo and the frontier. It was easy work. One of the gang would take a room in a town that they had scouted, maybe even a job, and wait until the relative absence of law-men and presence of cash—usually payrolls—hit the right balance. Then he would send a telegram in code to Ratnose: something clever like GERTIE EXPECTING MOMENTARILY STOP AWAITS YOUR RETURN WITH NO HARD FEELINGS. The gang, never more than six or seven men, badmashes all of them, would drift into town separately, arrange their getaway transportation, bust the bank or post office, hide out briefly in some safe cave or abandoned farm that the finger man had located, and then drift back home with no one the wiser.

It was a profitable, low-risk enterprise, until one day Mrs. Evelyn Marie Oates Ratnose accidentally in-tercepted one of the Gertie telegrams. Figuring that her hubby had gotten some poor girl in trouble out there in Stroudsville or Bantam Bottom or Keokuk, or somewhere, she converted all of her egg money into a certified check for $104.73 and sent it to the sheriff of the town in question along with a noble, self-reproachful night letter asking the lawman to give the money to poor, pregnant Gertie (she figured there couldn't be more than one poor, pregnant Gertie in a town that size), explaining that her husband worked hard and traveled a lot and was to be excused his lust, particularly as she, Mrs. R., was a failure as a wife in that she obviously could not keep her husband satis-fied.

There being no poor, pregnant Gertie in that town, nor yet a pregnant Abigail, rich *or* poor, the sheriff quickly put two and two together and stationed four deputies with shotguns in the bank, behind the teller's cage. When Ratnose and his boys came in, the shot-guns cut them all down except Ratty and Hunk, both of whom escaped fearfully wounded. Ratnose later found out the details of the accidental betrayal when the sheriff, who had become a sot, turned up in Ratty's saloon out in the Altyn Tagh a few years later. "Shot up like I was, I didn't dare go home after the am-bush," he said. "And by the time I was healed, there would have been no explaining my absence to Evelyn Marie Oates. Still, it was good to learn that she had betrayed me out of a noble motive. That made me feel better about not sending for her to join me. I doubt she could have stood the wanton, low-down nature of my life in those days.

I strung up the sheriff and skinned him out alive, then served him up for a year afterwards in the free lunch. I made souse out of his head, just the way you would a hog's. Cut it off, shaved the whiskers and hair, removed the eyeballs, and boiled it down in a big pot of salty water. You have to strain the meat good to get the little bones like the ear bones out; then you run the boiled meat through a meat grinder and let it all jell in a bread pan, along with some peppercorns and an onion, some cornmeal, and a table-spoon of sage. Best damned head cheese I ever et, though the rest of him didn't pickle too good. The jerky wasn't too good neither, as I recall. Well, like they say, you oughtn't to sneeze at free meat.

But Evelyn Marie Oates, I missed her there for a while. She was a steady woman, and a warm one, al-ways ready to blame herself for my failings and try to make up for it with love. I sure could have used her there during the months after the ambush when the buckshot was working its way out of me. Smarts like a son-of-a-bitch when one of them pellets is ready to pop, worse than any boil you ever had on your ass. Then, plunk, one day it falls down your pants leg and rolls away on the floor. I still got the scars from that little go-round, boys, yes I do." And he shows them to us.

27. He is afraid of lightning.

So that's all I can say for certain about Ratnose, in a factual way.

35

Winter ended. Nothing gradual—it just ended. The snow went down like the float in a flush toilet. The sun came up like a blowtorch. The guy who named the season "spring" in our neck of the woods might have called it "splat" if he'd lived on the upper Hassayampa. Or "squt," or "skluck." All of the snow just simply melted overnight, it seemed, and went rumbling off downhill carrying trees and toads and houses and dead horses with it—a steady, burbling flow of something in between water and mud, with hair on its back. When the ice went out, I thought we had gone to war, it was that much like gunfire. For a while we loved it. No longer did we have to go out behind the tepee on snowshoes to take a shit, straddling like an Olympic gymnast to keep the turds out of our webbing. But pretty soon it was just as tough crapping in the mud: you didn't know what you were stepping on when you stumbled away from the dump. Or even when you got back inside. The mud smelled like ripe compost.

We did have some fun on the rivers, though. Fric and Frac had an old canoe stashed away in one of the sheds, and when the streams started to rise we broke it out, patched up the holes with strips of hide from an elephant's ear, loaded the guns and the meat saws and a big burlap sack of rock salt into the middle of that rickety old birchbark, and off we went on a slaughter. We poured down those rivers like sixty, as Ratnose would say, with Fric in the bow and Frac at the stern paddle, while I sat on the salt bag in the middle with Hunky's .243 in my hands, whooping us over the haystacks and blasting every horned critter we found stuck in the mud. We ran down through a tumble of deadies the likes of which I never had seen:

giant oak trees rolling like rhinos in the mucky flow, tossing their roots at us from every angle, groaning and cracking, kicking up the sodden corpses of moose and aurochs—massive blue hulks with their eyes staring blue under the chocolate milk of the runoff, horns snatching at the birchbark as their heads and limp hooves lolled free, neck-broken, purple tongues; a scum of drowned chipmunks and marmots and rats bobbing bloated in the froth, while we ripped past, screeching and cursing. There were big brown chunks of rotten ice in the river, heaving like potato fields. And all the while the spring, splat, squt, skluck sun burning down through the webwork of the riverside trees.

We killed a ton of game every day, snagged some of it with our grappling hooks, and butchered out and salted down only a fraction of that amount at best. Yet in the two weeks of the runoff, we replaced all the meat that had been eaten by the band during the winter. It wasn't fat meat—not like the marbled red steaks and backstraps of the animals we killed in the late fall, after the rut, when they were building meat for the winter—but it was meat, and we were meat-eaters, and we liked it. I know it sounds cruel to you who are sportsmen, the way we killed those bawling, helpless cattle stuck up to their withers in the mud, but I, by God (or Ratnose), enjoyed it; we rode that rotten brown wave at our own peril and unthinking of our own peril, and shot those stupid fuckers where they stood, mired down in their own blind panic.

You might wonder how we dragged all that meat back to camp. Well, that was part of Ratty's genius. He had built the camp in the middle of a big horseshoe bend of the river, a bend that ran easily fifteen miles through the foothills. We put in on the uphill side of the river, about a stone's throw from the sheds, and ended up only a half mile away on the downhill side. When we got in with our meat at the end of the day, we just whooped—if they hadn't heard us coming already, which was easy enough, what with our shooting and singing and screeching—and the old ladies dragged the meat up to the smokehouse. God, how we preened ourselves on those returns! Fric balanced his paddle on the end of his nose and danced a jig step up the hill. Frac pole-vaulted over the stumps and paused from time to time and pretended to jerk off. I did gunfighter twirls with the .243 and made violent faces, followed by heavy winks to show I was just kidding. You never knew who might like to shoot you in that camp.

Twigan was always there with a steaming pot of mint-flavored crait when we arrived, and although she tried to make it seem that she was sharing it equally among us three great hunters, I knew right from the start that she meant the gesture for me. I think Ratnose knew as well. One evening he walked beside me up the hill, our boots *shlurp*-ing in cadence through the mud, and he put a hand on my shoulder. I could already feel the crait working—a slow, steady spreading of my sight and touch and hearing. The light was lime yellow; the time was tart and humming. Ratty's hand was the same.

"Ah, Runner," he said as we stopped. "Do you really appreciate this season, my boy? You and your buddies are so caught up in the running of water and the killing of meat that I fear you fail to appreciate the subtleties of spring."

I looked at him, and his one mad eye was just as playful as ever.

"The lowly crocus thrusting its pallid head through the newly liberated earth; the hillside trees stretching their limbs and yawning their buds as if in a slow awakening from winter's restful sleep; the stumbling bear cub emerging for his or her first glimpse of light, *first* taste of Father Sun's heady brew: do none of these events strike a sympathetic note within your murderous breast?"

I looked at him more closely, and he cut a fart.

"And the geese—"

A skein of honkers was moving overhead at that

very moment, riding high on the last of the sunlight. They were working toward a landing, and as the family groups reoriented themselves within the flight, they broke the V into an aerial alphabet far more complex than any I had ever memorized. Their yelps came down to us like those of wolves.

"—the hounds of heaven," continued Ratty: "do they not move you, Runner? Do not their constancies, their monogamies, their exquisite navigations—do not these loud miracles arouse your interest in the Godhead?

"No," he said, slapping my shoulder. "They intrigue you not in the least. Your interest resides in blood and fucking, in taking from the weak and humble, in defiling the crocus and slaughtering the bear cub. In humping the helpless women of my tribe. In riding that dirty goddam motorcycle of yours all over this lovely countryside. The only goose you understand is a tactile gesture."

By now the crait was all the way through me; it was pouring out of my thumbs. I knew what Ratnose had said, but I didn't know what he was saying—it was that different a thing. I sat down on a pine stump and unloaded the .243, testing the cartridges for grease before I pocketed them. Then the sound of the lever, clicking out the rounds, merged with the barking of the geese overhead. I looked up at them, shifting and sliding into their ever-changing alphabet that wasn't quite an alphabet, that had none of the easy, here-we-go-to-wisdom qualities of the alphabet. Goose. Mother Goose. Ratty had said something about a goose.

"The geese are flying calligraphy," I said finally.

"What do you mean by that, Runner?"

"I don't know. Just that they're flying a bunch of ideas that I can't read, I guess."

"But you'd like to kill them, and then go off somewhere and get laid, right?"

"I suppose so, but I don't know if the one thing has anything to do with the other."

"You're right it doesn't," Ratnose yelled. "You're

damned right it doesn't! Flying calligraphy, my ass!
You naughty boy. Study nature and learn!"

With that he stumped off up the hill, glaring back
at me from time to time with that peculiar monocular
menace of his. But none of it really reached me, really
penetrated my high. I was spread out on a wave of
crait that was as smooth and brown and bulging as
the river, and meanwhile the geese went to bed.

I don't know how long I meditated there, and I
don't even know if you could call it meditation. Finally, perhaps foolishly, I slung the .243 on my shoulder and hiked back up into camp. The fires were
glowing, spitting a few sparks, hissing at me like red-
and-yellow geese. Blondie stood before our tepee,
rolling her eyes and making suck-off sounds with her
smiling, toothless mouth. I walked into the tepee, giving her a hard shoulder that sent her weeping into the
dark, and picked up a blanket. Then I walked over to
the shed where I had parked the Husky. I kicked it
alive and blatted it for a while—harsh and angry, I'd
guess you might say. Twigan came out of the shadows, as I knew she would. The bike was warm now,
so I spread the blanket over her shoulders and reloaded the .243, slowly, keeping my eyes away from
Ratty's cave all the while, trusting the skin on my
backbone. Then I stuck the carbine into the boot and,
feeling Twigan's hands on my ribs and her weight on
the pillion, I dropped the bike into low and eased on
out of there. Just as I reached the last fire, I tipped
her up into second and came down hard on the throttle—that wicked yeah downward back-turning thrust
of skin on rubber that lifts your front wheel into the
sky and brings your back muscles up into your
skull—and we blew mud all over that campfire.

Okay, turbulence is the nature of spring, however
you call it. I balled Twigan turbulently all that night,
out there in the cold black humming muck of the Hassayampa. We set that goo to bubbling, she and I. Hot
it was, steam rising off of the bike where it stood there
in the webbed starlight, steam rising from Twigan's
twot and belly button. My prick was a steam shovel,

and at one point I retrieved a rock the size of a hen's egg from her cunt, where I'd shoved it as the result of too much root-hogging ardor. I never listened to her little whimpers of love and instruction, and she hardly heard my yelps of excitement. It was straight, plain fucking, with none of the refinements of thought that we later learned to suffer. The river was grumbling off there in the dark, and the hair on the back of my head stood stiff as my cock. I was fearless, yet I knew there was much to fear, and all the while the bike stood creaking and steaming beside us.

I got her up, finally, dog style, my hands all muddy on her waist. Her waist felt like a bundle of electric cable covered with glue and then again with silk. She looked back at me over her shoulder, under her coarse, hayrick hair, fearful, and I looked down at her bald ass hole and the gash beneath it. My eyes were an owl's eyes: I could see the cunt hairs twitching their calligraphy along the ridges of her slot. Whatever moon there was, and it wasn't much, glinted on the head of my cock. I stuffed it in there, into the slot already slippery with the madness of the night, that fishy steam bath. All the way up, my muddy hand spread on her narrow back, my balls slapping against her narrow thighs, her ass hole winking sideways at me, the long pale tube of my meat—*my own meat!* I remember chanting—slipping in and out of there, the bike chortling its metallic dance tune somewhere to the outside of my roaring eardrums; I tilted my head to the steamy sky that was already fogging my eyebrows and barked like a dog—I was Ratnose!

Much more than that, I know. Her little tits under my fingers, the nipples as long and tender as new peony shoots. Warm belly, cooled by the air, leading to the wiry nest of her box, electric. All of that, along with her smiles and her assurances that, believe me, kept me sane until the morning. How could we make love, *be* in love, without Ratnose approving of it? How could this passion arouse indignation? Ire? Murder? Yet I had ominous thoughts that night, slipping through the steam at the edge of my consciousness—

thoughts of head cheese in which the gristle of my ears, of my very own nose would provide the gelatin that others might favor. I could see Ratty ladling my ear bones out of the pot. I could see him picking his teeth with one of them. But then I would put my hand on Twigan's cunt, feel the juices cooling there over the volcano, and take courage from the geology of our love. "Oh, Runner," she said, toward dawn, "you in deep shit."

She was right. When we got back into camp that morning, with the cook fires smoking low and the smell of bacon fat already rancid in the nooning air, the whole tribe was awake. We grumbled in through the mud, watched by graybeards and babies, not a one of them with a smile for us. No sign of Ratty. His cave was shut tight, his shades drawn. Judging by the glum faces and tugged moustaches of the onlookers, everyone seemed to know that Twigan and I had cheated on Ratnose. Though how those immoral savages could judge us I sure didn't know. But even the bike seemed to agree. No sooner did we enter the compound than the Husky started hawking: out of gas. There was one more can in the shed, I knew, but I'd have to get more if I was going to retain my status with these people, and more importantly, with Twigan.

She scampered off to the girls' tent as soon as I parked. Cussing a blue streak, I wheeled the bike into the shed and grabbed the last gas can, one of the two that had been lashed to the side of the bike when Ratnose liberated it. The can had been full when I hefted it a few days earlier, but now it felt ominously light. I opened it and sloshed. Barely enough to get me back to the Hassayampa, if I rode light-handed all the way.

"We use petrol this morning to make our fires burn good," Hunk told me later. "That fog, it make the wood very damp." He kicked a tire and giggled. "Ratnose, he insist."

36

I wasn't worth much on the meat run that day. We slid down the river through fog and murmur, surprising a cow rhino and her calf, both of them belly-deep in the muck, their woolly locks clotted like tar, but I failed to kill either of them. I was shooting the late Chipper's .30-06 Mannlicher, and I took the cow through the shoulder hump—I could see the hair fly, along with a slab of raw, red hide—but the bullet only sped her on her way. She surged out of the gumbo like a long, black champagne cork, and her infant tripped lightly after her, my second shot splattering mud all over the baby's butt. When I worked the bolt for a third shot, it jammed.

"You must be fucked out," Fric said wonderingly.

"Naw," said Frac, "he just ain't woke up yet. Old Runner, he shoot good once he got the sleepy boogers out of his eyes."

I blew four more shots that morning—two on deer; one on an aged, lung-blown aurochs cow who reared back at the slap of my bullet a foot from her nose and spewed saliva to the treetops as she wheeled and fled. The last shot was at a bush pig, standing in profile beside a gnarled old beech tree teetering on the riverbank. The pig rooted contentedly in the beech mast, grunting a swinish little song to itself. Fric slowed the canoe, and Frac eased up to a stop alongside a waterlogged stump. I took a deep breath and shivered. It was an easy shot of no more than a hundred yards, with the river quiet in this backwater, gurgling assurance to me, it seemed, with the rifle barrel braced perfectly steady on the trunk of the tree—and when I squeezed off, I saw the bullet kick dirt well beyond the pig's shoulder. It looked up stupidly, stared for a long moment at the place where the dirt had jumped, and then went back to its song. I slipped another round into the chamber and took my rest again. I held the top of the leaf well down into the groove of the buckhorn; I took another deep breath and concentrated on bringing my pulse down to zero; I squeezed ever so gently as my eye burned a hopeful hole through the pig's shaggy, softly breathing hide, just back of the shoulder, but when the rifle went off—with that ever-surprising *whop* that a well-shot rifle utters—by Christ if the bullet didn't once again hit far over and beyond the target. This time the pig got the message. It humped into the brush before I could reload.

"Shit!" I said.

Fric and Frac said nothing, but exchanged meaningful glances. When we stopped for lunch, down near the bottom of the big bend, Fric allowed as how I was probably getting uptight as a result of no sleep and a series of misses with the rifle. Frac allowed as what I missed had nothing to do with firearms. I sulked. By this time, I had gotten to know them pretty well. Fric's real name was George P. Holmes, Jr., and he had grown up in Cincinnati, the son of a prominent hardware-store owner. Frac's real name was Edward Frattolini, out of Neenah, Wisconsin, father a fireman. They were both dropouts, and had met on a commune near Taos, New Mexico, where the living proved way too easy. They were ex-hippies, well versed in guitar playing and dope smoking, and they liked to argue about which one had had the clap more often. Frac always won, because he still had it. But Fric maintained that since he had also caught both the syph and the blue-balls, that put him ahead on degree-of-difficulty. Apart from screwing, rock climbing, skinny-dipping, dope smoking, dope dropping, dope shooting, and playing endless games of softball, the communards were into electronics in a big way. Their patron, a wealthy woman from Albuquerque whom they called Grass Widow, owned a big electronics-supply company and gave them everything they

wanted, from tiny transistors to a huge Moog synthe-
sizer. When the commune finally collapsed out of
boredom and the two ex-hippies took off in search of
Ratnose, Frac brought with him a bag full of electronic parts. Now, during the winter, and at odd moments when the spirit moved him, he was building an
Electronic Gun Dog. It had four stiff, clanking, robot-
like legs, a heat-sensitive nose that you could tune to
the body temperature of whatever game animal you
wanted it to hunt, and instead of eyes, two 12-gauge
shotgun barrels. To load it, you cocked the tail and
shoved the ammo up the Gun Dog's ass.

"What we need today is your goddam Gun Dog," I
said glumly as we munched our fried-maggot sand-
wiches.

"It wouldn't do any good," Frac said, shaking his
head. "He's crapped out right now. I need four D-
type batteries to get him going again, and we're fresh
out of them."

"Maybe they have some in Hymarind," Fric said.
"In the old Chinese market down there near the cala-
boose? I mean, they've got transistor radios and sew-
ing machines and shit like that; why not batteries?"

"Do they have gasoline in Hymarind?" I asked.

"Yeah," said Fric, "out by the ammo dump where
the Burma Road used to go through. Or at least, they
used to have gas there. That crazy doctor who came
to town last year was using it for his generator in the
hospital he built before the witchman poisoned him.
Maybe the doc burned it all up."

"I need gas for the Husky," I said. "Maybe we
ought to go into Hymarind and get us some batteries
and some gas."

Agreed. We gave up hunting for the afternoon and
bounced back to camp full tilt down the river. The
idea of going to town had infected us, had turned our
heads around so that we took the most dangerous
chances that the river afforded. We bounced on the
haystacks and roweled the white horses with our paddles so that it sometimes seemed the canoe was air-

borne, with only our blades touching the frothy water. And sure enough, as it so often happens when you're riding a wave of supreme confidence, luck looked after us. Not a hundred yards from the landing, we spotted a great cave bear digging in the bankside muskrat dens. He reared up on his haunches to get a better look at us, and swinging Chipper's rifle to my shoulder, I snap-shot and nailed him square between the eyes. Iron sights, from a canoe moving on white water, standing on my knees at a range of more than 200 yards, the best shot of my life. The bullet must have been fired from my eye, just like Frac's Gun Dog.

We left the bear for the women to butcher and ran up to camp. Ratnose's cave was still buttoned tight. I grabbed my saddlebags and threw in a bundle of jerky and a big bag of rice, along with a tea tin of crait makings and my old mess kit. Blondie was still sulking in the back of the tepee, so I pretended she wasn't there. I slung a bandolier of .30-06 rounds over my shoulder, threw a blanket over the other, and went out to rope me a horse. Twigan was standing by the corral, looking shy and hesitant.

"Listen," I said to her, "I killed a big bear just above the landing, on the other side of the river. You skin it out and tan the hide for us. I'll be back in a couple of days."

"Where you going, Runner?"

"Hymarind. We need gas for the Husky, so we can do some more riding like last night. Right?"

"Right," she said, and smiled. She grabbed her cunt and squeezed it, squinching her eyes together in a quick little mockery of anticipated sexuality. I didn't need any of that right now—not with Ratty probably looking down at us from his cave and plotting some wicked revenge. I told her to cut that shit out and went in to rope my horse.

37

It took us the rest of that day and the better part of the next to get to Hymarind, riding hard all the way and stopping only for a dinner of rice jerky and a breakfast of the same. But we were too eager for either fatigue or the dullness of the menu to blunt our fine edge. The crait helped some, too. When we finally reached the crest of the last ridge above Hymarind, our tails were dragging, so we stood there in the waning light, letting the horses catch their wind. The town lay like the hub of a broken wheel down there below us, with the four dusty, bent caravan routes leading into it like spokes and the late-afternoon sun gleaming on the corrugated-iron roofs at the center. A streamer of black smoke wiggled from the mouth of the smokestack that marked the site of the puffin factory. The smokestack was strictly ornamental, since the old women who worked in the puffin factory stitched their toy puffins by hand out of dragon-hide remnants and stuffed them with rice chaff before painting the ugly little birds with nail polish and boot blacking, imported at great cost from nearby Tor. Chang, the factory foreman, insisted on a smokestack, though, because he had seen pictures of the Industrial Revolution and felt that smokestacks were part of it. "Ah," sighed Frac, "home sweet Hymarind!"

The girls in the Costive Cowpoke Cocktail lounge were glad to see us. Not a single caravan had arrived yet that spring from the south, and the girls had spent the winter drinking tea, making those big bright Hymarind hooked rugs, and balling one another with the giant purple dildo that Hal McVeigh, the Costive Cowpoke himself, kept hanging on the wall behind the bar next to his framed dollar bill and the photograph, faded now, of Hal and his buddies in steel helmets and fatigues, posed beside their deuce-and-a-half truck back during the war.

"How's your bowels, Hal?" Fric asked. The Costive Cowpoke allowed as how they were tight enough.

"The winter was a real pisser down here," Hal said as he poured us our drinks. "Mean winds off the mountains and dust storms out of the desert, and the temperature never above zero. But no snow, thank Christ, or at least, none that stuck—it was all blown away before it could freeze. These damned chippies—every time the wind would get to howling, they'd come running into my room, whimpering like they do, and jump into bed with me. Six of the dizzy cunts, all grabbing at my dick and begging for help. How was it up at Ratty's camp?"

Quiet, we told him. But it sure wasn't quiet in there. The girls were getting stoned on company. They put on party hats and sang Christmas carols and snipped paper dolls out of the bar napkins. Gisela, the old redheaded circus whore who had come here all the way from Reeperbahn in Hamburg, snagged three pig's feet out of the jar behind the jukebox and started juggling them. (It was this Gisela, incidentally, who had nipped off old Beppo's nose—not with a shears, but with her teeth. "From little on," she told me, "I always had the urge to bite off the end of someone's nose.") Meiko, my favorite, a cuddly little number from Matsuyama on the island of Shikoku, played the comb and tissue paper for a while and then grabbed Fric by the groin, leading him upstairs with a coy smile. That was the signal for a mass orgy. Hal tried to whip them off with the dildo, but they were too strong for him, and too many. They dragged us up to the cribs like so many puffin dolls, and for an hour or so it was impossible to distinguish one body from another. It was all cockapuss and nipplebeard, slippery, hot, yelping, tangled, and confusing. At one point I could swear I saw Frac fucking Fric in the armpit. Then it all slowed down and sorted us out again into our original bodies.

"There was a gringo in here a couple of weeks ago asking about you," McVeigh told me. He had his chin on Meiko's pud and was twanging her nipples absentmindedly while he stared at me with his red, watery blue eyes.

"What did he look like?"

"A mean fucker. Big, with a droopy moustache."

"What do you mean, 'mean?'"

"Well, when little Carol tried to put the make on him, he pinched her tit and slapped her up against the wall. I came over the bar with the blackjack, but he pulled a gun on me."

"What was it?—the gun, I mean."

"I don't know: a Walther, maybe, or maybe a Luger. Or maybe one of those cheap Jap copies—no offense, Meiko."

"What did you tell him?"

"Nothing—or anyway, nothing about you or Ratnose. I told him Ratnose was a myth, a legend, like Pecos Bill or the Old Man of the Mountain. I told him I'd never seen any kid that looked like you. But I don't think he believed me."

"Why not?"

"Because these dumb broads kept giggling every time I denied there was a Ratnose. Finally the guy went away. He bought a couple bottles of bourbon off me and paid me in dragon's-tooth meth: good stuff, very fresh."

We paid for our drinks and entertainment with a couple of sable hides that Fric had brought along and then wandered down to the old Chinese market. A full moon was just rising, dirty orange behind the dust blowing in from the desert. Dogs and cripples whined at us from the doorways. The unemployment picture in Hymarind hadn't improved much since my last visit in the fall, and we saw a few humps of rags flapping in the shadows that had to be dead men.

So my father was looking for me. Maybe he'd given up and gone back down the river. I was pleased to think that he'd come this far, but uncertain about whether or not I hoped he was still on my trail. I'd gotten into Ratnose's camp on my own power, and I wanted to get out that way too, if I ever had to get out. Or at least using the Husky's power. That was my ace in the hole, that bike.

There was no gas in the Chinese market, though the old Chink did indeed have some D-type batteries for Frac's Gun Dog. He also had some beautiful dried seaweed—overpriced as usual, but I bought a bundle of it anyway as a present for Twigan. She loved seaweed in her crait, or even in her soup, for that matter. The old Chink didn't know if there was any gasoline out at the dump. He pulled at his moustache and avoided our eyes.

"Whatsa mattah you?" I asked him.

"Dumpee velly bad place," he said finally, when I stuck the muzzle of Chipper's Mannlicher under his goaty little chin. "Clazy mans out there, killum dead pinis byumbye. Killum plenty Chinaman last week."

"He's on the pipe," said Frac. "Either that or he's been selling stuff from the dump and don't want us clipping any of it for ourselves."

But Fric and I took the old man seriously. Fric questioned him in pidgin Mandarin and the old man chattered away for half an hour, drawing a cramped little map for us on the back of a cigarette paper, moaning from time to time, imitating gunshots with a high, hissing *clack* like Chinese firecrackers. Fric listened gravely, then offered the old man a handful of coins. The old man refused them gently and chattered something in a pleading tone. Fric shook his head.

"Let's go," he said. We walked back up the crooked street to the Costive Cowpoke. "The old guy says there's a man out there who kills anyone who stops at the dump," Fric told us. "Some of the locals think he's the ghost of World War Two. He wears old army fatigues and combat boots and carries a BAR. He is very righteous, like the Longnoses were during the Big War. Others say he is Tilkut, the Bear God, cousin of the Great Crow who lives north of the mountains and

spreads mischief and chaos down here by means of
his animal agents. They've seen him shuffling through
the dump as big as a bear, and very shaggy. Last
week he ambushed a party of Chinese merchants who
stopped to poke through the dump and killed them to
a man. Some of them he mutilated in a very peculiar
fashion, though the old man wouldn't tell me how.
When I asked him, all he said was 'Ngaa!' and pointed
to the mountains, Anyway, I don't think we ought to
go out there. It's probably some nut who's living off
the old C-rations and wearing the old clothes they left
there. No telling what he's up to."

I had a pretty good idea who he was and what he
was up to, but I didn't dare tell Fric and Frac. It was
probably my old man, holed up at the dump and
killing anyone who came through in hopes that he
would sooner or later nail Ratnose. He'd given me up
for dead by now and was out for revenge.

"Ah, it's just a crock of that old Hassayampan bullshit," said Frac. "They're all yellow up here, in more
ways than one. Except Ratty, and he's not really a
Hassayampan. Look at Hunk and Lump. There's
places in the mountains that they wouldn't go for all
the hemp in Hymarind—claim there's devils in there,
shaped like rocks or birds or waterfalls. I go into those
places all the time and nothing ever bothers me. If
anyone killed those Chinks, it was probably the old
man himself, that thieving bastard—he was a paymas-
ter in Chiang's army, that's what Hal says—or else
some of those Mao Mao who come up here every now
and then for ammo."

When we got back to the Costive Cowpoke, Hal
was too drunk to make much sense. He'd finally managed a good hearty crap and was celebrating with a
bottle of Old Overholt that he'd taken off the body of
a dead C-55 pilot in the winter of 1944 and had been
saving for a special celebration. Fric and I were dead
beat, so we bedded down—Fric with Gisela and I
with little Meiko. Frac stayed at the bar, drinking
with Carol and Hal. The last thing I heard as I

dropped off to sleep was the four of them singing, "Fuck 'em all, fuck 'em all, The long and the short and the tall . . ."

When I woke up in the morning, there was a note from Frac saying he'd gone down to the dump to get my gasoline and that we should be ready to ride out for the mountains by noon. "I took along Hal's Tommy gun," he added at the end of the note, "so don't worry about no Bear or Ghost Warrior gobbling me up."

38

A storm was brewing over the mountains as we rode down to the dump. Black clouds boiling over the dirty-gray peaks, and those long, bowling-ball rumbles of distant thunder that drowned out the sound of our gallop. Dust devils sucking up the desert and spitting it dry in our eyes. Even the wildlife seemed subdued in the aura of impending wrath that preceded the storm. We passed a small herd of what looked like onagers, huddled head down in a shallow gully, their tails snapping like whips in the brown wind. A ragtag string of ravens blew over us, helpless against the gusts, like the broken tops of so many black umbrellas, croaking with despair at their inability to navigate in this weather. They sounded just like Hal, who had come with us and was moaning all the while about his hangover and our stupidity in not telling him the night before when he was still sober that we wanted to go to the dump.

"I could of told you there was a madman down there," he kept saying. "One of those goddam killer-saints that wanders in here ever' now and then; maybe even that nut who was looking for you; but no—oooh, my head!—no, you gotta go and right away start messin' with my girls and get me drunk. Oh, shit, my *haid* just opened up and swallowed my *nose*. Oh, you dang dumb cork-soakin' kids that keep comin' around here, shit . . ." and on and on like that while we whipped the ponies on down the dusty, almost invisible caravan track that led past the dump a long weary way into China proper.

By the time we got to the dump, the storm was nearly on us. The light was eerie—that greenish-black gloom that is darker than night, and scarier too, what with the wind moaning through the picked carcasses of the old World War II trucks that stood there on their rusty tire rims with their hoods flapping over the empty holes where their motors had been before the local people had stolen them for idols in their churches, and the empty Quonsets creaking under the wind's fist, some of them giving off hollow howls where the wind blew flush past their open doors like a monster jug being puffed on by a giant, and the clatter of trash banging against the big, near-empty gasoline tanks, flaked and scarred by rust and time—the drums of a ghostly sky band. Frac's pony was tied to a dead bulldozer over near the guardhouse. The horse rolled its eyes and reared against the reins, and when we got close we could hear its sniveling over the rumble of the wind, but there was no sign of Frac.

There were two full jerry cans of gasoline near the pony, so Frac had gotten that far with it, anyway. I lashed the cans over the pommel of my saddle while Hal and Fric checked around the big tanks for sign. They moved very cautiously, with their rifles up and ready, their backs against the pitted steel, and sometimes I lost them in the clouds of dust that were getting thicker by the minute. If someone had taken a shot at them right then, even with a big automatic weapon, I wouldn't have heard it over the roar of the wind. But they came back finally, white-faced and solemn.

"Nothing," said Fric. "But anyway, the wind would have blown out his tracks even if he was only a minute ahead of us."

"Maybe he's in one of the Quonsets," said Hal. "He could be scrounging around in there for goodies, or something."

"I guess we'll have to look," Fric said.

We scouted the huts slowly, on tiptoe, each man taking a turn at poking his head in through the door while the others covered him. In the second hut, we found a crate of grenades—the frag models—and stuck some in our pockets just in case. The fourth hut had been a radio shack. It was creepy in there, with the old pinup posters smiling lewdly down on us from the walls, the girls looking incredibly faded and ancient except for their bright wet lipstick smirks that I suddenly realized meant the promise of blow jobs in an era that had never even said "fuck" out loud. And what did that cryptic phrase mean—KILROY WAS HERE?

It stayed in my mind as we stalked the other Quonsets, taking on the slow cadence of our steps: Kill-roy, kill-roy, kill-roy—then changing: pull-toy, pull-toy—then again: till-cut, till-cut, till-cut. You know how your head will do you when you're concentrating on your body: it will change things around in there, play a little crossword game with everything you know, or don't realize you know. Songs and prayers get mixed up, and somewhere along the way the mix will give you a spike of personal truth, for the moment.

Outside the hut that used to be the barracks, we found the bodies of the Chinese traders. They were still badly bloated, and the rats had been at work on them. The crows too, judging by their eyes. The wind kept the smell down, but I caught a whiff or two anyway. There were eight of them. Over near the road, their horses huddled in the lee of a wind-bent outhouse, nickering and stomping.

"The Leaning Tower of Pissed-Off," said Fric, yelling to be heard over the wind. I looked back toward town and could see the first line of rain just about to reach it—a shimmering white line that dropped from the gunmetal sky like a set of teeth twenty miles away. Then, it being my turn, I looked into the Quonset hut. Frac was in there.

At first I didn't see him. Then I saw him all too clearly. He was lashed hand and foot to the empty frame of a bunk, and from the way his head was bent I knew he was dead. There was a large pool of blood under his head, and a thick string of blood hung from the side of his mouth.

"Okay," I told the others. "Here he is."

We walked up slowly and checked him out. All of

his weapons were gone, even his belt knife. His eyes looked up and backwards toward the empty window, where the cobwebs were blowing, victims of the wind. There were no wounds visible through his clothing. Hal stuck a finger in Frac's mouth, which was full of blood.

"Still warm," Hal said. "And his tongue has been cut out."

Fric retched and turned away. Hal tilted Frac's head to the side and poured out the blood that remained in his mouth. I could see the stump in there beyond the gleam of Frac's nice white modern teeth.

Then Fric retched again, louder, and grabbed my shoulder. He pointed to the opposite wall. Leaning against it was an ultralight fishing rod that I recognized immediately, and at the end of the line, dangling from a shiny sharp Mustad 4/o hook, was Frac's tongue. Fric slumped back against the wall and sat down, retching and gagging on bile—we hadn't had any breakfast.

"Son of a bitch!" said Hal. "I haven't seen that since the War. The Jap Marines used to do that to their prisoners: stake 'em out and put a fishhook through their tongues, then just tug out the answers very gently. And when the guy had finally told 'em all he knew, they cut out his tongue and used it for bait."

We stood there for a long minute, thinking about that. Fric was sobbing now. Hal pulled out a hip flask and took a pull that gurgled in his throat. He passed it to me and I swallowed a mouthful of what might have been bourbon, though I wasn't tasting too sensitively right then. Suddenly I realized that the wind had died—the storm must have been about to hit—and the roar of the ghostly compound was gone. The silence dragged our minds away from the horror and turned us outward again. A crow began barking outside, not too far away, with those urgent doglike yaps they use to alert one another. And I remembered that my father was very good at birdcalls.

"Shit!" yelled Hal suddenly, his eyes wide with

panic. "I'm getting out of here."

He ran for the door, but the moment he stepped outside he flew sideways, and I heard the pounding of an automatic rifle. Then silence.

"What is it?" Fric asked. He had stopped crying and now looked quite alert.

"Hal got shot."

"Oh, Christ!"

The crow call was repeated. It was strange: I knew his voice, even when it was filtered through the language of a wild animal. He had tried to teach me the various crow calls, but my voice was too high. He liked to call the crows in, shoot the scouts, and then wait and laugh while the whole flock swirled around overhead, wondering what had happened to their lookouts. When he was a kid, he told me, he killed crows by the hundreds, but as he got older, he grew to like them so much that he couldn't bring himself to shoot. "They're a lot like us," he would say: "carrion eaters, group thinkers, too damned smart for their own good." But maybe my voice wasn't too high anymore. Maybe I could signal him and he would stop killing us.

I was about to give the yell when the storm hit—in full strength now, with horizontal sheets of rain and a wind that made the earlier one feel like a summer breeze. The lightning smacked down on us like the wrath of the devil. There was a stutter underneath it, and we saw a hot, orange flash much slower than lightning that ballooned outside the window from the direction of the big gasoline tanks.

"Shit," yelled Fric, "he's fired the gas tanks. He'll cook us in a minute!"

We ran for the door, but I got there first and held Fric back. I fumbled a grenade out of my pocket and threw it sputtering off into the glare in the direction where the shots had come from. When it blew, I ran, feeling the fire's heat like a slap in the face, vaulting Hal's body and keeping low until I had the Quonsets covering me. Fric was at my heels—I could hear his boots splatting the mud, or maybe that was just bullets—and the herd of Chinese horses was moving with us, apparently taking us for other, wiser horses. Through the gaps between the Quonsets I thought I could see a large, lightning-lit figure stalking us, bulbous and hairy, at about a hundred yards' distance. The Bear God. Till-Cut. I slipped and fell over a ditch, but on the other side I found my rifle at my shoulder and snapped off a shot in the direction where I'd seen him last. Kill-Roy!

Under the chuffing of the wind and fire I thought I heard the crow call. I tried to answer it, but I had mud in my throat. Then the lightning flashed once again. Backlit he stood there, close and huge, bristling, with the bear's ears like horns on his head. The shadow of his moustache, the shine of his teeth. Fire all around him, front and back. Cawing at us, *haw haw, haw haw*, and the long shiny BAR coming up to his shoulder. I knew he was strong enough to shoot that weapon offhand—any weapon. He would boast about how he had shot the big 16-inch guns when he was a kid in the Navy. He still knew all the drill, could do the gun captain's ballet; they had shot those monster naval rifles in twenty-seven seconds, he told me time and again. And then the BAR cut loose, very loud that close, and with bits of wadding sparking around the blast, and in the muzzle flash I could see his eyes, I thought, full of rage and joy behind the fire, and I wanted to yell at him that I was his son, spare me!—but instead I was pulling the ring on another grenade, and my arm came across, and he must have seen the fire in the fuse, because when the blast came he wasn't there. Or maybe he saw my arm swing. But then I was up behind the next hut, and around it, and onto my pony, riding. We rode out low, with the Chinese horses all around us. That's the only way I can explain how he missed us.

39

Except that he was too good a shot to have missed us, even in that bad light. And he was clever, now that he had slipped into madness and murder. Why kill us when he could trail us back to Ratnose's camp? Even if Frac had told him where the camp was, it would be easier and quicker to trail us back and then kill us when we got there. I didn't think of that right then, though. I was too spooked, shaking with fear as we pounded the horses back up the road to Hymarind, with the fire roaring behind us and Fric's pony ahead of me throwing clumps of mud into my face so that I had to ride blind with my cheek against the horse's wet, lathery, sweet-smelling neck. But it occurred to me later while we were standing around in Hal's saloon, telling the weeping girls about the Bear God's ambush. Fric by now had recovered from his case of the horrors and was all bluster, swearing vengeance and showing his teeth in wicked snarls. He'd get together a posse, by God, just as soon as the storm was over, by Christ, and then they'd by Jesus ride down there and slaughter that yellow-bellied mammy-jammin' bushwacker—no, they'd take him alive and string him up and then skin him out real slow; they'd cut off little bits of him and cook the bits over a fire and make him eat them . . .

"Listen," I told him finally, "you know you're not going to get any posse together in this town; they're all too spooked of that guy. And you know that Frac must have told him where Ratty's camp is. And if we don't get moving right now, he's going to be somewhere along the trail back, waiting to ambush us again. Let's haul ass."

A little flicker of the fear came back into his eyes.

"You're right," he said.

We had to kick the whimpering whores away from our stirrups to get out of there, with Fric promising to bring back Ratnose and wreak revenge, and them not listening but only begging us to stay and protect them from Tilkut, but finally we were out of town and riding. The air after the storm was light and sweet, and the country smelled fresh, tangy with mud and rivulets. A thick, yellow-brown column of smoke rose straight into the sky, miles high, from the burning dump. It remained in sight over our shoulders until nightfall. We rode hard. There was new snow at the higher elevations, and we cursed it because it would give Tilkut an easy track to follow, but we stuck to the streambeds as much as possible, even though the heavy runoff threatened to spill our ponies. We rode all that night as well, eating jerky and cold rice out of our saddlebags, zigzagging to make best use of the bare ground and throw Tilkut off the trail. At least, we were making him work.

Toward dawn I must have fallen asleep in the saddle, because the next thing I knew I was waist-deep in the stream we'd been following, spluttering and cursing while my horse tried gamely to kick my head off. When I remounted, Fric took the reins and led my pony at a walk while I alternately shivered and dozed. Shortly after dawn, I did the same for him. By now we were into the timber, and the chances of ambush were that much greater. But we never saw the Bear God, nor did we cut his track, which was good because it meant he might not be ahead of us, lying up on some boulder with that damned BAR of his, waiting to cut us down. I could imagine him, though, humping along on a ratty pinto pony with that bearskin draped over his head and shoulders, the bear's withered muzzle acting as a sun visor, his automatic rifle across the pommel and the Luger stuck in the back of his waistband, the way he always liked to carry it because a Mexican narc and gunfighter he once knew had carried his piece that way, and I could see his eyes under the bear's muzzle, green and mean like when he was going to spank me, only this time he meant to kill my ass. . . .

A deer crashed out of a willow brake ahead of us, and we both nearly died of heart failure. Then we saw her flag—a big, barren doe—as she skipped up the ridge through the snowdrifts and disappeared on the far side. We were both about to say something in relief—Fric had a silly grin on his face now—when we heard a shot from the direction in which the doe had disappeared. Just a hollow *clap* it was, gunfire doesn't carry far in these mountains.

"Oh, shit," Fric said, his face falling.

But when we bellied up over the ridge, we saw that it was one of our own hunting parties—Hunk and Korti were gutting the deer, while three of the older men whose names I could never remember sat their horses and looked glum. I thought of them all as Grumpy, from the Seven Dwarfs. Their expressions didn't change even when Fric and I came whooping down the slope toward them, skidding and falling in the snowdrifts in our relief at finding friends. Hunk, who had stripped off his shirt for the messy business of cutting the deer's windpipe from the inside, withdrew his arm from the steaming chest cavity and stood up bare-chested, reaching for his rifle. He was red to the shoulder, his arm studded with gleaming, purple-black clots of the deer's shattered lungs, and his stubble-bearded face looked deadly. But it relaxed into a grin at the moment he recognized us. It suddenly struck me as funny that I should be running with joy toward so savage and gruesome a figure—running away from my own father into the protective embrace of a blood-stained bandit. It must have been hysteria, because I couldn't stop laughing even while Fric was telling them about Frac's death, and the Bear God who was stalking us all.

We hopscotched back to Ratty's camp, always leaving two men in ambush on our backtrail as the rest of us rode cautiously ahead in stages, then waited in a defensive perimeter while the rear guard caught up.

Hunk led us on a sinuous course that kept us in the open as much as possible, so that we could steer clear of the most obvious ambush sites and keep our back-trail in view as long as possible. For most of that bright, tense afternoon it seemed that his precautions were unnecessary. We saw no sign of Tilkut, and I began to hope that maybe he had satisfied his lust for revenge back there at the dump. But then, just as we were nearing camp, he killed two of the Grumpys who had been left as rear guards, and we never even heard him do it.

We had waited on a knoll not far from camp for the Grumpys to catch up. When they didn't show after about half an hour, Hunk ordered us to fan out and retrace our track, very cautiously. We moved back at a painful crouch, slow, our rifles at high port, locked and loaded. Back where the Grumpys had set their ambush, we found a wide blood trail in the snow, and we followed it down a gully to a big snowdrift. The bodies of the two Grumpys were stuck head-down into the drift, with only their limp, rag-wrapped, moccasined legs protruding. The bodies felt strangely light as we dragged them out of the snow, and then we saw why. They were headless.

Hunk studied the single set of tracks that led away from the bodies, but at that moment none of us was brave enough to follow it out. Our courage had frozen like the blood on those raw stumps. Fric and I dragged the bodies back to the place where we had picketed the ponies while Hunk, Korti, and the surviving Grumpy fanned out around us, ready to return fire. As we approached the knoll, we could hear the ponies whinnying to one another in that strident tone they use when they're scared or hurt. Near the top of the rise, two faces stared at us—the faces of the dead Grumpys. The heads were stuck on stakes just over the rim of the hill, so that they were glaring down at us as we climbed, their mouths glummer than ever above the stiff, red roaches of their bloody, frozen beards.

All the horses had been hamstrung, except for the packhorse that had carried the butchered deer meat, and that horse was gone. Hunk methodically shot the crippled ponies, and we gutted them out, so that at least their meat would not go to waste. I unlashed the gas cans from my pony before Hunk shot him. Then we hiked, leg-weary and numb with cold or fear, down into camp. It was dark when we got there.

Ratnose took the news calmly enough. He even smiled during Fric's account of how Frac had been tortured—a knowing, nodding grin—and flicked his eye in my direction. "That Tilkut sounds like a bad operator, hey, Runner?" he said. It was the first notice he had taken of me since the night with Twigan, and I relaxed a bit for the first time since then. But not for long.

"I wonder what brings him to us, don't you, Runner? Could it be that he's queer for toy dump trucks, the way you were when you first joined our merry band? Or does he covet our women? Could it be something that simple?" He laughed his croaking kingfisher laugh.

"Well, there's nothing we can do about him tonight: no moon; we couldn't track him safely in this kind of darkness. And the snow will still be there tomorrow. We'll post a heavy watch tonight and take after him first thing in the morning." Ratnose fingered the scar on his throat, coughing delicately as he often did when the old wound bothered him. "And when we catch him, we'll have some entertainment along with our revenge."

I got out of Ratty's cave as quickly as I could after the meeting broke up and took the two cans of gasoline down to the shed where the Husky was parked. I still hadn't seen Twigan since our return—actually, I'd been too uptight and excited to look for her in the crowd—but she showed up while I was pouring gas and oil into the bike's tank. Even in the half-light of the campfires I could see that she had been beaten up. Her right eye was black, and her nose looked puffy.

Her upper lip was thick and scabbed.

"Hey," I said as she sidled into the shed, her eyes downcast, tentative, as was her style. I slipped my hand under her long, cool hair and rested it on the nape of her neck. Her neck was warm and smooth, almost fragile.

"I skinned out the bear like you told me, Runner," she said. "The hide is drying, but with the storm and all, it is taking longer than I . . ."

"Cut it out," I said. I pulled her up close to me, feeling the knots in my stomach loosening as her body came up against mine. Strange, I thought: when I came here last year, she was just my height; now I'm a head taller than she is.

"Who beat you up?"

"Nobody. I fell down a cliff during the blizzard."

"Come on," I said, "was it Blondie, or was it . . . him?"

"I'm so sorry about Frac dying," she said. "I missed you while you were gone, Runner."

"If it was Blondie, I'll kick her ass up to her shoulder blades."

She leaned back and looked up at me, her teeth shining under the fat lip.

"And what if it was Ratty?"

"I'd still do it," I said finally. "But I'd have to wait awhile and pick my shot." She laughed, but it was a kindly laugh.

I finished fueling the bike, and then we walked up to the cave that Fric and Frac had shared. It was totally dark inside. When I lit the fat lamp, I saw Fric lying in his bunk, staring up at the roof. He pretended that we weren't there. The air in the cave smelled sickly sweet with grass fumes, and there were three thick roaches spread fanwise in the stone ashtray that rested on Fric's belly.

"You hungry?" I asked him. He didn't say anything.

"Well, Twigan will fix us something to eat. I'd like to stay here tonight, if it's okay with you."

"Okay," he said slowly. After a while he giggled.

Twigan went down to the communal cookpot and came back with a pail of steaming-hot stew. Then she sliced some bread from a dark loaf she had under her arm. While she ladled the stew into a couple of skull bowls, Fric sat up; the smell of the stew must have finally penetrated his dopey haze. I hadn't realized how hungry I was, and I scoffed down two bowls, along with half the loaf of bread. The stew was delicious, the meat tender and sweet.

"Jeezus that's good," I said at last. "What is it?"

"Puppy meat," Twigan said. "While you were gone, Ratnose took up a new sport. He uses that big fly rod he got from the Indian, Johny Black, and he casts for puppies. When he hooks one, he plays it in like you would a big salmon and then strangles it for the stewpot. He says we have too many puppies anyway, and he needs the practice for the fishing season."

Fric groaned and pushed his bowl aside, then rolled another bomber.

40

Our tracking party, twenty men strong, rode out of camp at first light. During the night the wind had veered around to the southeast, and now you could smell summer on it—warm, wet, and woody. The sky was clear, and we would have to work fast, because by the time the sun reached noon the snow would all be gone from the south-facing slopes, and with it the Bear God's tracks. At the site of the previous day's massacre, Ratnose ordered Beppo and five other men to butcher out the horses and then pack the meat, along with the bodies of the two dead Grumpys, back to camp. A skunk had been there during the night, and both heads were already badly gnawed.

"I want Runner and Hunk on the point," Ratnose told us as our horses milled around, twitchy at the smell of death. "You two are our best riflemen, and we may just get a long shot somewhere up ahead. I want the automatic weapons at the middle of the column, ready to spread out in case we're flanked or enfiladed. What weapons does he have besides the BAR?"

"Probably grenades," Fric said. "We found plenty of them at the dump."

"He could have a light mortar, too," I said. "I saw a couple of cases of mortar rounds in one of the Quonsets."

"If he had a mortar, he'd probably already have dumped a few rounds into camp," Ratnose said. "And packing a mortar along would require another horse, most likely, which would slow him down some. If he does have one, he'll be planning to take a stand somewhere and drive us into a perimeter defense, then unload on us before we can scatter. One man against a dozen: he wouldn't stand a chance."

Ratty had his eye on me, looking for an objection,

but I kept quiet. Hunk and I moved down off the knoll, where Beppo's meat saws were already growling, and followed the tracks of the man and the packhorse down into a stand of lodgepole pines. There we found where he'd tethered his riding horse. He had wasted no time, but had mounted up and lined it on down the draw toward the southwest. With the warming effect of the wind, the tracks were already melting into plate-sized depressions with soft, rounded edges—easy to follow. We rode about a hundred yards ahead of the main body. It was warm so I took off my hat and stuffed it into a saddlebag. That way, I thought, if he is up there waiting to zap us, he might recognize me and not shoot.

Though I really doubted that he could recognize me now. I had grown a lot in the months since I ran away. My whiskers had come in, and now I wore a seedy black beard and moustache. My hair was shoulder-length and clubbed back with a strip of rawhide. Wind and sun had burned me darker than I had ever been back home, or even on the Hassayampa in midsummer. I was dressed all in skins, like the rest of Ratty's men. Even up close, he would be hard put to recognize me as his only begotten son: my nose, which had been broken in that crazy ride on the bronco, lay over to one side under a pronounced bump. My voice was different, too—not just naturally deeper, but gravelly: the result of my unconscious imitation of Ratnose. And my carriage had changed as well. I rode and walked with a mountain man's painful slouch—the result of too much time on horseback and of the many sprains and bruises picked up as a matter of course in that kind of a life. If he shot me out of the saddle for a bandit, I couldn't really blame him. Because I was one.

Judging by his tracks, though, it looked like ambush was the last thing on his mind. He had headed straight down through the hills toward the high desert, moving at a trot most of the time and pushing his horses into a canter on the few level stretches.

"Tilkut have good weather nose," Hunk said after an hour or so of tracking. "Afraid we track him out if stay close with snow down. Smel̃ warm wind coming. Ride out far, far from camp, then come back in when ground clear."

Already the snow was nearly gone. The sun was past the equinox, hard and hot. We saw crocuses flowering through the thin white crust on the southerly slopes, and the shadbushes along the streams were fat with flowers about to burst. Dwarf willow and osier stitched the wet spots yellow and red, and there were waterfowl on all the sloughs—vast, cackling, barking, squalling sheets of ducks and geese, swirling up into the air like multicolored feathery tornadoes as we trotted past. The grouse were already drumming up on the ridges, and from time to time they spooked us with their sudden, chain-saw roar. Most of the white was gone from the rock ptarmigan. At the lower levels, we saw suckers as long as a man's leg bellying their way up the muddy riffles to spawn.

"Ah, yes, Runner, the cruellest month," said Ratnose as we halted, about noon. He wheeled his pony up next to mine and scrutinized the barely visible track. The sun had sucked up the snow, and already the faint arcs of the horseshoes were crumbling into caked mud. "Memory and desire . . . I will show you fear in a handful of dust." He smiled his brown little smile at me and slapped me on the shoulder. "But you don't know Eliot, do you? I'm remiss in your education. I should send you back to school. How would you like that?"

"This is school enough for me," I said.

"But your father wouldn't agree to that, would he? Your father wouldn't like to see you out here riding with a bunch of nasty outlaws. Your father wouldn't like to think of you scrambling your brains on cannabis and spending your nights diddling a thirteen-year-old whore? Living on a diet of bugs and dog meat? Getting shot at by a psychopathic sniper? Going for days on end without brushing your teeth or changing your underwear? Hey?"

"I don't think he would mind it one bit," I said, feeling stiff and flushed with anger all at once. "He always thought I was too soft."

We rode out into the desert, following the trail that grew ever fainter. I had never been this far south of camp before. To our right was the low chain of hills that marked the course of the Hassayampa. Behind us, the Altyn Tagh rose like a blue-black wall topped with white. Ahead of us, about a day's ride, another ridge of hills erupted from the flats—dry hills, dark and treeless, with no snow on the crest. Off to our left, the desert sloped flat into a tan and featureless infinity.

Soon the mud gave way to long stretches of wind-smoothed rock, and we had to circle outward, quartering to pick up the odd set of hoofprints. The warm wind from the southeast grew hotter, with grit in its teeth. We rode with our hat brims down and our eyes squinched tight. Then we lost the trail completely.

"He'll need water, so he must be swinging toward the river," Fric said.

"There's water in the Jawbone this time of year," Ratnose said, pointing to the bare hills due south of us. "If you know where to look."

"Yeah, but does he know that?"

"We have to assume so. And the Jawbone is honeycombed with caves—very good defensive ground. During daylight, he can see anything coming from this direction for miles. And he has plenty of meat."

"So what do we do?"

"We go in there and root him out."

41

We pushed on until well after dark, eating and dozing in the saddle, swinging to the west after sundown so that we might intercept the edge of the Jawbone at the point where it came closest to the Hassayampa. When the ground began to rise, Ratty sent Hunk ahead to find a wadi where we could hole up for the night. He found one that had a little surface water in it. We dug a shallow well for the horses and then made a fireless camp, rolling up in our saddle blankets against the wind, which had lost all its warmth with the setting of the sun. The night sky was moonless, starless, humming with a sandy wind that felt out the gaps and seams of our blankets as cleverly as a pick-pocket. Still, it had been a hard day's ride under the blinding sun, with the tension building all the way, and soon most of the band were snoring. I dozed off myself, fitfully, waking from time to time with a start from some nightmare which immediately faded from my consciousness. Around about midnight, I snapped awake again, but this time the nightmare was real: Ratnose was standing over me, grinning.

"Let's take a walk, Runner," he whispered. "Just you and I and the wind."

We walked down the wadi and out into the flatland, Ratnose leading the way. Behind us the Jawbone rose, blurred through the grit in my eyes so that it appeared as some low black cloud, spreading against the charcoal sky. Ratnose stopped in the lee of a boulder and sat down carefully.

"There are scorpions out here," he said, "and the worst sort of snakes. But they aren't as mean as what's up there." And he gestured at the Jawbone. "Who is he, Runner?"

I said nothing. The wind worked its fingers down

the nape of my neck and sandpapered my spine.

"Come on, Runaway, I asked you a question."

Nothing.

"All right, let me suppose, then." He reached behind him and pulled his toadstabber; I caught the glint of it in the murky light. He began to clean his fingernails, his head down and his voice as grating as the wind. "Let me suppose that a man and his boy are coming up the Hassayampa, up from the cities on a hunting-and-fishing expedition. Let me suppose that the man is wise, that he has heard of Ratanous, of the bandit's evil ways. Let me suppose as well that the man has even *met* Ratanous—shot at him, hurt him, killed some of his men. But that was long ago, and the man assumes Ratanous is dead, or gone, or both.

"But let me suppose that the higher he gets on the river, the weaker this assumption grows. After all, the river has a way of eroding false assumptions, doesn't it, Runner? It rots them like meat in warm water and flushes them away. So the man waxes fearful. Ratnose is there, Ratnose is around him, somewhere. Ratnose has designs on the man's life. Or perhaps on the life of his son. The man decides to press his luck no further. He will leave the Hassayampa.

"But the boy doesn't want to leave—not just yet. He knows nothing of Ratnose, or perhaps he knows only the good things about Ratnose—that Ratnose is wild, willful, free, mean, all-knowing . . ."

"Fuck you," I said. "I never thought you were all-knowing."

"Aha! The Runaway speaks! What did you think of me, then?"

Nothing.

"Just so. But you were interested, curious, compelled to learn more about this romantic bandit leader of whom naught but ill was spoken. And when the Indian stole your things and sold them to Ratnose, you decided to continue even though your father wanted to go home. Laudable pluck, Runner. Well done! You walked right into my trap."

"What trap?"

"You think that Beppo is the great trapper around here, don't you? Well, everything Beppo knows, I taught him. *I* am the trapper. Not of mere animals, but of men, Runner, of men and boys. I bait my traps with the two most effective lures known to man—curiosity and challenge. No man can resist the chance of knowledge or the threat of death."

"Bullshit," I said. "You sound like my father—all that pompous baloney about challenge. I came because . . . because I like the country and I wanted my stuff back."

"Keep that in mind, Runner. It's interesting that you should compare me to your father. Keep that in mind, too. But what I'm going to tell you now is the main reason I asked you out here for this little chat. We're going to kill that madman up there." He pointed the knife at the Jawbone—a darting thrust that seemed to impale the blackness and open it to the light. "You and I, Runner, we're going to capture him and make him pay for what he's done to our friends. *Our* friends, Runner. Because that madman is nothing to you anymore. You are one of us, now. Forever. And we kill our enemies."

I thought about that for a long, loud moment. The wind had increased in volume. The sand lashed at our boulder. To the east, a pumpkin moon was rising, orange through the dusty sky. I imagined my father, there on the dark height of the Jawbone, huddled in his bearskin against the wind. His eyes are bright with blood. He mutters curses against the wind and the darkness. His voice, in the grainy howling of the wind, sounds like Ratnose's. . . .

"I don't know what I'll do," I said finally. "I think you're mad at me because I dared to take Twigan away from you. I think you want to make me pay for that by helping you kill my father. Okay, I feel bad about what he did to Frac, and to Hal McVeigh, and to those old men he chopped, but not bad enough to wish him dead. Up here, death doesn't seem to mean that much. But the main thing, Ratnose, is that I don't give a damn if I offended you by taking Twigan. I took her because she was willing, and even if she hadn't been willing, I would have taken her eventually anyway. You taught me how to do that."

Ratnose smiled and sheathed his knife. He stood up and squinted his eye against the sand and the moonlight.

"All right," he said. "Twigan is yours. Tilkut is mine."

We walked back into the wadi.

42

I slept poorly and awoke in the false dawn, sneezing and shivering, with the image of the bear inside my eyelids. My teeth crunched with the night's dirt, and my eyes were glued shut with a mud composed of sand and tears. When I finally cracked them open, I could see the others shuffling around in the half-light, yanking at bellybands and cursing the horses and oiling their weapons. Fric gave me a pull from his canteen. It was cold tea spiked with crait, and in a little while I felt much better. The images of the night faded as the day spun closer.

We rode up the wadi, slumped low in our saddles. The wind had died, and the air smelled of crushed cactus. My first clear view of the Jawbone came as we emerged from the wadi into the full light of the sun. It rose above us like an enormous scab—swollen, pitted, crumbling, the color of old blood. Actually, it was lava from some ancient, cataclysmic eruption. Over the centuries, the wind and the weather had sculpted it into a shape that roughly resembled a dead man's mandible. It was full of caves and crevices, but empty of life.

"How in the hell do we hunt that kind of country?" asked Fric.

"Slowly," said Ratnose, "and on foot."

Leaving two men to watch the horses at the mouth of the wadi, Ratnose divided the remaining dozen of us into two-man teams. I was paired off with Korti, a tall, hollow-chested guy with gray hair and enormous forearms. He never talked much, but when he did, it was in broken English. Frac had once told me that Korti was an ex-Legionnaire who had split from Dienbienphu before it fell and just kept walking north. He had two women back at camp—his A team and his B team, he called them—and a nice string of horses. He and I were to hunt up the middle of the rockpile, over its highest point.

"I want this Tilkut taken alive, if at all possible," Ratty said before we moved out. "We could have some fun with him back at camp. But don't take any chances that could get you killed too easily. Shoot to maim if you see him run."

Nice, clear orders, I thought. All we had to do was climb up this crumbling, convoluted hunk of rotten lava without breaking our ankles or our skulls, locate a madman sharpshooter who could be hidden in any one of a few thousand caves, flush him out without getting zapped ourselves, and then shoot him in the leg. I looked over at Korti and saw by the focus of his eyes that he had already erased Ratty's orders from his mind: he would shoot to kill. He checked the selector switch on his AK-47 and flicked it to full automatic.

Well, I couldn't blame him, and he hadn't lived that long through all those slaughters by playing the noble hero, but what was I going to do? I hefted the Mannlicher, cracking the bolt to make sure I had a round in the chamber. The rifle had been too heavy when I first tried to shoot it. Lately, though, it felt right for me: not exactly a feather, but balanced and solid, the iron sights lining up automatically—almost eagerly, it seemed—when I brought it to my shoulder. I could hit with it, I knew; when I was relaxed and cocky, I could hit with it at 300 yards from a rest and at 200 off the shoulder. But when I was nervous, the muzzle swung all over the place, my finger slapped the trigger like it was a shotgun, and I couldn't hit my foot if I was leaning on it. And right now, as we started up the Jawbone, I was nervous.

It was like climbing up into one of those nightmares where the ground is glue and your eyes don't work, where everything is slow but panic, the earth too dark and the sky too bright. Chunks of lava like misshapen heads cracked and slid beneath our feet. We could hear the clatter of rocks kicked loose by the other parties echoing all around us. The black rock radiated heat, and within fifty yards I was slick with sweat. There were small, spiky cactuses growing in the creases of the rock, brightly flowered in this season, red and yellow and blue, but every time I lost my balance, my hand seemed to fall on one. Pulling out the spines with my teeth, I thought of the nature lovers back home, "Flower Sniffers," my father called them. They would love the Jawbone. They would twitter and chirp over its "craggy beauty," sigh over its "infinite mysteries." Well, naturally enough, I guess. They wouldn't have to worry about a .30 caliber bullet turning their chest into a pot of lung soup at any moment.

Korti was ahead of me, nearly to the crest, when we heard the first shots. A rapid, distant popping, masked by the rock. Then silence for a space of perhaps five heartbeats. Then a heavier, louder burst, punctuated by the door-slamming bang of a rifle. Korti flattened against the rocks and I sat back quickly into a convenient crevice, picking up the inevitable cactus in the butt. Korti motioned me to swing around to my right, toward a broken outcropping that might give a view of the action. I waited until I heard another burst of automatic-weapons fire and then scrambled over to the outcropping. As I hunkered down behind the rock, concentrating on the sounds of the firefight over the hammering of my heart, something leaped out of the shadows—a gray, mottled lizard nearly a yard long that skittered down the slope quicker than my eye could follow. A caprizond, the leopard lizard of these hills. It scared the heart out of me. I slumped back in the rocks, feeling tears sting at the back of my eyes.

When I looked up over the outcropping, I saw Korti just then disappear over the crest of the ridge, heading for the fight. I could see the mouth of a big cave about a third of the way down the slope on the far side of the crest, and then I saw the wink of muzzle

blast in the dark of the cave's mouth. A short burst—
dut-dut-dut. Heavier fire answered from the rocks
beneath the cave. Tilkut was in the cave. Some of our
guys were pinned down on the lower slope. Then
something came flying out of the cave and fell into
the rocks below with a bright, flat crack: a grenade.
Another burst of automatic fire from below and two
furry figures tried to run up the hill to the cave under
its cover. Tilkut chopped them down not ten yards
from the mouth, and the bodies bounced back down
the hill.

God damn it, he was killing a lot of my friends!

But it looked like Ratnose had him pinned down in
there, all right. It was only a question of time, now.
We had more ammo than he did. We had men enough
to resupply ourselves and still keep him from moving.
When dark came on, Ratty would ease his riflemen up
closer to the cave mouth and either shoot or dynamite
the Bear God out of there. Then I heard Ratty yelling
from the rocks below the cave.

"Tilkut! Tilkut! *Speak* to me, Tilkut!" I could imagine Ratty snickering at that.

Another grenade came *crump*-ing down.

"Don't be that way, Tilkut! Listen to reason! We
have you surrounded. No escape. I have more men
coming, more than you can ever kill. Tilkut?"

Silence.

"Let's end this ugly war! I have done you no harm,
and you have done much to me. We are harmless
country folk, woodcutters and trappers. We don't
know why you have chosen to pick on us. But we
want no more killing. Come out and eat with us, talk
with us, smoke with us, join our tribe. We want no
more deaths, though we will accept them if we have
to in order to kill you if you won't come out. Tilkut?"

Silence. But then I saw movement beyond the cave
and just above it. Korti had circled about Tilkut's den
and was easing his way down to the cave mouth, the
assault rifle ready in his hand. Ratnose must have seen
him too.

"Tilkut," he pleaded, "have you no feeling for this

wonderful country? This unpolluted paradise where
man and rock and water and all God's creatures live
in meaningful harmony? Why splash it with blood?
Why sully its silences with loud noises? Why befoul
its air with the stink of gunpowder? You see, Tilkut, I
am like you a man of sensitivity, a man in love with
nature and nature's God, a peaceful man who seeks
no gain from the earth or its creatures, great or small.
Like that, Tilkut. Tilkut? Come out of there, you
fucker, or we'll blow you out!"

Silence. By now, Korti had reached a ledge at the
lip of the cave. He stood there for a moment as Ratnose finished his tirade. Then he seemed to take a
deep breath. He jumped into the cave mouth with the
AK-47 roaring even as he landed. He disappeared into
the cave.

Silence. After a minute, two more figures rose from
the rocks below and started up slowly, bent-kneed, rifles at the ready, toward the cave. As they came
closer, I saw that they were Hunk and Fric. When
they reached the entrance, they yelled in for Korti,
but got no answer. Then they went in. Down below,
I could see Ratty peering over the top of a boulder.
We waited.

"Ratnose!"

The yell came from the crest of the Jawbone, directly above the cave but a hundred feet higher.
Tilkut stood black against the sky. He lifted a body
by its hair and threw it down the cliff, crashing and
bouncing on the rock, starting a small landslide. The
body bounced over the mouth of the cave and flapped
limp and broken down to Ratty's boulder. Korti, sure
enough.

When I looked back to the ridge, Tilkut was gone.
He must have found a chimney at the back of the
cave, hidden in it, killed Korti and dragged him up to
the top. But as I was figuring that out, I heard rocks
clattering to my left, coming down the ridge. I swung
the rifle around to cover the route Korti had taken to
the top. Tilkut was coming.

He burst on me with a speed that seemed impos-

sible, leaping down the steep slope in twenty-foot
jumps, huge, black-faced beneath the stiff bear snout,
the BAR with its bipod rattling as he skidded into
sight, snarling deep in his throat, only his teeth shining in a face dark with beard and rage and mud. As
he roared past, he saw me and began to swing the
BAR, but I slammed it out of his hand with the muzzle of my rifle and then poked it against his chest,
hard. He staggered back, and his other hand went behind him for the Luger.

"Leave the Luger where it is," I said, jabbing him
again with the muzzle.

His eyes walked up the rifle barrel to my face, and I
could see them come into focus. His chest was
pounding under the green, wet uniform. The bearskin over his shoulders seemed to have a life of its
own, but slowly that life died. His eyes narrowed,
and the madness went out of them. I eased the tension on the trigger.

"I thought you were dead," he said.

There was a clattering in the rocks behind us, and
then Fric and Hunk dropped down on either side.
Hunk kicked the BAR out of my father's reach and
then removed a knife, four grenades, and the Luger
from various parts of his clothing. Fric looked on,
white-faced and quivering.

"Ah!" came Ratnose's voice from behind us. "What a
pleasant sight."

He was standing on the rocks overhead, his legs
straddled and his eye joyous. He clicked the safety on
his rifle.

"A father and a son," he said, "reunited at last!"

Part 3

43

Tilkut's irrationale.

My madness was total: sublime, ecstatic, unmarred by any doubts or sulks. At no point during the months I roamed that mean, lean country, killing for food and pleasure, do I recall one moment of reason, one instant of unhappiness. It was as if a caldron of liquid laughter had come to a slow, steady boil behind my eyes, perking joyfully there, sending shots of giggly steam down my nostrils and up my throat, exploding from time to time in scalding, superheated guffaws that left my vocal cords raw and aching with delight. I felt no fear, no hunger, no worry—only the immense, ridiculous power of my freedom.

At first, when the boy failed to return, I was desolate—sane with concern. How could I ever explain his absence, his death, to his mother or his friends, or even to myself? Yes, much worse, to myself? I ranged out in ever-widening circles from the camp, searching for sign. The country was immense, empty. It cackled at me with rain and wind. At the foot of a hill, it would seem certain that he must be visible from the crest; from the height of the ridge, equally certain that he was behind me, circling back to camp, or perhaps lying up with a broken leg in some ravine on the far side of the river. I would dash back down the hill, heading in precisely the opposite direction to that which I had chosen for the day's hunt. And then I would stop, ponder, panic, scoot off in yet a third direction, the country hooting with scornful laughter at my indecision. Still, as long as I was moving I had the illusion of accomplishment: I was doing something, getting somewhere, applying reason to a situation that only reason could resolve. But then, as the days progressed without any sign of him, any single clue, reason demanded that I go mad. A slow sour hint at first, easily dismissed with a wry chuckle. Then a hoarse whisper at night beside the dying fire: He's gone, you won't find him; if he's not dead in a gully or already digested in the guts of a carnivore, he's fallen among murderers, tortured and skinned out and devoured by Ratnose.

Or else just gone, zip, like that. It had happened so often to other men in big country. One would read about it in the literature: "He headed out of camp that morning to fetch the rest of the elk he'd cached up in the box canyon, and it wuz a clear day, warm, & never cum back. . . ." I had seen it myself once, or part of it, up in the Skalkaho Country of the Bitterroots, where Lewis and Clark nearly starved on their outward journey. We had organized a deer drive, down a simple valley. My friends stood near me on the crest. We waved at each other and started down. A cloud blew over, burying us. At the bottom, one man failed to appear. We fired shots, we hooted and whooped, we tried to track him out. Nothing. No sign, no blaze, no smoke. It was as if the fog bank had absorbed him. The panic in my gut spread and strengthened like a fire on a west wind; it was worse than being lost oneself, because there was nothing more we could do. Finally, just at sunset, he emerged from the woods at the base of the mountain, sheepish and dehydrated. He ate a couple of apples and then vomited. No, he never heard our shouts or our shots, never saw the sun, never cut the stream that might have told him where he was. He just got turned around, that's all. Happens to everybody sooner or later, doesn't it?

But—how horrible! There beside the campfire, with Reason insisting in a cold, clear voice that my son was gone, with Reason insisting that there was nothing more I could do in a reasonable way to find him, that he was gone for good, dead one way or another, for neither Reason nor I could even conceive the possibility that the boy had actually, willingly, gone forth to

join Ratnose, my nemesis, my dread; with Reason insisting that nothing more could be done for me—like
a reasonable mechanic in a garage one trusts, to
which one has taken one's automobiles for most of an
adult lifetime, insisting that the car is done, finished,
can't be fixed, shifting his eyes away, embarrassed
that he can no longer offer hope; or perhaps like a
trusted family physician saying, Yes, it's terminal,
looking away, offering no hope, hope being after all, a
finite phenomenon, and we're out of it right now;
there beside the cheerful hickory logs, hopeless, Reason suggested a sojourn—just a brief visit, mind you,
nothing permanent—with his pal. Madness.

Sure, why not?

But Madness is coercive, concentrated, special, like
an old friend one hasn't seen in many years, an old
college roommate perhaps, a shipmate, an old buddy
with whom one drank and wrestled and went to parties, to whom one confided all the conquests and dis-
mays, then didn't see again for quite a while. When
you get back together with Madness, the only place to
go is on a binge. A freedom binge—yeah, man, let's
hang one on! Let's really rip it off, man, all that shit
that's happened since we seen each other: fuck the
job, fuck the responsibilities, fuck the old lady sulking
at home and laying plans to make us suffer some more
for our few, timid dashes at freedom. And the laughter boils up behind the eyes. The laughter paints the
sleazy saloons with a golden varnish, spikes the booze
with a belly-warming strength, erases the age, the
stench, the cosmetics, the crevasses of calculation
from the faces of the doorway trollops, unmans the
muggers and sends them scuttling into their garbage
cans like so many bubonic rats afraid just yet to nip.
And then time stops, the night stands still, tomorrow
is so distant as to appear absurd—a laughing dream, a
projection that must be suffused with laughter:
golden, no sweat, no remorse, not even *there*.

And when the cop comes up to you, finally, his
hand swinging tentatively near the pistol butt, you

look at Madness and Madness looks at you, and you both start laughing uproariously as you grab the cop and pound his head against the curb and then, pulling the pistol in one easy, greasy gesture, as smooth as any signature your hand ever wrote while dismissing tomorrow's debt to a flimsy credit-card chit, you or Madness, or perhaps both of you, blast the cop's head into a broken pumpkin, except for his blue Irish eye that stares into the gutter. Freedom!

So we drifted through that country on the Upper Hassayampa, my buddy Madness and I, killing whatever crossed our path, and killing it with impunity. The big meat critters froze at our approach, goggling, petrified. We walked right up to them, giggling, blessed, and patted them on the brow, aurochs and elk alike, before shooting them. Snakes lay quiet in our presence, flicking their tongues to taste our untoward odor. I came upon a bear that could have—should have—charged and torn me to bits. I walked right up to it where it stood frozen in appreciation of me and my Madness and scratched it behind the ears. I lifted its lips to study its teeth, laughing joyfully at their white, strong symmetry. I tugged on its mane and placed the muzzle of my pistol against its temple, growling obscenities and threats into its tick-swollen ear. But finally I spared it, for a laugh.

Madness and I were delighted with the Dump. It brought back all the joys and giggles of that War—the last one we could love or envy. The one in which Four Freedoms implied a fifth: the freedom to kill in a good cause, with no regrets; the freedom to hate without reservation and kill in the same joyous mood, as we were killing now. We loved the faded posters, the naked, naive graffiti. We spent long evenings in the dark, musty barracks discussing girls we had known back then, with their bright mouths and pompadours and seamed stockings leading up to cunts that were actually fertile. We fondled the ancient weapons: Thompson submachine guns and Garands, Browning Automatic Rifles that had real walnut for their stocks and fore ends, bayonets heavy with stale cosmoline but, once cleaned, bright with a vicious purpose that pared away guilt—after all, they were meant for Nazis and Monkey-Men. And when the late few travelers came through, we killed them with a godlike joy, our nostrils twitching, swooning in the incense of burned gunpowder.

I laughed when I killed the hippie. The fishhook trick was Madness's idea, but I must admit I loved it. I laughed at the hippie's outrage, his horror, at his pain, at the blood that filled his mouth—I admit now that it was an act of unconscionable cruelty, but after all, Madness made me do it, and he laughed harder than I did. And the kid was an enemy, an *Enemy!* A real, certified, honest-to-badness villian: otherwise why did he slink so fearfully at the sight of **our weap**ons, cry so piteously when caught, protest so vehemently under torture, refuse so staunchly to reveal the whereabouts of Ratnose's enclave? Why did he lisp with the hook through his tongue?

Burning the Dump, killing another Enemy, then trailing the rest back into Ratnose's country and killing a few more—all of that was joy unbounded, easy, natural. And the ride down the melting mountain. It never occurred to me to hide my track, to puzzle the pursuit that both Madness and I knew must now follow from Ratnose's camp. Madness required a straight line to the cinder heap where he and I would make our stand and slaughter the savages, and we would have killed them to the man—we had it all figured out. I was halfway up the chimney in the back of the cave which Madness had pointed out to me, which I had known about from previous visits, when the skinny gunman shot his way in. Madness smiled at me in the dark, only his eyes and his broken teeth flashing yellow-white like some phosphorescent fungal growth, before he broke the skinny gunman's neck with a single blow of his fist, and then bit off the skinny gunman's ear for good measure—my buddy Madness worked well in the dark.

Madness knew where they kept their horses. After
throwing the skinny gunman down to them—that
would keep them busy for a while—we headed down
to kill the horses and the horse guards, Madness and I
chattering away to each other as we ran down the
lava slope, as unconcerned about silence as we had
been about disguising our trail, knowing we were in-
vulnerable as we had been with the bear. But then as
I came round the rock, as I came round the rock and
the kid was standing there, as I came round the rock
and the kid jammed that rifle barrel in my chest and
my hand slid around for the Luger to blast his lungs
up through his nostrils, and my eyes hit his face, hit
his own eyes, and—zip!—he was there again, alive,
my son . . .

Whoops, said Madness. I gotta split. My mother's
calling . . .

And Madness was gone.

And another voice piped up, a creaky old voice,
calm, measured, dry . . .

Uh, well, it seems we made a mistake, said Reason,
clearing his throat and knocking the dottle from his
briar. He adjusted his pince-nez and straightened his
starched white doctor's smock. Yes, it seems that it
isn't terminal after all . . .

Oh, but it *is* terminal. Or at least, it will be very
soon. Ratnose and I must have our little meeting, our
tête-à-tête, our two-man encounter-group session from
which only one of us will emerge even partially cured.
Yet the prospect of our fatal confrontation does not
frighten me as much as I thought it would. After all
these years of worry, all those gum-footed nightmares
in which his hideous face served as focus and cathar-
sis, I find I rather like the man. Perhaps it's because
he is a charmer, literate, adept at putting one at one's
ease, the antithesis of brute rage or cowardly hysteria.
Nor is he as ugly, in close-up, as he appears at long
range. There is a quiet, calm, almost heroic quality to
the way he carries himself. His eye is deep, and although it can roar black with scorn and purpose, more

often it reflects a wise, umber amusement. The grit in his voice lends density to his words, as if they were boulders shifting on an ancient slope that has been prone to avalanche. Altogether a very imposing man. If I had friends, real friends, I would be happy to count Ratnose among them.

At a deeper level, of course, I like him because I know I can kill him. Now that Madness has left me and Reason is again my hired consultant, I realize that I have matched Ratnose in cruelty, perhaps (in the business of the hippie's tongue) even exceeded him. After all these months alone in the mountains, I am stronger than he, more thoroughly inured to pain and danger, quicker, darker, uglier. To be sure, he may very well be a better dresser, a better dancer, a better conversationalist in mixed company; but none of those factors will apply in the contest he has chosen to settle our fate, and that of my son. Because my son is my real weapon: my strength and my hope, the catalyst from and through which I can, and shall, draw all my skill when the moment comes. And more.

Ratnose will die.

44

Yes, the fly rods—that was the brilliant stroke, of course. They were the best of the breed: H. L. Leonard rods, built of split Calcutta cane, tall and slim and elegantly balanced, their nickel ferrules snug as a hand in a velvet glove, the guides wrapped off impeccably in silk and finished with the sparest strokes of lacquer. Rods with backbone enough to bend the spirit of the strongest trout, yet with grace enough not to break it. Aristocratic rods, shaped carefully, calmly, lovingly by the sure though withered hands of dry old men in cozy workrooms, the teakettle piping on the stove, while through the riffles of memory there flowed again the fast, clear waters of streams now dammed and gone—Neversink, Esopus, Rondout—or else befouled past reclamation—Connecticut, Kennebec, Androscoggin: alive again in the taper of these rods, the long black shadows finning again over the gravel. Yes, the cryptic movement of the great, clean, sullen monsters, preliterate messages, translatable only through the subtle twitches and electric surges of the fly rod, and then at best inarticulate—inarticulable, like the dreams of dry old men in cozy workrooms.

And of course, it was Ratnose's notion. Pistols or knives? Pah! Plebeian! But a duel to the death between angling gentlemen (and here he snickered) using *fly rods!* That was more like it. That would be death with style!

Ridiculous! snorted Tilkut. How could you possibly kill a man with anything as small and innocuous as a trout fly?

Flies kill men in nature, Ratnose rejoined. All it takes is the proper poison. And Ratnose had it: a gummy, resinous concoction extracted from the milky sap of the ketwai tree (a relative of the *Hevea*, or rubber plant). Before the advent of firearms, Hassayampan warriors had always dipped their arrowheads in ketwai, and some still used it on their knives. The sticky white sap was boiled slowly over a low fire until it turned thick and brown, almost black. Once it entered the bloodstream, paralysis swiftly ensued.

Thus, the locale of the combat would be quite important. Ratnose had in mind a place high in the Altyn Tagh, where the Hassa and the Yampa flowed together to form the headwaters of the great river itself. The tributaries, fast and frigid enough to induce paralysis without the aid of ketwai, poured in whirlpool fashion down a monstrous, mile-deep granitic gullet known locally as the Suck Hole. The combatants would stand 100 feet apart—one in the Hassa, the other in the Yampa—facing each other across the whirlpool. They would be naked, so that clothing might not serve as armor against the poisoned flies, their only weapons the elegant, aristocratic fly rods. The aim, of course, was to hook the other man and then, as the paralyzing ketwai went to work, drag him into the grip of the Suck Hole. To preclude any desperate attempt at biting oneself free of the hook, wire-cored leaders would be used.

All right, said Tilkut reluctantly, as if he had a choice in the matter, but what about the selection of line? Would that be left to the individual?

Ratnose laughed. Of course not. Both would use double-tapered, sinking lines. That way, the unfair advantage in speed inherent in a weight-forward, "shooting" fly line would be nullified. The highest premium would be placed on precise, economical long-distance fly-casting ability, as it should be in a combat to the death between angling gentlemen.

And the choice of flies?

Ah, that might just as well be a matter of individual preference. No special advantage or disadvantage would accrue in this regard, provided the combatant did not stupidly penalize himself with some gaudy, feathery, air-resistant and hence slow-moving abortion like an Umpqua Red Brat or a Coles Comet. Ratnose assumed that Tilkut would choose something small but flashy, something symbolic, a wet fly like the Grizzly King or perhaps the Silver Prince.

Tilkut stiffened at the insult. No. He would rely on his old standby at this season, with its olive wool body and its dark ginger hackle and its wing of gray duck quill. The Cowdung was good enough for him; it suited the prey.

Ratnose chuckled. For himself he would tie his own favorite of deer hair, cream and ginger. The Rat-Faced MacDougall.

45

The nearest ketwai tree was located a two days' journey to the south of Ratnose's camp, in a region of sandstone hills and hot springs draining into the Hassayampa. Runner was dispatched on his motorcycle to fetch the sap from which the poison would be distilled. He took Twigan with him. While he was gone, Ratnose and Tilkut tied their fatal flies in the bandit leader's cave. Both were experts with vise and forceps, dubbing needle and hackle pliers, and both were willing conversationalists. Their dialogue, though technical and at times rambling, is nonetheless of some interest.

RATNOSE: Pass me that peacock herl, will you please, Tilkut?

TILKUT: Here you go.

RATNOSE: Thanks. I think I might try a little more color in the body on this one. . . . You know, that's a fine kid you've got there, Tilkut.

TILKUT: Grumph . . .

RATNOSE: He's not a whiner, like so many of the punks that we get up here from Downriver. I don't know what you're doing down there anymore, but you're sure producing a bunch of sniveling softies. Except for Runner, that is. The rest of them get up here and immediately start muttering about "They." You know the song. "They want us to study, they want us to work, they want us to fight, and what do we get out of it? Old is all we get." Or else: "They won't let us fuck, they won't let us smoke dope, they won't let us lie around and dream, and still they envy us because we're young." Oh, they're great at screwing and doping and dreaming, all right, but when I try to put them to work in between times, they usually take off. And lump me along with "They" at the next place they stop, I suppose.

TILKUT: If the kid's smart, he'll keep that motorcycle going when he gets to the ketwai tree.

RATNOSE: Why? I mean, why the hell should he? I've got nothing against him. I used him to bait you in, that's all. Not his fault that his father loves him, or wants to avenge him. Most natural thing in the world, I'd guess. No, if he stays here he stands a chance to inherit the tribe. If you kill me up at the Suck Hole, my man Hunk takes over, and Hunk is getting a bit long in the tooth, I guess you've noticed. Hunk thinks the world of Runner, and when Hunk goes, Runner takes charge.

TILKUT: Hand me that thread wax, okay?

RATNOSE: It's over there under the tinsel. But goddammit, Tilkut, you're avoiding the issue—no pun intended. You assume because I want to kill you that I want to kill your son—or hurt him, anyway. Why should the one follow the other? I mean, however it happened, you sent me a fine kid, and I've made him better. I'd be a damned fool to throw that away, wouldn't I?

TILKUT: What is this, summer camp? I sent you a fine kid and you made him better—you sound like some kind of a pussy camp counselor. And why the hell should I want my kid to end up a bandit leader? What's the future in that? Blood on his hands and a price on his head. When they come in here with planes and cavalry . . .

RATNOSE: Forget it—they tried. It doesn't work. This is Outlaw Country—always has been and always will be. The one part of the world where the outlaw is regarded as an endangered species. "Live and let kill." You knew that or you wouldn't have brought him up here.

TILKUT: Okay, yeah, I knew it, and I wanted him tougher; I wanted to see the test, having flunked my own when I was a kid. But that doesn't mean I want him to end up a loser here in the mountains. Down below he can get rich, he can gain power, he can manipulate people and take more from them than their lives. It's like domestic cattle: you've got to realize that by keeping them going you get more out of them than just by killing and eating them. And you've got comfort while you're doing it—houses with central heating, woolen blankets, refrigerators, cars that smell like a million bucks, pâté de foie gras, the theater, silk suits and perfumed cunts, television—and sure, I know it sounds silly to you, but those things mean a lot to a lot of mean people. . . .

RATNOSE: Too clever, Tilly. You put the lie to your argument with your own trite cuteness.

TILKUT: Just trying you out, Ratty. Do you want some tea? I'm going to have another cup.

[Tilkut rises from the vise bench, stretches, walks over to the tile oven where the crait pot is warming. Tree frogs are singing from the wooded slope across the stream. Only one bonfire is blazing in the dark down below. A few figures are gathered around it, wrapped in furs against the chilly mountain night. The kid they call Fric is playing his guitar. Tilkut pours two cups of tea and returns to the bench.]

RATNOSE: I wish I had some good mandarin flank feathers for these wings, or some wood duck. A nice, healthy, prime drake in autumn plumage, when it's faded a bit with the summer sun; that almost invisible sheen they get—you know?

TILKUT: You don't need those for your Rat-Faced MacDougall.

RATNOSE: Oh, I'm tying flies for later. Once I've dropped you down the Suck Hole, I'm planning to spend the next month fishing. [Chuckles]

Tilkut sucks his tea, grimaces, sulks, scratches his crotch.

Ratnose peers through a magnifying glass at the tiny fly in his vise. His eye is as big and bright as an eggplant. The fly, up close, is a wonder of shifting colors and electric tendrils, the steel of the finely tempered #34 wire hook sending off explosions into the night.

TILKUT: Who was that . . . girl, that went off with him on the bike?

RATNOSE: Little flat-chested slope-head? Worn-out

leather pants and a bear-hide cape?

TILKUT: Yeah, that one.

RATNOSE: Oh, that's Runner's old lady. You didn't know that, did you—that he had a woman now? I suppose he kept it from you. Well, he would, I guess. We call her Twigan—means something like Horsefly in Hassayampan. You'll get a kick out of this: she was my girl before Runner aced me out.

TILKUT: Your girl! You mean *one* of your girls, don't you? That's another reason I don't want my kid hanging around here. What you're running here is nothing more than a fuck farm, like those damned hippie-dippie communes they have where everyone rolls around with everyone else, all covered in vegetable oil. What you've got here is a commonist society, and what's wrong with commonism is that it's *common!* It's not one bit swell or special or different—it's just plain *common!*

RATNOSE: It's an extended family, as opposed to a nuclear family. The nuclear family is passé.

TILKUT: I understand what you mean about extended families versus nuclear families, and I must admit there's something attractive about a loose, flexible grouping of like-minded people living together without all the nervous-making strictures and rigid roles that the traditional daddy-and-mommy-and-baby thing demands. But none of them seem to last—or at least, very few of them do. Not just because the people are lazy and undisciplined, but because they get bored; it's too smooth, too gentle, too goddam *benign!* It's like when I was a kid and I'd get to thinking about Heaven. An eternity of niceness! Well, I figured if I ever got there, I'd cut Choir sure enough, but even at that, what would I end up doing forever and ever amen? Fishing? That would pall a bit after the first eight billion lunkers, each one taken on the first cast with my three-foot, half-ounce ultraextrasuperlight rod with the half-pound tippet. Hunting? Look, you know it ain't no fun if you hit 'em every time, particularly if they don't run both ways, and I'm sure all the grizzlies in Heaven have rubber teeth. The same with everything else—sex, child rearing, business, art, philosophy, science: no conflict, no doubt, no collisions, no fear, no triumph, everything nice. . . . You know what really makes me want to puke, Ratnose? When a parent says to his child, "Make nice to the doggie, Gretchen." Make nice to the doggie! And the little sticky soft hand dawdles away from the ripe smell of prunes turned to shit and awkwardly pats the dog on the head, and little Gretchen gets this nicey-nicey little baby-goo smile on her face, and everyone claps their hands. And the dog, Ratnose, the fucking *dog!* he *loves* it! His tongue hangs out between those big white choppers and he goes huffa-huffa-huffa with his eyes squinched shut! Make nice to the doggie. Isn't that what they teach us about everything?

RATNOSE: It's not what I teach. It's not going to be so nice up at the Suck Hole.

Tilkut ponders that for a moment, fiddles with the dubbing needle. He gets up and walks to the window. He spreads his arms, stretches. Ratnose watches the big, wide back. He had never realized before how big Tilkut was. Tilkut's face is small, pinched in with his many confusions, but his back is gigantic, wide and flat as a barn door. Tilkut stretches for a long time, his joints creaking and his mouth uttering high-pitched squeaks and groans. Then he reaches for a hunting knife on the windowsill—a smooth, swift reach that precludes interception—and whirling, he slams the knife, point first, into a beam across the room. The knife *thunks* and hums, its point buried two inches deep in cured white oak.

TILKUT: Oh, it'll be nice up at the Suck Hole, all right. It'll be nice for me. I could have killed you just then, like I could have killed you anytime I wanted in the past few hours. And you know it. I could have finished you and eased on out of here without anyone knowing. But I'm going to kill you up on the mountain, where my son can see me do it, and then I'm

going to take him out of here and bring him back
home. He'll go back to school and learn his sums and
his takeaways. He'll learn to wear a coat and a tie
again. He'll get a job, finally, and a wife, and a sec-
ondhand car, and a house. Maybe he'll get fat and
bored and drunk like so many of us down at the end
of the river, but at least he'll have a chance to grow.
And a chance to play while he's growing; he'll play at
power and at love—subtle games, full of machina-
tions, maybe, but the kind of play that can turn him
into something more complex than a mere killer and
fucker. Your way of life, with its orgies of blood and
sex, seems free at first glance—captivating, even—but
it produces simple machines. That's why I'm going to
kill you and bring my son out of it.

RATNOSE: I don't kill that easy. I don't have to die.
For anyone.

TILKUT: We'll see. We'll see as soon as the kid gets
back.

It was like back home, Runner thought, when they used to tap the maple trees. There were eight big sugar maples across the stream, behind the house, and when the snows of February had turned crusty—rotten, really, because the seasons die their deaths too—he and his father and his sister would take the sap buckets and the galvanized iron spigots and a hammer and the big, red-knobbed auger and walk down through the rotting snow across the rotting oaken bridge to the sugar bush. His father would crank the auger, watching first the gray elephant-hide bark turn out along the bright steel bit and then the fresh, wet, white, tender wood, boring deep into the tree's veins. Then Runner would tap the spigots home, *tink-tink-tink*, and his sister would hang the buckets.

At each tree they waited, until the sap began to run, *drip, drip, drip* into the buckets—cloudy at the beginning with chewed wood and then finally clear, cold, with only a hint of the syrup and sugar to come. Then each day after school, he and his sister would run galumphing in their overshoes down to the sugar bush and pour the sap into a big pail, and between them lug it up, sloshing and unwieldy, with a mind of its own like that of all liquids whether contained in cups or oceans, into the kitchen, where their mother would boil it down to syrup. The redwing blackbirds would have returned by then, grating their metal cries through the willows that flanked the stream. A few early trout hung in the murky boils under the bridge. Coming in from the raw, sour smell of spring, breathing the cured, sweet steam of new maple syrup, Runner and his sister felt very snug. The prospect of Mom's pancakes hung rich in the house. It promised a happy future.

But this was a poison tree, promising only death. Runner and Twigan lay on a bed of hides and swamp grass near the ketwai tree. The Hassayampa groaned at their backs, fat and uncomfortable with the spring runoff, clearing its throat from time to time of the logs and skulls that were its seasonal burden. Runner wondered what his sister was doing right now. This had always been the best time of the year between them, when the testy side of nature came clear. The squirrels chasing each other through the trees, some to fuck and some to fight, or both. Even the birds went weird in the springtime, the female downy woodpeckers chasing the other females from the suet feeder while the males, with their red-dotted skullcaps, chased after the fight. Back then, before he had learned about sex, Runner enjoyed chasing his sister through the mud, or being chased by her, mocking and in a way emulating, envying, the birds and the squirrels.

His hand lay on Twigan's naked belly, relaxed, just above the wisp of her skimpy bush. He wondered if his sister had gotten into fucking yet. She was older than he was, so probably she had. His hand on Twigan's belly got a little nervous at the thought: Am I now or have I ever been unconsciously incestuous? The sap from the ketwai tree dripped slowly but noisily into the tin bucket which he had hung beneath a hand-carved willow-wood spigot. Already he had filled two canteens with the sap, and this bucket would complete a third. That was all Ratnose had said he needed, so by tomorrow morning they could head back to camp. Actually, they could leave tonight if they wanted—the moon would be full, and the sky promised clarity. But Runner was not all that sure he wanted to return. He dreaded the duel: not out of any sense of squeamishness—no, blood didn't bother him anymore—but because he could not decide which man he wanted to win. More than that, he realized now, watching the sap drip: he could not decide which man he wished to become.

If Ratnose won, Runner would stay with the band—remain forever on the Hassayampa, hunting and killing and balling and scrambling his brains, never seeing his old pals again or his books or his softball mitt or his model rocket collection. Or his mother and sister, either. He would never again have the chance to lie around eating fudge and watching a monster movie on the late show, while a sleet storm howled outside. No jetliners, no museums, no ball games, no chance to win a trophy for motorcycle racing. No choice, really. In Ratnose's world, you were plain and simply a man. He could feel the simplicity most sharply in his imagination. A man worked, screwed, and fixed things. Nothing more. Even the stories that Ratty's people told were all the same, after you got through the first excitement of blood and transformation. Sure, the crait helped some, by making the rocks and the trees and the river and the animals seem somehow deeper than they were, but finally they all ended up being Stone Age people, Ratnose's people, simple. Okay, Runner thought, recalling a line from a song his sister loved, 'tis a gift to be simple. But for how long?

On the other hand, if his father won, Runner would leave the Hassayampa. No more wolf howling with Twigan; no more Hunk; never again the mad, screaming scrambles after wild cattle, with the raw, red heart meat hot and smoking in the winter mornings. No more orgies denying the night, crazy couplings, bombed out of his gourd so that the sun when it finally rose seemed to sing a prayer in a wondrous, loving language. No more leather against his skin, strange heads, the eyes glazing slowly into death, into rot. Only plastic clothes, tame meat, reconstituted orange juice. School buses and homework, the deadening discipline that promised "freedom" at the end. Partial pruderies. His guns would be locked in a gun cabinet, and he could not turn them on another man without the threat of legal action. He would not be allowed to race his bike without the muffler—things like that. What, after all, was the choice they promised you? The freedom to accept restrictions? Not much more. Oh, the freedom to make a pile of money and own the niftiest toys—sure, I'd love a brace of matched Purdeys, a Ferrari 365 GTB-4, a Land-Rover, an MV Agusta 500, Payne rods and Hardy reels galore, a cellarful of vintage Dom Perignon to mix with my fresh-squeezed Lebanese orange juice every morning, and a kennel full of blooded Bouviers to stand in contrast to my scarred lion dogs—but where and how would I use them? In play, against subtle men who think of hunting and fishing as games, like squash or golf, where the dead are merely markers.

But if he went home, Runner thought, there would be work as well. It wasn't all play. He could study at natural history, maybe look deep into the ocean and see what it was like down there, help it stay alive. Or maybe look the other way—into space—because there was always the chance of new, unspoiled worlds beyond the time barrier. . . .

"Who do you want to win?" he asked Twigan.

"Tilkut," she answered without hesitation.

"Why?"

"He's your father."

Runner rolled his eyes and groaned. No help from that direction. He wiggled a fingertip in Twigan's belly button and got to his feet, pulling on his pants and his boots but leaving his shirt off. The sinking sun still shed a delicious warmth. He walked over to the ketwai tree and checked the sap bucket: nearly full. Another hour or two. The tree was immense, its trunk green and black and shiny, like a snake's back. Appropriate. He poured a cup of crait from the smoke-blackened pot over the cook fire and stirred some honey into it. Might as well get a little high, he thought. Plenty of time before we move out. . . .

Maybe I should go back and kill the both of them. It would be easy enough. I still have a few of those grenades. Wait until they're both in Ratty's cave, bull-shitting each other the way they like to do, then pull the pin and let the spoon fly clear and toss the smoking ball right in there; plug my ears; *kapow!* No more problems.

But there *would* be problems. If I kill Ratnose, I might have to face off against Hunk, and that wouldn't be much fun. And even though my father deserves to die, that prick! Killing my buddy Frac that way, the rotten bastard! Even though he deserves it, that miserable mammy-jammer, even so, he *is* my father. He cares for me. He brought me up here because he loves me, though it's a strange way to show love, I guess; he probably thought it would make a man of me, hacking around up here with a bunch of robbers and mean animals.

I wonder if any kid ever really wanted to become a man? It's a silly concept anyway—Be a Man! What else are you after you sprout hair on your balls and your voice changes, if not A Man? Well, some of them are pretty soft back there downriver, the ones with their suits and ties and righteous faith in the perfectability of humankind, their tired tears for the oppressed, and some of them are downright womanly with their vicious little digs and backbiting, sneaky, afraid to come right up to it and face it and fuck the consequences—yeah, like me right now: afraid to face it, the choice. Afraid of the country, too: its silence, how it never answers you—only stands there, old, old, so very old and changing so very slowly; rock, water, air, energy, matter, all ticking away forever and ever, the one thing changing gradually into the other and then back again or into a third thing while we emerge and change so fast, like one of those biology movies, seed into beanstalk into decay in three seconds flat.

That would be a hell of a scary movie: the history of man compressed into a couple of hours, the sloping foreheads bulging fast and steady like a bubble-gum bubble; zip, they're wearing clothes now! Cities rising and falling before your eyes like bellows. Armies raised and wiped out in the snap of a finger. Man and his works spreading like spilled oil over the earth.

First smoke, then rockets arcing into the sky. The
oceans muddying suddenly, as if some giant fish had
flirted its tail at the bottom of a shallow pond. The
splutter of mushroom clouds. The earth covered with
men and shit like a glazed doughnut at a picnic, ant-
eaten. Then the end of man, the oil slick gathering
back in on itself, the skies clearing, the seas clearing,
nothing left but ice and bare rock. And then, slowly
but fast enough so that its inevitability is obvious, the
rock flaking into dirt, the dirt pushing up plants, the
protocrab crawling out of the sea, studying the plants,
nibbling one . . . Christ, the earth!

Stoned on time and doubt, Runner rose from his
seat beside the fire. A tremendous awe filled him, an
awe of the earth. He walked over to the Husky and
kicked it into life. The desert—threat or promise, he
would whip it or die trying. Without a glance at
Twigan, he toed the gear shift, popped the clutch,
and screwed down hard on the throttle. The bike
leaped out like a charging grizzly, vaulted a hillock,
and screamed off into the desolation. Twigan watched
it go. Then she got up and began packing their gear
and the last of the ketwai sap. She shouldered the
pack and picked up the spare gasoline can. She hiked
away from the river, following the ripped and studded track of Runner's knobbies. As she walked, she
sang a little song to herself, a song of the Hassayampa:

> Once I saw a thunderstorm
> That tore the sky with thunder
> And shore the rocks with lightning
> And rained in the fierceness of nature.
> The world is crying, and I will sing
> A song that speaks of everything. . . .
>
> Once I saw the ocean,
> With gray, foaming waves
> That beat the strand unending
> And sprayed my face with salt.

The world is crying, and I will sing
A song that speaks of everything. . . .

Once I saw a lake.
It was green as the grass, an emerald.
I saw my face,
and worlds underwater.
The world is crying, so I will sing
A song that speaks of everything. . . .

47

Runner wrestled with the earth in much the same way
he had wrestled with his father when he was a little
boy. The earth's weight, if you could put it on a scale,
would come to about 6 sextillion 588 quintillion short
tons. Runner and his bike weighed 392 pounds 7
ounces. The earth's speed, flat out at the equator, is
roughly 1,040 miles an hour. Runner's top speed, in
the straights with his belly tight along the tank and
his feet on the back pegs and the grip screwed tight,
was 89.664 miles an hour.

Runner didn't give a damn about the odds.

I'll whip your ass, you mother, he yelled silently to
himself as he tore across the desert. His dope-crazed
flesh had become one with the motorcycle, his eyes
knobbed rubber, his tendons coiled steel, his lymph
and blood now oil and gasoline. The violent vibra-
tions of motor and earth blended into a fine, steady
roar, a tingle punctuated with shocks, that climbed his
spine and infected his brain, both feeding and refining
his inchoate rage, honing it down to an awl of metal
and fire that punched through the wasteland with
aimless resolution. No next, no then: just now.

A hill before him, he climbed it—flew in its face,
split its lip, singed its moustache, scoured snot from
its nose with his flailing tires.

A draw beneath him, he violated it—wrenched its
bush, tweaked its twot, scattered slime and water
with a raging blast of his exhaust.

He leaped crevasses, vaulted boulders, kissed the
hard shoulders of cliffs with his knees; he slid through
spiky thickets of thorn and puckerbush, sinuating,
squashing snakes and feeling the bite of wood in his
naked chest, his arms, his brow. Blood flew behind
him in a thin pink contrail; pink spit streamed from

his mouth; he swallowed blood, loving it, feeding on it.

The earth raced to meet his eyes—tan, tough, warped, and strong in its infinite variety, outrageous in its disregard. He met that hard neutrality with his own skill, imagining the challenge even as he imagined and, a split second later, put into action its solution. And as he raced across the desert, across the face of his adversary, he slowly began to realize that the wounds he was inflicting were not wounds at all, only tracks, temporal; that the earth itself was unconcerned with his transgression. That the earth is the original sadomasochist, meting out pain and accepting it with equal aplomb.

His rage began to fade even as his skill began to fail. He no longer was one with the machine. A boulder reared before him—popped right out of the ground, it seemed—and in that split-second change of his head, he lost it, lost it all; the bike (insensate now) bounced, bent itself like a bronco, the roar of the engine sickening, dying, and Runner flew through the air. . . .

Twigan trudged along in the waning light, swinging the gas can and watching the trail. She poked at the crushed snakes and lizards with a stick. One of them, a rattler, was still alive. She watched it trying to crawl away, unaware that its squashed guts, in combination with a hot sun, had glued it to the rock where Runner's wheels had surprised it. The snake writhed irritably, searching for a better purchase, for a traction that was impossible, given the drag of its own congealed flesh and body fluids. She watched it for a long time, taking a swig from the canteen, enjoying her rest. The snake finally became aware of her presence. It buzzed its rattle and shot its tongue, attempting to coil but unable to do so except imperfectly, owing to its wound. Its bright eye searched for her. She sat quietly, curious. Finally the snake calmed down and once again concentrated on getting under way: it was almost night; it needed warmth. She left it wriggling busily, unaware of its own already patent death.

A little farther on she found Runner, sitting next to the bike. He was covered with scabs where the thorns had ripped him, and his nose was twice its usual size. She handed him his shirt, and he winced as he put it on. He took the gas can and refilled the bike. The sun was gone, but an afterglow remained. The moon was just rising. Runner put his hand on the back of her neck and looked at her very closely.

"I know it now," he said. "You don't have to beat it."

48

Only the ill and the old stayed behind when Ratnose's gang ascended the Altyn Tagh. There was a carnival air to the march. Children scampered around the horses, skittering between their legs even as they climbed, gaudy gadflies, squealing and chirping excitedly. The women were dressed in their holiday finery—headbands and shawls of red, yellow, green, orange, purple. The men wore their talismans of bear claws and elks' teeth, aurochs horn and ivory, dragon's eyes and mummified human fingers. Some tied fangs and feathers to their trigger guards. A mixed, unorchestrated chorus of bells accompanied the group, surrounded it, preceded it. Camel bells, yak bells, reindeer bells, cowbells, carabao bells, elephant bells, sleigh bells.

Slay bells, thought Tilkut, riding beside Ratnose near the head of the ragged column. His confidence had waned a bit since Runner's return. Ratnose had quickly brewed a vat of the ketwai poison and then tested it on the puppies in the compound. Tilkut watched, stone-faced but impressed, while Ratnose fed the heavy line out through the guides with a practiced double haul, the line hissing ominously through dozens of false casts (Ratnose was showing off his strength of wrist), then laying out neat and straight, the leader with its deadly fly pausing just for an instant over the stupid, grinning puppy face, then dropping in to sting. A yelp, a moment of frantic, puzzled scratching, and then the puppy went limp—its eyes glazed; fleas crawling on its fat, soft belly. Ratnose killed six that way in half an hour. "Enough for breakfast stew," he said, smiling.

Tilkut chose not to practice on the puppies. He had no stomach for killing dogs. In fact, the killing of any

animal was beginning to pall on him—any animal but
man. He took his fly rod and waded down the river to
practice on fish, with an unpoisoned, barbless fly.
Standing waist-deep in the icy spring water, naked to
test himself against the cold he would have to endure
on the Altyn Tagh, he worked his arm and his eye
back into shape. As he cast, he thought about killing.
Yes, man was his meat now. As a boy, even as a young
man, he had enjoyed killing game. The *splat* of bullet
on flesh had given him a godlike sense of power, an
awe at his own skills, at the fact that it was *his* choice
these creatures should die. But as he grew to know
more about wild animals and their ways of life, their
guilelessness, their simple and thoughtless courage,
the god role had gradually come to feel obscene. At
the same time, he was coming to detest man, the in-
ventor of gods. Man the filthy, man the self-delusory,
man the pompous, the grinning, the smart-ass, the
sanctimonious, the greedy, the cowardly. Snivelers
who beshat the earth. He came to feel that he could
kill most men with no more compunction than other
men would feel in killing rats. Not all men. Some
were still worth saving—the few who were tough
without posing, honest without self-congratulation,
faithful to their wives and friends without the usual
smarm of guilt. . . .

A fish slammed the fly, leaped, then took off downstream while the reel chattered. Tilkut checked the
fish just above the next riffle, turned it finally, stripped
in line like a mad masturbator. The fish paused for a
moment, shaking its head. Then it raced off again
while the rod bowed, an anxious servant. Tilkut followed, up to his armpits now in the numbing water,
his bare feet skidding on the slick boulders. He
checked it again, turning the fish into the back current
along the far bank. A belted kingfisher flew over,
peering curiously at the action. Tilkut retreated to the
shallower water. The fish was under control. He
played it as gently as the tippet would permit, knowing that with the barb pinched down on his fly, he

could give it no slack. With most of the line back on the reel, he was breathing confidently for the first time when the fish rolled just fifteen yards out. It was a huge rainbow, scarred and bent-jawed, and as it rolled, it slipped the fly. Tilkut watched it sink, finning and working its gills, its eyes on his, out of sight. . . .

Now, riding beside Ratnose toward the Suck Hole, Tilkut felt uneasy. His wrist was strong, his eye was sharp, but his luck was uneven. Hell, his luck was downright rotten. His son had not spoken to him, except in the most routine manner, since his return from the ketwai tree. Maybe the kid planned to stay even if Ratnose died. Right now he was chugging along on the dirt bike, with his girl friend riding behind him, squirting ahead every now and then to the delight of the women and children, cutting doughnuts in the pea gravel, vaulting ruts and logs. He was a young hero in these mountains. Down in the flats he would be just another beginner. Everything he had learned here was useless down below. Hunting, tracking, trapping, fishing, shooting—all of those things were anachronisms, sentimental vestiges, child's play. Even his skill on a bike, honed to perfection up here, was worth little more than fool's gold at the far end of the Hassayampa. With good luck, a rider might earn $80,000 in one season, then lose his kneecap the next. With bad luck, he might punch a hole in a concrete retaining wall and be remembered awhile for his bloodstains. "Yeah, that's where Runner died—hit the wall at a hundred and twenty and went right on through. They scraped him off Speedway Avenue with a pancake turner. There were bits of his pecker in the carburetor . . ."

Fuck the judgments, Tilkut thought. The kid can do what he wants to do. I've got to concentrate on the job at hand. Killing Ratnose. Relax, enjoy the scenery. And he did: the waning of the timber as they climbed; the stunting of the shrubbery; the gradual accession of the mosses and lichens. Eagles turned on the ground wave of rising air. Dwarf deer scampered up the rocky draws—olive-colored creatures no larger than dogs. Rills and rivulets sparkled in the sun. A family of sheep, drawn by the bells, stared down at them from an impossible cliff, the ram with a curl and a half of heavy, frowning bone on his brow. Runner borrowed Hunk's .243 Browning and sighted in on the great, grave ram, taking a rest across the seat of his bike. He squatted there, concentrating death through the scope.

"Don't," said Tilkut.

Runner looked around at him. Their eyes met. Tilkut could feel the outrage in his son's eyes, and his own rose to meet it. They stared at each other.

"Do you need the meat?" Tilkut asked.

"I want the trophy."

"A windfall trophy? A trophy you just happened to luck into? You didn't *hunt* the bastard, you *stumbled* onto him. Why don't you save yourself the climb and buy that big head off of Ratnose—the one he uses for a backrest?"

Runner handed the rifle back to Hunk. He shrugged to Twigan: The old man's nuts.

So much for fuck-the-judgments, Tilkut thought. So much for letting him do what he wants to do. Well, anyway, he still values my opinion of him. Relax, enjoy the scenery.

They heard the Suck Hole long before they saw it: first a murmur, then a growl, finally a graveled, grating roar. Mist hung thin and rainbowed over the rocks. The children ran ahead, excited by the sound. When the main body of horsemen came up, the children were throwing stones and driftwood into the whirling vortex. It was bigger than Tilkut had imagined, frightening in its slow, inexorable acceleration. The two tributaries swept down from the peak of the mountain in a shallow V, seemingly innocuous with their borders of pink and purple lichen, their blanched boulders and glinting rapids.

One of the children threw a piece of driftwood into

the exact confluence of the streams, perhaps a hundred feet from the Suck Hole itself. A dog—a shaggy, happy collie bitch who had followed along from camp—leaped in to retrieve the stick. She paddled strongly, angling downstream to intercept it. She took it in her jaws and turned to struggle back toward the bank. She made no headway. Panic entered her eyes. She was pulled backward, her ears peaked as if they might by themselves draw her to safety, while everyone watched. Some of the women laughed, and the children followed suit—all but the child who had thrown the stick. The collie bitch kept scrambling even when the whirlpool caught her, turning her around and around, still holding the stick in her jaws as she disappeared into the guttural, mumbling mist. The children laughed and laughed.

Ratnose chuckled and poked Tilkut in the ribs. "As I said, it's not so nice at the Suck Hole."

They dined that night on dog stew and roast aurochs, head cheese and broiled trout—fresh-speared from the Yampa, where a long, cold pool held hundreds of fat rainbows. Brown rice, boiled roots, watercress. Tilkut had to admit that Ratty's people ate well. He himself was not hungry. He nibbled a side of trout, chewed a sprig of watercress. He stayed away from the crait, which was bubbling merrily in its customary, inevitable castiron pot over the men's fire. Let them scramble their brains; he wanted his hardboiled.

Pretty soon they all started guzzling, then giggling, then rushing off to their saddlebags to fumble for their nose flutes and jew's harps and mandolins. Or whatever they called them. In a little while, the music threatened to drown out the sound of the Suck Hole. The nightly orgy got under way. Tilkut watched it through hooded eyelids, his mouth curled in contempt under his moustache. All that groping, stroking, poking, whooping, swapping, sucking, grouping—and in front of the children!

He saw two little kids—no more than four years

old, he guessed—trying to imitate the grown-ups. The little man on top couldn't get it up. He shook his tiny dong and yelled at it in Hassayampan. No go. The little man laughed—a katydid's chirrup in the dark— and rolled away. When the kid underneath stood up, Tilkut saw that it was another boy. Tilkut was tempted to go over there and tell them what was what, but he didn't have the words. He saw Runner and Twigan balling at the edge of the firelight. Runner was doing all right, he thought. A good, steady stroke, plenty of hip action, no fears of premature ejaculation . . . What the hell am I doing? he thought. What place is this? How can this be?

A woman came over and sat down beside him. She was toothless, round-eyed, with hip-length blond hair. She flashed her gums at him and reached for his groin. She flipped a tit out of her blouse. It was long, veined, scarred in places with stretch marks, culminating in a nipple that looked like the face of a pug dog. Stunned, Tilkut let her take his hand and place it under her skirt. Horrified, he felt his fingers working of their own volition. Amazed, he found himself palpating those slippery walls, twanging that rigid thumblet. Flabbergasted, he realized vaguely that his own dong was feeling the breeze, stiff and eager, with a mind of its own, responding like an eager gun dog to the toothless woman's caresses. Unbelieving, he discovered himself mounted upon her, into her, fucking away like a veritable demon—like his own son, by God—humping and thrusting with the toothless woman all agroan beneath him, yelping her crait-stained breath into his nostrils, her legs wrapped around his ears, her voice rising to a crescendo of whoops and howls that erased the disbelief from his brain just as the music had drowned out the death song of the Suck Hole. . . .

"Hey, Pop, pretty good!" said Runner, staring down at him with the first smile he had seen on his son's face since they had been reunited. Runner was standing there with Twigan and Ratnose and the rest of them, gathered in a circle around Tilkut and Blondie where they lay in the scuffed and scattered gravel. Everyone was smiling—even the two misguided four-year-old pederasts. They had never seen a Bear God screw before. Or so Tilkut thought, laughing.

49

"Look," he asked Ratnose the next morning, "do we have to go through with this?"

They were naked in the chilly mist. The sun, still red and huge, had not yet burned away the cold. The rest of the gang huddled on the boulders of the riverbank, wrapped in quilts and skins, staring glumly at the two combatants who stood just short of the water with their poisoned fly rods in hand. Ratnose put a hand on Tilkut's shoulder.

"No other way," he said. "You hurt me years ago. You killed some of my men quite recently. I stole your son. I tried to pervert him to a way of life alien to what you had planned for him. Moreover, my people expect an entertainment."

A dog yapped on the bank.

"It's not that I'm afraid . . ."

"I know that," Ratnose said. He smiled and gripped Tilkut's shoulder.

"I don't want to kill you," Tilkut said. "I never wanted to kill you—at least, not back then when we shot up your gang down on the lower river. I brought my son up here this time because, in a way, though I fear you—or feared you back then, before we left—I felt we could learn from you, from being near you. You've taught him a lot, and taught me a lot, too. I admire you. . . ."

"I'm a cruel man, Tilkut. A killer. A thief. A believer in torture and revenge. A believer in entertainment. Food, fucking, song, blood, sleep, contests— things like that. I stole your son."

"If he wants to stay, he can stay. That possibility was implicit in my decision to bring him up here; I know that now. But I don't want to kill you."

"I don't die that easily," Ratnose said, grinning

again. "And anyway, death doesn't hurt. Living can hurt, if you live wrong. But let's get it on. The people are waiting."

They waded into the stream, plodding slowly so as to keep their footing on the slimy boulders of the bed, drawing farther and farther apart as the water rushed between them and they approached their designated stations at the edge of the whirlpool. At one point, Ratnose yelled something to Tilkut, but the noise of the water drowned it out. Tilkut shrugged, smiled his incomprehension, and kept on wading. The water had reached his balls now, and he felt himself shrink from it: entering cold water was always a torture. He caught the thrust of the river against the small of his back, braced against it, found his stride, and plodded on. A trout skittered out from its holding place behind a large, pink boulder and brushed against his thigh—quickly electric. It spooked him for a moment, and he paused, the rod held high overhead so that none of the gummy poison would wash from the fly, clinched tight in the wire half-circle above the cork butt. Then he waded forward.

When he came to his station, he turned and stared back through the mist. Ratnose was a small, distant figure—a head, two arms, a chest above the water, nothing more. The figures on the bank blurred in the fog. There was no sound other than the roar of the whirlpool. He realized that, because of his greater height, he offered a better target to Ratnose than Ratnose did to him.

That tricky bastard!

He felt the old rage light off in his belly now, paranoid kindling, better than none. He waded out a few more steps, until the water reached his nipples. It was numbingly cold, but nothing he couldn't tolerate. He planted his feet in the rocks, gripping the gravel with his toes, finding a comfortable purchase. Then he unhooked the poisoned cow-dung fly and held it carefully in his left hand while he stripped the leader clear of the guides and brought the nail knot and the

first few feet of fly line clear. He began to false cast,
working fly line out and up—eleven o'clock, pull back
to one o'clock, open the wrist, drift, forward again to
eleven, the power stroke—the line seeming to slice the
fog with a wet snicker, then lashing ahead in its easy
sinuations until he could no longer see the knot.

He false-cast for a while, staring through the mist
toward Ratnose, who seemed to be motionless in the
distance. He kept the line moving; good—his arm was
still strong, no fear of going dead this early in the
game. Then the light suddenly increased, as if someone had turned up a rheostat, running quickly up
from blue to gray to green to gold to silver, and he
heard a hiss near his ear. The sun popped clear. The
fog was gone. The hiss repeated itself, and—turning
his eye—he saw a yellow stripe of line flick past, followed by the glint of a leader and, at the end, a
blurred black speck.

Ratnose's fly.

He glanced back toward the place where he had
last seen Ratnose, standing motionless in the chest-
deep water. He focused more closely, and his stomach
clenched.

Shit! A false Ratnose!

A tree stump!

His eyes swung frantically, right and left. The real
Ratnose was masked against the shore: close—much
closer than Tilkut had thought—so close that he rose
huge and toothy like a monster from the gravel pit. I
missed him in the fog, goddammit, Tilkut raged; the
fucker, he conned me. . . .

But Tilkut's own fly was still airborne, reaching out
toward the false Ratnose, the tree stump up the river,
now—with the fog gone—so patently a tree stump,
with its snaggy roots resembling arms, its bark scarred
and peeling: a tree stump washed down river in the
night, goddammit. . . . My line's too far out, Tilkut
raged, stripping it in, trying to work it around toward
Ratnose even as he heard Ratnose's fly buzzing near
his ear. . . . Cursing as his fly ticked the water—

There goes some poison, bloody hell!—his arm twitching back and forth like the big hand on a clock gone berserk—eleven, one, drift, eleven, push, eleven—realizing suddenly that he had stripped in more than he needed—his fly flickering short of Ratnose now—stepping forward in a rush to bring it closer—hearing a *snick* behind him, and feeling the spray of water on his neck from Ratnose's fly where it had missed, then hearing Ratnose's line hit the water beside his leg . . .

He saw his line straighten out above Ratnose's head. He saw it settle for an instant. He saw Ratnose's face, grinning, teeth clenched, the eye on him as hollow as a bullet hole. He struck. He felt his fly hang home, saw Ratnose's head tip forward, the twitch of hair on Ratnose's head where the fly had snagged him, and he stripped in line as fast as he could, straightening the slack, exultant . . .

And felt the bite on his ankle. Just a nip. A sharp, stinging tug in his right ankle that scarcely shifted his balance on the shifting bottom, scarcely penetrated the numbness of the river's cold. But he was hooked, and he knew it. A thrill of horror shot through his gut. A double hookup—he had Ratnose, and Ratnose had him. Already the poison was working. The toes of his hooked foot cramped painfully, briefly, then went dead. A numbness far colder than that of the river began to spread upward from his ankle.

But I have him by the scalp, Tilkut thought, and for the poison it's a shorter trip from scalp to brain than it is from the ankle. He leaned back against the strain of the line, the rod bent and throbbing with Ratnose's struggles, trying to drag Ratnose off his feet and into the grip of the current; but Ratnose shook his head, still grinning, then thrust his head forward, hoping to gain some slack, his hand fumbling at the back of his head, trying to unseat the poisoned barb. But I have him good now, Tilkut exulted, he's got to fall, he's got to fall! He redoubled his efforts to pull Ratnose off balance. The numbness had reached his knee by now;

his thigh muscles were fluttering. He planted his good leg against a boulder and surged once more against the rod.

And Ratnose came—slowly, ever so slowly, still shaking his head, like some great shark hooked deep in the gullet, shaking his head to the dim, dawning realization that he has swallowed something strange: he has swallowed death. And Ratnose came slowly, slowly out into the current. His face, wet with spray or sweat, began to crumble, to dissolve like clay in the rain. His eye seemed to spread like a pool, like the ink of a squid dissolving in the water. Ratnose came out into the deeper water, and the current caught him by the waist, dragging him slowly, then a bit faster, then faster still, into the race. The tension of Ratnose's line against Tilkut's ankle began to ease—there was slack. Tilkut reached down into the water and felt his way down the leader to the fly, then ripped, ripped again—and the fly came loose. Free!

Ratnose spun into the edge of the whirlpool, his head up, rolling. His eye was still on Tilkut. He went around the edge of the whirlpool, around again, closer to the vortex. Then he began to sink. His eye seemed to grow beneath the water. It was still fixed on Tilkut. Ratnose sank, his jaws working, into the heart of the whirlpool, out of sight. . . .

Tilkut watched the line melt off his reel, accelerating with the momentum of Ratnose's body as it fell down the Suck Hole; watched the backing race and blur; braced himself for the shock when the line would part—*snap!* Then, using the fly rod as a wading staff, he started for the shore.

His son stood on the bank, next to the motorcycle. The engine was turning. He had the Luger in his hand and his eyes on the crowd. Some of the women screamed. Tilkut saw that Twigan was crying. Hunk's face was impassive, but his hands were empty of weapons. Only Fric had a rifle. His face was bone-white and his hands trembled on the stock.

"Don't try it, hippie," said Runner. "I'll blast your guts out your ass hole."

He swung a leg over the saddle. Tilkut crawled up behind him.

"Can you handle the Luger while I ride?" Runner asked.

"Kuh, kuh, kuh, kuh . . ." said Tilkut.

"Okay," said Runner, "I can do both. Let's get out of here, Pop. I'm not much for long good-byes."

He let in the clutch, and the bike jumped away from the river.

50

They ran the ancient game trails that flanked the Has-sayampa—the rutted, dusty routes of bison and mastodon, aurochs and elk. Game flushed ahead of them in panic or else stood frozen, wide-eyed, in the thickets as they passed. The manticores watched sternly from their perches in the drowned, dead trees beside the river. The boy did not see them—he was too busy, too happy with the ride. He threw his body into the corners, leaped the wallows, vaulted the ruts, playing the gearbox like a church organ. The man did not see them either. His eyes were locked out of focus, at zero or infinity, he did not know which. All of his concentration was directed to the act of breathing, which had now become a work of the will. He knew his arms were wrapped around his son's waist and that his feet were on the pegs, but he could not feel it. So he did not worry about balance. He worried about breath. Could he get it in this time? Slowly, aching, cold. Then, could he get it out this time? Just as slowly, just as cold.

He lived inside his lungs, down there with the bright blood and the bellows roar of diaphragm and alveoli, a world of tubes and flowages. He grew familiar with the gurgle of his heart, imagining somewhat whimsically that it approximated the sound of the river past which he was flashing without sight or sound. Was it day? Was it night? All the same to him. He knew he was probably sweating as his body tried to pump away the poison, that he had probably voided his bladder in unconscious obedience to the orders of his kidneys, but he felt neither wet nor dry. Somewhere along the way he vomited, feeling rather than tasting the faint sting of bile at the top of his nostrils. It did not matter. What mattered was air—

elusive air; neutral, impartial air—a substance that could not be begged or bought or coaxed, but could be gained only by concentration, by hard work. He worked at it.

Then, after years of hard labor, his nerves began to awaken. Gradually at first, just the faintest of tingling in his wrists and along his legs. His jaws began to ache, as if he had eaten a mountain. His eyes accepted the light; his optic nerves screamed like a fire victim. Then his larger muscles. Someone was lashing them with nettles, shoving nettles down his throat, up his nose, pulling them through his arteries. Another someone had skinned his head and was pouring alcohol over it, was now skinning out his back, his arms, his legs, pouring the fire over his raw flesh. He could not bring himself to scream. He yelled curses instead.

But that too went away. He was left with a gnawing ache in his ankle, the ankle that had been bitten by the poisoned fly. It was dark. His son was feeding the campfire, and the rumble of the Hassayampa underlay the crackling of the flames. The bike was parked not far away, glittering red and silver in the firelight. A game bird turned and sizzled on a greenwood spit.

"Peacock," his son said. "He flushed off the trail up into a tree just before dark. I headed him with the Luger and figured we might as well stop here for the night and eat him."

"How long have we been . . ."

"A week tomorrow morning."

"Then we must be nearly home."

"We're about a day's run by the bike, but I'm down into the reserve already. No more gas after that. We'll have to steal a boat."

"You can stash the bike and come back for it later with some more gas. But I don't think we'll find a boat around here, and my ankle feels kind of septic."

The boy looked away. Then he busied himself with the game bird. Then he looked at his father's legs, wrapped and lumpy under the bearskin.

"Well," the boy said, "I better tell you now. I had to take it off. Your right foot, halfway down the shinbone."

The man sat there for a long, long minute. He wiggled his ghost toes. He was afraid to look under the bearskin.

"Shit," said the man.

"It was that or your whole leg when we got home," the boy said. "Or probably your life. The goddam gangrene was in there. You didn't seem to be feeling anything—I slapped you around some and stuck you a bit with the knife—so I figured it was as good a time as any."

"Shit," the man said again. "Oh, shit. Oh, dear."

"Well, it's done," the boy said hotly. "It's better than having your tongue cut out."

"I didn't mean that; it's just . . ."

"I know, I know."

"I mean, what I should be saying is 'Thanks.' How the hell did you do it?"

"I figured it out. It was pretty easy, actually. Do you want the details?"

"Sure."

"Well, getting through the skin and the muscles was a cinch—do you know how many muscles you have in there, in the calf? You've got about six of the bastards, all of them tough—but I had a good edge on the knife. I'd cranked on a tourniquet just below your knee, really wound that baby down tight. There was a lot of blood at first, but it all drained out. You were moaning and rolling around, so I had to tie you down. Still, that ketwai poison was a pretty good anesthetic. I don't think you were feeling much pain—maybe just having bad dreams."

"I was living in my lungs, I think."

"The bone was tough. Bone is a lot tougher than you'd imagine. And the shinbone is a tricky sonofabitch, a lot of angles to it. But there was still a good bite to the meat saw. You know that Swedish wire job you use on big game? I remember how I nearly threw up the first time I watched you using it, on the bear I killed up the river there. The sound of the wire going through bone. But it didn't bother me a bit this time. In fact, there were a few little splinters when I finally got through it, and I filed them down with the file we use on the ax."

"Christ."

"But the tricky part was how to close off the blood vessels. They were staring at me like so many little mouths, waiting to be filled with something. I remembered from my books that back in the days of the Napoleonic Wars and the American Revolution, they would stick the stump in a bucket of boiling tar to sear the arteries and seal them. But we didn't have any tar close at hand. Then I thought of a red-hot bar of steel, but I couldn't find anything big enough to cover the surface of the stump at one shot. Until I thought of the bike."

"How's that?"

"I ran the bike like crazy, burned up a quarter of a tank of gas doing it, and when the tailpipe was so hot that it popped water when I sprinkled some on it, I rolled your stump against it. I figured there couldn't be any bacteria on the pipe, not at that heat. It seared the arteries and veins just as neat as you'd please."

"I'll be damned."

"You know what it smelled like?" the boy said, grinning. "It smelled just like roast pork." He laughed.

"You're a hard sonofabitch," the man said.

"Damn right," said the boy. "You made me that way."

51

The bike ran dry just before noon the next day. It was hot and buggy on the lower stretch of the river, so after he had hidden the motorcycle as best he could in a canebrake well above the high-water mark, the boy cut his father a crutch and helped him to a promontory where the breeze would keep the mosquitoes and blackflies down. Then, sticking the Luger into his waistband at the small of his back, he started downriver looking for a boat. He was lucky. Not an hour from the point, he came upon two fishermen in an aluminum canoe. He hailed them and they paddled over, helpful concern on their faces. As they came closer, the boy could see they were city dudes, wearing fancy fishing vests and expensive wool shirts, with gaudy flies in their caps.

When they had beached the canoe, he drew the Luger and ordered them to start walking away from the river.

"You rotten little hippie!" said one of the men, a fat, red-faced fellow with a pencil moustache. "I told you, Willie, these fucking . . ."

The boy stared hard at the man and made a gesture with the Luger. He wondered what the man would say if he shot him in the kneecap. The men stalked off, muttering and looking back anxiously over their shoulders. The boy emptied the canoe of their fishing tackle, but kept the stringer of smallmouth bass they had caught. There were no tents or sleeping bags or axes or gas stoves in the canoe, so they must have a camp somewhere nearby. If they couldn't find it, they deserved to die. At least, they wouldn't be out anything for the canoe; it was rented.

The boy paddled the canoe back upriver to the place where his father lay snoring among the bullrushes. He built a fire and cleaned the bass, then fried them and woke his father. After they had eaten, they pushed off. There was still an hour or so of daylight. . . .

As they slid back down the river the next morning, the boy felt his heart sicken. So many changes while he was gone! Not just in him, but in the river itself. Opposite Kurlander, where his father had first hunted aurochs, the pink and blue of a trailer park spread on the banks of the Hassayampa. Power shovels and backhoes stood in orderly yellow ranks near the first pilings of a bridge that would soon span the river. He saw two boys about his own age throwing rocks at an oil drum that was drifting, half submerged, in a backwater near the left bank. The boys wore cutoffs and tie-dyed tank shirts, and they flipped the bird at the canoe as it went by.

They met a ski boat—a powerful, buzzing Campbell—trailing a woman in a black bikini whose hair whipped behind her in the wind: long, black hair like Twigan's, but the woman had something glittering around her throat, maybe diamonds. The driver waved at them, a beer can in his hand. The woman tried to jump the wake, but fell in a great splash, laughing.

The Hsien-ho Gorges had been tamed and renamed. A dam was rising at the bottom, and the place had new management, a recreation group that called itself Big Skid. The worst of the rapids had been dredged and rechanneled, and for only $150 a year it was possible to buy a season's ticket that entitled the canoeist to membership in the Skid Club ("Free Skid Flicks Every Night!"), transportation for canoe and party from the foot of the gorges back to the put-in dock, and a bonus crash helmet sporting the club's colors (International Orange and green). A campground capable of handling 1,200 vehicles had been cleared and hot water piped in at the confluence of the Buffalo and the Hassayampa. Its motto: "The couple that woos together canoes together." The

World Whitewater Championships would be held at Big Skid later that summer.

"How'd your dad lose his foot?" the attendant at the put-in dock asked when the boy was ready to leave the store.

"Split it with a hatchet, chopping firewood," he answered, hefting his bag of groceries. "You sure you haven't got any fruit rolls?"

"Not a one," said the attendant. "We only stock the essentials, for real outdoor livin'."

They camped one night at the edge of the Porcupine Mountains. A new highway had come through during their absence, so the boy hitchhiked over to see old Otto, the onion farmer. When he returned, shortly before dawn, the man awoke.

"What happened? How's the old man?"

"He's dead. Got run over by a snow plow sometime last winter. They're putting up a development where he had the farm."

"What about What's-her-name—you know, the fat laundry lady? Helgard."

"Gone."

The man lay silent for quite a while. He could smell the beer on the boy's breath.

"Did you bring me a beer?"

"Sure." The kid handed a beer to his father, but it was warm. The man drank it anyway.

"Dead and gone," he said, finally, "dead and gone. All the good part of it, that is. Like my foot, for instance. Hey, I've been wanting to ask you, what finally happened to . . . it? I mean, what did you do with it?"

"I threw it over in the bushes, and something came along in the night and took it. I think it was a coyote. I could hear it growling and crunching on the bones all night long."

"Well," the man said, "they like rotten meat."

The man sipped his beer. Dead and gone, he was thinking.

"Even Ratnose," he said finally.

"What do you mean?"

"Dead and gone. A damned shame, in a way. He was a tough bastard, old Ratanous. I got to like him there, towards the end."

"I liked him too."

The man threw a few more sticks on the fire and poked at the coals. It was a clear night, but he did not want to look at the stars. He wished he had another beer.

"Do you have another beer?" he asked the boy.

"Not a one," the boy said. "But I've got some crait."

"Give us a slug," the man said. The boy went over to the canoe and came back with a canteen. The man unscrewed the cap and took a long pull from the neck. "Ah," he said, "that's just fine. Listen, before I get too high on this stuff, there's something I wanted to ask you. Maybe it's not the right time, and maybe I even know the answer already. But I want your words on it. Why did you leave there? Why did you take me out of there? Why did you leave your girl and your— well, position? You were a hero up there, and Ratnose himself told me you would ultimately become the chief. Down here . . ."

"Yeah," the boy said, "down here. I don't know. A lot of it had to do with Ratnose. At first I really was scared of him, and then later I saw that he was trying to help me, so I got to liking him. And then I got to liking his woman—or girl, I guess you'd say—Twigan. And then I felt I had to take her away from him, I wanted her that badly. Or maybe I just wanted to show him something. But whatever it was, I got her, and then I knew that sooner or later I'd have to go up against him. I didn't like that notion. It was easier to go up against you, and I did. Then *you* went up against Ratnose. So in a way, I copped out: I let you do my fighting for me. I owed you that. And besides, you're my father."

The man sat silent, washed in a wave of sadness. For a moment there, he had been Tilkut again. The Bear God. Huge, omnipotent, fearsome in his righteous, blessed madness. Now the feeling was gone, drained away, like the waters of the Hassayampa itself, pouring tame through the freshly dynamited channels of the Big Skid. He knew it would never return. Taking his crutch, the man limped down to the riverbank and watched the Hassayampa roll past. Far upriver he could see storm clouds gathering, a black wall ticked with lightning that spread slowly over the sky. Idly, he cursed his missing foot: no more Tilkut, no more hunting, no more wading the high trout streams in the early spring, with the redwing blackbirds bouncing on the naked branches, the smell of warm mud and willows . . . What was it Ratnose had said? A man is the sum of his scars.

He limped back to the campfire. His son held up something bright for him to see: the dump truck. "She gave it to me as a memento," the boy said. "How do you like that?" The man could see he had been crying.

"It's raining upriver," the man said. "The water will be up by morning, very fast. We'll be home by suppertime."

52

The following morning, the river was very fast indeed—fast and high and commensurately safe. They ran with the runoff from the storm, which still grew behind them, slow-moving and grumbling with fire in its belly. They swerved like a silver leaf through the uprooted trees, borne on the boiling brown water, through scum lines of junk—beer cans, Clorox bottles, popsicle wrappers, old shoes, wrecked piers, wayward outhouses. They swept past the mouth of the Menomonee, where the man had trapped muskrats and raccoons so long ago. A gutted, abandoned Cadillac lay hung up on a tangle of driftwood at precisely the point where the smaller river joined the larger one. It rolled on the conflict of currents like a stranded, sunburned whale.

The swamp where they had shot ducks on their way upriver had by now been drained. Concrete culverts diverted the river past a vast shopping center, from which the sounds of Muzak reached them above the distant rumbling of the storm, and drainpipes set in the concrete walls poured colorful waters into the Hassayampa. They paddled through rainbows of oil. What looked like the corpse of a baby, stiff and bloated in a drift line farther downstream, proved to be only a rotten rubber doll.

Even the Indian reservation had changed. The stands of mature white pine along the river's bank had receded, or else been transmuted during their absence into the sprawl of low, rustically modern summer homes that now stared wide-eyed at the raging Hassayampa, as if the dwellings themselves were fearfully certain of being swept away to join the flow of flotsam.

They beached the canoe briefly where they had

cached the mastodon tusks on the way upstream. The
logs with which they had built the cache were slimy
with mud and dying algae, and mice had gotten to
the ivory during their absence. The man studied the
tusks, fascinated with the random, delicate scrimshaw
work left by the rodents' teeth. When he squinted, it
almost seemed that he could read the tusks—as if
some ancient historian at the dawn of ideography had
left a message for him here, a code of nips and
slashes. But the storm was still visible upstream,
thumping in the distance, and questions of legibility
would have to wait. They loaded the ivory and
pushed on with the strength of the river at their
backs.

Then the Hassayampa widened, approaching its
mouth. It seemed to slow. The storm was well behind
them now, so fast had they run the chutes. They had
even outrun the runoff: here at the river's end, the
water was clear. The boy, paddling at the bow,
braked the canoe to a swirling halt. He pulled a fly
rod from his pack and began to assemble it.

"What are you doing?"

"We can't come home empty-handed," the boy said.
"Not after all this time."

The man stared down through the glassy surface.
Fleets of bluegills maneuvered through the weed. A
largemouth bass lay solid and heavy in the shadow of
a sunken log. Turtles sunned themselves on the
stumps near the shore, where a great blue heron stood
silent and steady, waiting for frogs.

The boy fished for an hour, while the storm drew
nearer. He caught bluegills, yellow perch, a white
crappie and one fair-sized bass. When the string was
of a respectable size, they beached the canoe and unloaded their gear. Not much of it, when they stood
back and looked at the pile. The man stuck the Luger
into his waistband, at the small of his back, and then
draped the bearskin over his shoulders. Better to hide
the weapon: he didn't want to scare the neighbors.
The tusks worked well as crutches. The boy carried

the fly rod in one hand and the string of fish in the other.

They walked slowly away from the river, toward home.

Epilogue

Hunk squatted on his heels in the dark beside the Hassayampa. The rain had swept through, though the lightning still illuminated the wet cliffs and the racing river from time to time. Hunk kept his eyes on the water. Anytime now, he thought. He had squatted there all day, impervious to the weather, watching the flotsam spin past. Trees, bones, bloated carcasses of the drowned. Now he saw a flash of white in the darkness upstream.

It flashed again, closer.

Hunk walked into the river and waited. It was the body of a man. He grabbed its wrist as it rolled by and dragged it up onto the skull-sized stones of the shore. He laid it on its back and straightened as best he could the broken, rock-torn limbs. Then he waited some more.

The thunder boomed, rolling away downriver.

The eyelid flickered. The nostrils flexed. The chest rose, fell, rose again. Then the lid lifted completely and the black eye swam into focus.